Maisey Yates is a *USA TODAY* bestselling author of more than seventy-five romance novels. She has a coffee habit she has no interest in kicking, and a slight Pinterest addiction. She lives with her husband and children in the Pacific Northwest. When Maisey isn't writing she can be found singing in the supermarket, shopping for shoes online and probably not doing dishes. Check out her website: www.maiseyyates.com

USA TODAY bestselling author **Catherine Mann** has won numerous awards for her novels, including both a prestigious RITA® Award and an *RT Book Reviews* Reviewers' Choice Award. After years of moving around the country bringing up four children, Catherine has settled in her home state of South Carolina, where she's active in animal rescue. For more information, visit her website, catherinemann.com

Also by Maisey Yates

Copper Ridge
Take Me, Cowboy
Hold Me, Cowboy
Seduce Me, Cowboy
Claim Me, Cowboy
Want Me, Cowboy
Need Me, Cowboy
Gold Valley
A Tall, Dark Cowboy Christmas
Unbroken Cowboy

Also by Catherine Mann

The Baby Claim
The Double Deal
The Love Child
The Twin Birthright
The Second Chance
The Rancher's Seduction
The Billionaire Renegade
The Secret Twin

Discover more at millsandboon.co.uk

RANCHER'S WILD SECRET

MAISEY YATES

HOT HOLIDAY RANCHER

CATHERINE MANN

MILLS & BOON

First Published in Great Britain 2019
by Mills & Boon, an imprint of HarperCollinsPublishers,
1 London Bridge Street, London, SE1 9GF

ISBN: 978-0-263-27197-3

1119

MIX
Paper from
responsible sources
FSC™ C007454

RANCHER'S WILD SECRET

MAISEY YATES

One

The launch party for Maxfield Vineyards' brand-new select label was going off without a hitch, and Emerson Maxfield was bored.

Not the right feeling for the brand ambassador of Maxfield Vineyards, but definitely the feeling she was battling now.

She imagined many people in attendance would pin the look of disinterest on her face on the fact that her fiancé wasn't present.

She looked down at her hand, currently wrapped around a glass of blush wine, her fourth finger glittering with the large, pear-shaped diamond that she was wearing.

She wasn't bored because Donovan wasn't here.

Frankly, *Donovan* was starting to bore her, and that reality caused her no small amount of concern.

But what else could she do?

Her father had arranged the relationship, the engagement, two years earlier, and she had agreed. She'd been sure that things would progress, that she and Donovan could make it work because on paper they *should* work.

But their relationship wasn't…changing.

They worked and lived in different states and they didn't have enough heat between them to light a campfire.

All things considered, the party was much less boring than her engagement.

But all of it—the party and the engagement—was linked. Linked to the fact that her father's empire was the most important thing in his world.

And Emerson was a part of that empire.

In fairness, she cared about her father. And she cared about his empire, deeply. The winery was her life's work. Helping build it, grow it, was something she excelled at.

She had managed to get Maxfield wines into Hollywood awards' baskets. She'd gotten them recommended on prominent websites by former talk show hosts.

She had made their vineyard label something *better* than local.

Maxfield Vineyards was the leading reason parts of Oregon were beginning to be known as the new Napa.

And her work, and her siblings' work, was the reason Maxfield Vineyards had grown as much as it had.

She should be feeling triumphant about this party.

But instead she felt nothing but malaise.

The same malaise that had infected so much of what she had done recently.

This used to be enough.

Standing in the middle of a beautiful party, wearing a dress that had been hand tailored to conform perfectly to her body—it used to be a thrill. Wearing lipstick like this—the perfect shade of red to go with her scarlet dress—it used to make her feel…

Important.

Like she mattered.

Like everything was put together and polished. Like she was a success. Whatever her mother thought.

Maybe Emerson's problem was the impending wedding.

Because the closer that got, the more doubts she had.

If she could possibly dedicate herself to her job *so much* that she would marry the son of one of the world's most premier advertising executives.

That she would go along with what her father asked, even in this.

But Emerson loved her father. And she loved the winery.

And as for romantic love…

Well, she'd never been in love. It was a hypothetical. But all these other loves were not. And as far as sex and passion went…

She hadn't slept with Donovan yet. But she'd been with two other men. One boyfriend in college, one out of college. And it just hadn't been anything worth upending her life over.

She and Donovan shared goals and values. Surely they could mesh those things together and create a life.

Why not marry for the sake of the vineyard? To make her father happy?

Why not?

Emerson sighed and surveyed the room.

Everything was beautiful. Of course it was. The party was set in her family's gorgeous mountaintop tasting room, the view of the vineyards stretching out below, illuminated by the full moon.

Emerson walked out onto the balcony. There were a few people out there, on the far end, but they didn't approach her. Keeping people at a distance was one of her gifts. With one smile she could attract everyone in the room if she chose. But she could also affect a blank face that invited no conversation at all.

She looked out over the vineyards and sighed yet again.

"What are you doing out here?"

A smile tugged at the corner of Emerson's mouth. Because of course, she could keep everyone but her baby sister Cricket from speaking to her when she didn't want to be spoken to. Cricket basically did what she wanted.

"I just needed some fresh air. What are *you* doing here? Weren't you carded at the door?"

"I'm twenty-one, thank you," Cricket sniffed, looking…well, not twenty-one, at least not to Emerson.

Emerson smirked. "Oh. How could I forget?"

Truly, she *couldn't* forget, as she had thrown an absolutely spectacular party for Cricket, which had made Cricket look wide-eyed and uncomfortable, particularly in the fitted dress Emerson had chosen for her. Cricket did not enjoy being the center of attention.

Emerson *did* like it. But only on her terms.

Cricket looked mildly incensed in the moonlight. "I didn't come out here to be teased."

"I'm sorry," Emerson responded, sincere because she didn't want to hurt her sister. She only wanted to mildly goad her, because Cricket was incredibly goadable.

Emerson looked out across the vast expanse of fields

and frowned when she saw a figure moving among the vines.

It was a man. She could tell even from the balcony that he had a lean, rangy body, and the long strides of a man who was quite tall.

"Who's that?" she asked.

"I don't know," Cricket said, peering down below. "Should I get Dad?"

"No," Emerson said. "I can go down."

She knew exactly who was supposed to be at the party, and who wasn't.

And if this man was one of the Coopers from Cowboy Wines, then she would have reason to feel concerned that he was down there sniffing around to get trade secrets.

Not that their top rival had ever stooped to that kind of espionage before, but she didn't trust anyone. Not really.

Wine-making was a competitive industry, and it was only becoming more so.

Emerson's sister Wren always became livid at the mere mention of the Cooper name, and was constantly muttering about all manner of dirty tricks they would employ to get ahead. So really, anything was possible.

"I'll just run down and check it out."

"You're going to go down and investigate by yourself?"

"I'm fine." Emerson waved a hand. "I have a cell phone, and the place is heavily populated right now. I don't think I'm going to have any issues."

"Emerson..."

Emerson slipped back inside, and out a side door, moving quickly down the stairs, not listening to her sister at all. She didn't know why, but she felt compelled to see who the man was for herself.

Maybe because his arrival was the first truly interesting thing to happen all evening. She went in the direction where she'd last seen the figure, stepping out of the golden pool of light spilling from the party and into the grapevines. The moonlight illuminated her steps, though it was pale and left her hands looking waxen.

She rounded one row of grapevines into the next, then stopped, frozen.

She had known he was tall, even from a distance. But he was…very tall. And broad.

Broad shoulders, broad chest. He was wearing a cowboy hat, which seemed ridiculous at night, because it wasn't keeping the sun off him. He had on a tight black T-shirt and a pair of jeans.

And he was not a Cooper.

She had never seen the man before in her life. He saw her and stopped walking. He lifted his head up, and the moonlight caught his features. His face was sculpted, beautiful. So much so that it immobilized her. That square jaw was visible in even this dim light.

"I… Have you lost your way?" she asked. "The party is that way. Though… I'm fairly certain you're not on the guest list."

"I wasn't invited to any party," he said, his voice rough and raspy, made for sin.

Made for sin?

She didn't know where such a thought had come from.

Except, it was easy to imagine that voice saying all kinds of sinful things, and she couldn't credit why.

"Then… Forgive me, but what are you doing here?"

"I work here," he said. "I'm the new ranch hand."

* * *

Damn if she wasn't Little Red Riding Hood delivered right to the Big Bad Wolf.

Except, she wasn't wearing a scarlet cloak. It was a scarlet dress that clung to her generous curves like wrapping paper around a tempting present.

Her dark hair was lined silver by the moonbeams and tumbling around naked shoulders.

He could picture her in his bed, just like that. Naked and rumpled in the sheets, that hair spread everywhere.

It was a shame he wasn't here for pleasure.

He was here for revenge.

And if he had guessed correctly based on what he knew about the Maxfield family, this was Emerson Maxfield. Who often had her beautiful face splashed across magazine covers for food and wine features, and who had become something of an It Girl for clothing brands as well. She was gorgeous, recognizable… and engaged.

But none of that would have deterred him, if he really wanted her.

What the hell did he care if a man had put a ring on a woman's finger? In his opinion, if an engaged or married woman was looking elsewhere, then the man who'd put the ring on her finger should've done a better job of keeping her satisfied.

If Holden could seduce a woman, then the bastard he seduced her away from deserved it.

Indiscretion didn't cause him any concern.

But there were a whole lot of women and a whole lot of ways for him to get laid, and he wasn't about to sully himself inside a Maxfield.

No matter how gorgeous.

"I didn't realize my father had hired someone new," she said.

It was funny, given what he knew about her family, the way that she talked like a little private school princess. But he knew she'd gone to elite schools on the East Coast, coming back home to Oregon for summer vacations, at least when her family wasn't jet-setting off somewhere else.

They were the wealthiest family in Logan County, with a wine label that competed on the world stage.

Her father, James Maxfield, was a world-class visionary, a world-class winemaker…and a world-class bastard.

Holden had few morals, but there were some scruples he held dear. At the very top of that list was that when he was with a woman, there was no coercion involved. And he would never leave one hopeless, blackmailed and depressed. No.

But James Maxfield had no such moral code.

And, sadly for James, when it came to dealing out justice to men who had harmed someone Holden cared about very much, he didn't have a limit on how far he was willing to go. He wondered what Emerson would think if she knew what her father had done to a woman who was barely her age.

What he'd done to Holden's younger sister.

But then, Emerson probably wouldn't care at all.

He couldn't see how she would *not* know the way her father behaved, given that the whole family seemed to run the enterprise together.

He had a feeling the Maxfield children looked the other way, as did James's wife. All of them ignoring his bad behavior so they could continue to have access to his bank account.

"I just got here today," he said. "Staying in one of the cabins on the property."

There was staff lodging, which he had found quaint as hell.

Holden had worked his way up from nothing, though his success in real estate development was not anywhere near as splashed over the media as the Maxfield's success was. Which, in the end, was what allowed him to engage in this revenge mission, this quest to destroy the life and reputation of James Maxfield.

And the really wonderful thing was, James wouldn't even see it coming.

Because he wouldn't believe a man of such low status could possibly bring him down. He would overlook Holden. Because James would believe that Holden was nothing more than a hired hand, a lackey.

James would have no idea that Holden was a man with a massive spread of land in the eastern part of the state, in Jackson Creek.

Because James Maxfield thought of no one but himself. He didn't think anyone was as smart as he was, didn't think anyone was anywhere near as important.

And that pride would be his downfall in the end.

Holden would make sure of it.

"Oh," she said. She met his eyes and bit her lip.

The little vixen was flirting with him.

"Aren't you meant to be in there hosting the party?"

She lifted a shoulder. "I guess so." She didn't seem at all surprised that he recognized who she was. But then, he imagined Emerson was used to being recognized.

"People will probably be noticing that you're gone."

"I suppose they might be," she said. She wrinkled her nose. "Between you and me, I'm getting a little tired of these things."

"Parties with free food and drinks? How could you get tired of that?"

She lifted one elegant shoulder. "I suppose when the drinks are always free, you lose track of why they're special."

"I wouldn't know anything about that."

He'd worked for every damn thing he had.

"Oh. Of course. Sorry. That's an incredibly privileged thing to say."

"Well, if you're who I think you are, you're incredibly privileged. Why wouldn't you feel that way?"

"Just because it's true in my life doesn't mean it's not a tacky thing to say."

"Well, I can think of several tacky things to say right back that might make you feel a little bit better."

She laughed. "Try me."

"If you're not careful, Little Red, wandering through the wilderness like this, a Big Bad Wolf might gobble you up."

It was an incredibly obvious and overtly sexual thing to say. And the little princess, with her engagement ring glittering on her left hand, should have drawn up in full umbrage.

But she didn't. Instead, her body seemed to melt slightly, and she looked away. "Was that supposed to be tacky?"

"It was," he said.

"I guess it didn't feel that way to me."

"You should head back to that party," he said.

"Why? Am I in danger out here?"

"Depends on what you consider danger."

There was nothing wrong—he told himself—with building a rapport with her. In fact, it would be a damned useful thing in many ways.

“Possibly talking to strange men in vineyards.”

“Depends on whether or not you consider me strange.”

“I don’t know you well enough to have that figured out yet.” A crackle of interest moved over his skin, and he didn’t know what the hell was wrong with him that the first time he’d felt anything remotely like interest in a hell of a long time was happening now.

With Emerson Maxfield.

But she was the one who took a step back. She was the one whose eyes widened in fear, and he had to wonder if his hatred for the blood that ran through her veins was as evident to her as it was to him.

“I have to go,” she said. “I’m… The party.”

“Yes, ma’am,” he said.

He took a step toward her, almost without thinking.

And then she retreated, as quickly as she could on those impractical stiletto heels.

“You better run, Little Red,” he said under his breath.

And then he rocked back on his heels, surveying the grapevines and the house up on the hill. “The Big Bad Wolf is going to gobble all of this up.”

Two

"Emerson," her dad said. "I have a job for you."

Emerson was tired and feeling off balance after last night. She had done something that was so out of character she still couldn't figure out what she'd been thinking.

She had left the party, left her post. She had chased after a strange man out in the grapevines. And then…

He had reminded her of a wolf. She'd gone to a wolf sanctuary once when she was in high school, and she'd been mesmerized by the powerful pack alpha. So beautiful. So much leashed strength.

She'd been afraid. But utterly fascinated all at once. Unable to look away…

He worked on the property.

And that should have been a red light to her all the way down. An absolute *stop, don't go any further.* If the diamond on her finger couldn't serve as that warning, then his status as an employee should have.

But she had felt drawn to him. And then he'd taken a step toward her. And it was like suddenly the correct instincts had woken up inside of her and she had run away.

But she didn't know why it had taken that long for her to run. What was wrong with her?

"A job," she said blankly, in response to her father.

"I've been watching the profits of Grassroots Winery down in town," he said. "They're really building a name for themselves as a destination. Not just a brand that people drink when they're out, but a place people want to visit. We've proved this is an incredibly successful location for weddings and other large events. The party you threw last night was superb."

Emerson basked in the praise. But only for a moment. Because if there was praise, then a request couldn't be far behind.

"One of the things they're offering is rides through the vineyard on horseback. They're also doing sort of a rustic partnership with the neighboring dude ranch, which sounds more like the bastion of Cowboy Wines. Nothing I want to get involved with. We don't want to lower the value of our brand by associating with anything down-market. But horse rides through the vineyards, picnics, things like that—I think those could be profitable."

Emerson had met the owner of Grassroots Winery, Lindy Dodge, on a couple of occasions, and she liked the other woman quite a lot. Emerson had a moment of compunction about stepping on what had clearly been Lindy's idea, but then dismissed it.

It wasn't uncommon at all for similar companies to try comparable ventures. They often borrowed from each other, and given the number of wineries beginning to crop up in the area, it was inevitable there would be crossover.

Plus, to the best of her ability Emerson tried not to look at the others as competition. They were creating a robust wine trail that was a draw in and of itself.

Tourists could visit several wineries when they came to Logan County, traveling from Copper Ridge through Gold Valley and up into the surrounding mountains. That the area was a destination for wine enthusiasts was good for everyone.

The only vineyard that Maxfield Vineyards really viewed as competition was Cowboy Wines. Which Emerson thought was funny in a way, since their brand could not be more disparate from Maxfield's if they tried.

And she suspected they *did* try.

She also suspected there was something darker at the root of the rivalry, but if so, James never said.

And neither had Wren, the middle sister. Wren's role in the company often saw her clashing with Creed Cooper, who worked in the same capacity for his family winery, and Wren hated him with every fiber of her being. Loudly and often.

"So what is the new venture exactly?" Emerson asked.

"I just told you. Trail rides and picnics, but we need a way to make it feel like a Maxfield endeavor. And that, I give over to you."

"That sounds like it would be more Wren's thing." Wren was responsible for events at the winery, while Emerson dealt more globally with brand representation.

"I think ultimately this will be about the way you influence people. I want you to find the best routes, the prime views for the trips, take some photos, put it up on your social media. Use the appropriate pound signs."

"It's a… It's a hashtag."

"I'm not interested in learning what it is, Emerson. That's why I have you."

"Okay. I can do that."

She did have a massive online reach, and she could see how she might position some photos, which would garner media interest, and possibly generate a story in *Sip and Savor* magazine. And really, it would benefit the entire area. The more that Maxfield Vineyards—with its vast reach in the world of wine—brought people into the area, the more the other vineyards benefited too.

"That sounds good to me," she said.

"That's why I hired a manager for the ranching portion of the facility. I need him to oversee some new construction, because if we're going to have guests in the stables, everything needs to be updated. I need for him to oversee the acquisition of a few horses. Plus, the rides, etc."

"Oh," she said. "This…person. This man you hired. He's…tall?"

James shrugged. "I don't know. I didn't consider his height. Did you?"

"No," she said, her face flaming. She felt like a child with her hand caught in the cookie jar. "I just… I think I saw him last night. Down in the vineyard. I left the party to check and see what was happening." Total honesty with her father came as second nature to her.

She tried to be good. She tried to be the daughter he had raised her to be, always.

"You left the party?"

"Everything was well in hand. I left Cricket in charge."

That might be a stretch. But while she was as honest with her father as possible, she tended to leave out some things like…her feelings. And this would be one of those times.

"I met him briefly, then I went back to the house. That's all. He told me he worked on the property."

"You have to be careful," her father said. "You don't want any photographs taken of you alone with a man who's not Donovan. You don't need anything to compromise your engagement."

Sometimes she wondered if her father realized they didn't live in the Victorian era.

"Nothing is going to compromise my engagement to Donovan."

"I'm glad you're certain about it."

She was, in spite of her occasional doubts. Her father might not understand that times had changed, but she did. She felt certain Donovan was carrying on with other women in the absence of a physical relationship with her. Why would she assume anything else? He was a man, after all.

She knew why her father was so invested in her marriage to Donovan. As part of his planned retirement, her father was giving ownership stakes in the winery to each of his daughters' husbands.

He felt Donovan would be an asset to the winery, and Emerson agreed. But she wasn't sure how that fit into a marriage.

Clearly, Donovan didn't much care about how that fit into a marriage either.

And she doubted he would be able to muster up any jealousy over her behavior.

"Image," her father said, bringing her back to the

moment. "It isn't what you do that matters, Emerson, it's what the world *thinks* you're doing."

There was something about the way her father said it, so smooth and cold, that made her feel chilled. It shouldn't chill her, because she agreed that image was important in their business.

Still, it *did* chill her.

Emerson shifted. "Right. Well, no worries there. Image is my expertise."

"It's all about the brand," he said.

"I tell you that," she said.

"And you've done it well."

"Thank you," she said, nearly flushed with pleasure. Compliments from James Maxfield were rare, and she clung to them when she got them.

"You should head down to the stables. He'll be waiting for you."

And if that made her stomach tighten, she ignored the sensation. She had a job to do. And that job had nothing to do with how tall the new ranch manager was.

She was as pretty in the ridiculously trendy outfit she was wearing now as she'd been in that red dress.

She was wearing high-cut black pants that went up past her belly button, loose fitted through the leg, with a cuff around the ankle, paired with a matching black top that was cropped to just beneath her breasts and showed a wedge of stomach. Her dark hair was in a high bun, and she was wearing the same red lipstick she'd had on the night before, along with round sunglasses that covered her eyes.

He wished he could see her eyes. And as she approached, she pushed the glasses up to the top of her head.

He hadn't been prepared for how beautiful she was.

He thought he'd seen her beauty in the moonlight, thought he'd seen it in photographs, but they didn't do her justice. He'd been convinced that the blue of her eyes was accomplished with some kind of a filter. But it was clear to him now, out in the bright sun with the green mountains surrounding them, and her eyes reflecting that particular blue from the center of the sky, that if anything, her eyes had been downplayed in those photographs.

"Good morning," she said.

"Good morning to you too. I take it you spoke with your father?"

It took all of his self-control for that word to come out smoothly.

"Yes," she said. "I did."

"And what do you think of his proposition?"

In Holden's opinion, it was a good one. And when he was through ruining James and sinking his brand, Holden might well buy the entire property and continue making wine himself. He was good at selling things, making money. He could make more money here.

"It's good. I think a few well-placed selfies will drum up interest."

"You're probably right. Though, I can't say I'm real up on selfies."

That was a lie. His younger sister was a pretty powerful influencer. A model, who had met James Maxfield at one of the parties that had brought their type together. He was angry at himself for the part his own money had played in all of this.

Because Soraya had been innocent. A sweet girl from a small town who had been catapulted into a lifestyle she hadn't been prepared to handle.

Holden could relate well enough.

He certainly hadn't known how to handle money in the beginning.

But he'd been helping his family dig out of the hole they'd found themselves in. The first thing he'd done was buy his mother a house. Up on a hill, fancy and safe from the men who had used her all throughout Holden's childhood.

And his sweet, younger half sister… She'd tumbled headfirst into fame. She was beautiful, that much had always been apparent, but she had that lean, hungry kind of beauty, honed by years of poverty, her backstory lending even more interest to her sharp cheekbones and unerring sense of style.

She had millions of people following her, waiting to see her next picture. Waiting to see which party she would attend.

And she attended the wrong one when she met James Maxfield.

He'd pounced on her before Holden could say "daddy issues." And James had left her devastated. Holden would never forget having to admit his sister for a psychiatric hold. Soraya's suicide attempt, the miscarriage… The devastation.

It was burned in him.

Along with the reality that his money hadn't protected her. His money had opened her up to this.

Now all that was left was revenge, because he couldn't make it right. He couldn't take her pain away.

But he could take everything away from the Maxfield family.

And that was what he intended to do.

"I don't think we've officially met," she said. She stuck her hand out—the one that didn't have the ring on it. That one angled at her side, the gem sparkling in the sunlight. "I'm Emerson Maxfield."

"Holden Brown," he said, extending his own hand.

If James Maxfield weren't a raging narcissist, Holden might have worried about using his real first name.

But he doubted the older man would ever connect the younger model he'd used for a couple of months and then discarded with Holden. Why would he? James probably barely remembered Soraya's first name, much less any of her family connections. Holden himself wasn't famous. And that was how he liked it. He'd always thought it would be handy to have anonymity. He hadn't imagined it would be for reasons of revenge.

He closed his hand around hers. It was soft, desperately so. The hand of a woman who had never done hard labor in her life, and something in him suddenly felt desperate to make this little princess do some down and dirty work.

Preferably on his body.

He pulled his hand away.

"It's nice to meet you, Holden," she said.

"Nice to meet you too." He bit the pleasantry off at the end, because anything more and he might make a mistake.

"I have some routes in mind for this new venture. Let's go for a ride."

Three

Let's go for a ride was not sexual.

Not in the context of the ranch. Not to a woman who was so used to being exposed to horses. As she was.

Except, she kept replaying that line over and over in her head. Kept imagining herself saying it to him.

Let's go for a ride.

And then she would imagine herself saying it to him in bed.

She had never, ever felt like this in her entire life.

Her first time had been fine. Painless, which was nice, she supposed, but not exactly exciting.

It had been with her boyfriend at the time, who she'd known very well, and who had been extraordinarily careful and considerate.

Though, he'd cared more about keeping her comfortable than keeping her impassioned. But they had been young. So that seemed fair enough.

Her boyfriend after that had been smooth, urbane and fascinating to her. A world traveler before she had done any traveling of her own. She had enjoyed conversations with him, but she hadn't been consumed by passion or lust or anything like that.

She had just sort of thought she was that way. And she was fine with it. She had a lot of excitement in her life. She wasn't hurting for lack of passion.

But Holden made her feel like she might actually be missing something.

Like there was a part of herself that had been dormant for a very long time.

Right. You've been in the man's presence for...a combined total of forty minutes.

Well, that made an even stronger case for the idea of exploring the thing between them. Because in that combined forty minutes, she had imagined him naked at least six times.

Had thought about closing the distance between them and kissing him on the mouth no less than seven times.

And that was insane.

He was working on the ranch, working for her father. Working for her, in essence, as she was part of the winery and had a stake in the business.

And somehow, that aroused her even more.

A man like her fiancé, Donovan, knew a whole lot about the world.

He knew advertising, and there was a heck of a lot of human psychology involved in that. And it was interesting.

But she had a feeling that a man like Holden could teach her about her own body, and that was more than interesting. It was a strange and intoxicating thought.

Also, totally unrealistic and nothing you're going to act on.

No, she thought as she mounted her horse, and the two of them began riding along a trail that she wanted to investigate as a route for the new venture. She would never give in to this just for the sake of exploring her sensuality. For a whole list of reasons.

So you're just going to marry Donovan and wonder what this could have been like?

Sink into the mediocre sex life that the lack of attraction between you promises. Never know what you're missing.

Well, the thing about fantasies was they were only fantasies.

And the thing about sex with a stranger—per a great many of her friends who'd had sex with strangers—was that the men involved rarely lived up to the fantasy. Because they had no reason to make anything good for a woman they didn't really know.

They were too focused on making it good for themselves. And men always won in those games. Emerson knew her way around her own body, knew how to find release when she needed it. But she'd yet to find a man who could please her in the same way, and when she was intimate with someone, she couldn't ever quite let go… There were just too many things to think about, and her brain was always consumed.

It wouldn't be different with Holden. No matter how hot he was.

And blowing up all her inhibitions over an experience that was bound to be a letdown was something Emerson simply wasn't going to risk.

So there.

She turned her thoughts away from the illicit and forced them onto the beauty around her.

Her family's estate had been her favorite place in the world since she was a child. But of course, when she was younger, that preference had been a hollow kind of favoritism, because she didn't have a wide array of experiences or places to compare it to.

She did now. She'd been all over the world, had stayed in some of the most amazing hotels, had enjoyed food in the most glamorous locales. And while she loved to travel, she couldn't imagine a time when she wouldn't call Maxfield Vineyards home.

From the elegant spirals of the vines around the wooden trellises, all in neat rows spreading over vast acres, to the manicured green lawns, to the farther reaches where it grew wild, the majestic beauty of the wilderness so big and awe-inspiring, making her feel appropriately small and insignificant when the occasion required.

"Can I ask you a question?" His voice was deep and thick, like honey, and it made Emerson feel like she was on the verge of a sugar high.

She'd never felt anything like this before.

This, she supposed, was chemistry. And she couldn't for the life of her figure out why it would suddenly be *this* man who inspired it. She had met so many men who weren't so far outside the sphere of what she should find attractive. She'd met them at parties all around the world. None of those men—including the one her father wanted her to be engaged to—had managed to elicit this kind of response in her.

And yet… Holden did it effortlessly.

"Ask away," she said, resolutely fixing her focus on

the scene around them. Anything to keep from fixating on him.

"Why the hell did you wear *that* knowing we were going out riding?"

She blinked. Then she turned and looked at him. "What's wrong with my outfit?"

"I have never seen anyone get on a horse in something so impractical."

"Oh, come now. Surely you've seen period pieces where the woman is in a giant dress riding sidesaddle."

"Yes," he said. "But you have other options."

"It has to be photographable," she said.

"And you couldn't do some sexy cowgirl thing?"

Considering he was playing the part of sexy cowboy—in his tight black T-shirt and black cowboy hat—she suddenly wished she were playing the part of sexy cowgirl. Maybe with a plaid top knotted just beneath her breasts, some short shorts and cowgirl boots. Maybe, if she were in an outfit like that, she would feel suitably bold enough to ask him for a literal roll in the hay.

You've lost your mind.

"That isn't exactly my aesthetic."

"Your aesthetic is… *I Dream of Jeannie* in Mourning?"

She laughed. "I hadn't thought about it that way. But sure. *I Dream of Jeannie* in Mourning sounds about right. In fact, I think I might go ahead and label the outfit that when I post pics."

"Whatever works," he said.

His comment was funny. And okay, maybe the fact that he'd been clever a couple of times in her presence was bestowing the label of *funny* on him too early. But it made her feel a little bit better about her wayward hormones that he wasn't just beautiful, that he was fascinating as well.

"So today's ride isn't just a scouting mission for you," he said. "If you're worried about your aesthetic."

"No," she said. "I want to start generating interest in this idea. You know, pictures of me on the horse. In fact, hang on a second." She stopped, maneuvering her mount, turning so she was facing Holden, with the brilliant backdrop of the trail and the mountains behind them. Then she flipped her phone front facing and raised it up in the air, tilting it downward and grinning as she hit the button. She looked at the result, frowned, and then did it again. The second one would be fine once she put some filters on it.

"What was that?"

She maneuvered her horse back around in the other direction, stuffed her phone in her pocket and carried on.

"It was me getting a photograph," she said. "One that I can post. 'Something new and exciting is coming to the Maxfield label.'"

"Are you really going to put it like that?"

"Yes. I mean, eventually we'll do official press releases and other forms of media, but the way you use social media advertisements is a little different. I personally am part of that online brand. And my lifestyle—including my clothes—is part of what makes people interested in the vineyard."

"Right," he said.

"People want to be jealous," she said. "If they didn't, they wouldn't spend hours scrolling through photos of other people's lives. Or of houses they'll never be able to live in. Exotic locations they'll never be able to go. A little envy, that bit of aspiration, it drives some people."

"Do you really believe that?"

"Yes. I think the success of my portion of the family empire suggests I know what I'm talking about."

He didn't say anything for a long moment. "You know, I suppose you're right. People choose to indulge in that feeling, but when you really don't have anything, it's not fun to see all that stuff you'll never have. It cuts deep. It creates a hunger, rather than enjoyment. It can drive some people to the edge of destruction."

There was something about the way he said it that sent a ripple of disquiet through her. Because his words didn't sound hypothetical.

"That's never my goal," she said. "And I can't control who consumes the media I put out there. At a certain point, people have to know themselves, don't they?"

"True enough," he said. "But some people don't. And it's worse when there's another person involved who sees weakness in them even when they don't see it themselves. Someone who exploits that weakness. Plenty of sad, hungry girls have been lost along that envious road, when they took the wrong hand desperate for a hand up into satisfaction."

"Well, I'm not selling wild parties," she said. "I'm selling an afternoon ride at a family winery, and a trip here is not that out of reach for most people. That's the thing. There's all this wild aspirational stuff out there online, and the vineyard is just a little more accessible. That's what makes it advertising and not luxury porn."

"I see. Create a desire so big it can never be filled, and then offer a winery as the consolation prize."

"If the rest of our culture supports that, it's hardly my fault."

"Have you ever had to want for anything in your entire life, Emerson?" The question was asked innocuously enough, but the way he asked it, in that dark, rough voice, made it buzz over her skin, crackling like electricity as it moved through her. "Or have you always been given everything you could ever desire?"

"I've wanted things," she said, maybe too quickly. Too defensively.

"What?" he pressed.

She desperately went through the catalog of her life, trying to come up with a moment when she had been denied something that she had wanted in a material sense. And there was only one word that burned in her brain.

You.

Yes, that was what she would say. *I want you, and I can't have you. Because I'm engaged to a man who's not interested in kissing me, much less getting into bed with me. And I'm no more interested in doing that with him.*

But I can't break off the engagement no matter how much I want to because I so desperately need...

"Approval," she said. "That's...that's something I want."

Her stomach twisted, and she kept her eyes fixed ahead, because she didn't know why she had let the word escape out loud. She should have said nothing.

He wasn't interested in hearing about her emotional issues.

"From your father?" he asked.

"No," she said. "I have his approval. My mother, on the other hand..."

"You're famous, successful, beautiful. And you don't have your mother's approval?"

"Yeah, shockingly, my mother's goal for me wasn't to take pictures of myself and put them up on the internet."

"Unless you have a secret stash of pictures, I don't see how your mother could disapprove of these sorts of photographs. Unless, of course, it's your pants. Which I do think are questionable."

"These are *wonderful* pants. And actually deceptively practical. Because they allow me to sit on the horse comfortably. Whatever you might think."

"What doesn't your mother approve of?"

"She wanted me to do something more. Something that was my own. She doesn't want me just running publicity for the family business. But I like it. I enjoy what I do, I enjoy this brand. Representing it is easy for me, because I care about it. I went to school for marketing, close to home. She felt like it was…limiting my potential."

He chuckled. "I'm sorry. Your mother felt like you limited your potential by going to get a degree in marketing and then going on to be an ambassador for a successful brand."

"Yes," she said.

She could still remember the brittle irritation in her mother's voice when she had told her about the engagement to Donovan.

"So you're marrying a man more successful in advertising in the broader world even though you could have done that."

"You're married to a successful man."

"I was never given the opportunities that you were given. You don't have to hide behind a husband's shadow. You could've done more."

"Yeah, that's about the size of it," she said. "Look, my mother is brilliant. And scrappy. And I respect her. But she's never going to be overly impressed with me. As far as she's concerned, I haven't worked a day in my life for anything, and I took the path of least resistance into this version of success."

"What does she think of your sisters?"

"Well, Wren works for the winery too, but the only thing that annoys my mother more than her daughters taking a free pass is the Cooper family, and since Wren makes it her life's work to go toe-to-toe with them, my mother isn't quite as irritated with everything Wren does. And Cricket… I don't know that anyone knows what Cricket wants."

Poor Cricket was a later addition to the family. Eight years younger than Emerson, and six years younger than Wren. Their parents hadn't planned on having another child, and they especially hadn't planned on one like Cricket, who didn't seem to have inherited the need to please…well, anyone.

Cricket had run wild over the winery, raised more by the staff than by their mother or father.

Sometimes Emerson envied Cricket and the independence she seemed to have found before turning twenty-one, when Emerson couldn't quite capture independence even at twenty-nine.

"Sounds to me like your mother is pretty difficult to please."

"Impossible," she agreed.

But her father wasn't. He was proud of her. She was doing exactly what he wanted her to do. And she would keep on doing it.

The trail ended in a grassy clearing on the side of the mountain, overlooking the valley below. The wineries rolled on for miles, and the little redbrick town of Gold Valley was all the way at the bottom.

"Yes," she said. "This is perfect." She got down off the horse, snapped another few pictures with herself in them and the view in the background. And then a sudden inspiration took hold, and she whipped around quickly, capturing the blurred outline of Holden, on his horse with his cowboy hat, behind her.

He frowned, dismounting the horse, and she looked into the phone screen, keeping her eyes on him, and took another shot. He was mostly a silhouette, but it was clear that he was a good-looking, well-built man in a cowboy hat.

"Now, *there's* an ad," she said.

"What're you doing?"

He sounded angry. Not amused at all.

"I just thought it would be good to get you in the background. A full-on Western fantasy."

"You said that wasn't the aesthetic."

"It's not mine. Just because a girl doesn't want to wear cutoff shorts doesn't mean she's not interested in looking at a cowboy."

"You can't post that," he said, his voice hard like granite.

She turned to face him. "Why not?"

"Because I don't want to be on your bullshit website."

"It's not a website. It's... Never mind. Are you... You're not, like, fleeing from the law or something, are you?"

"No," he said. "I'm not."

"Then why won't you let me post your picture? It's not like you can really see you."

"I'm not interested in that stuff."

"Well, that stuff is my entire life's work." She turned her focus to the scenery around them and pretended to be interested in taking a few random pictures that were not of him.

"Some website that isn't going to exist in a couple of years is not your life's work. Your life's work might be figuring out how to sell things to people, advertising, marketing. Whatever you want to call it. But the *how* of it is going to change, and it's going to keep on changing. What you've done is figure out how to understand the way people discover things right now. But it will change. And you'll figure that out too. These pictures are not your life's work."

It was an impassioned speech, and one she almost felt certain he'd given before, though she couldn't quite figure out why he would have, or to who.

"That's nice," she said. "But I don't need a pep talk. I wasn't belittling myself. I won't post the pictures. Though, I think they would have caused a lot of excitement."

"I'm not going to be anyone's trail guide. So there's no point using me."

"You're not even *my* trail guide, not really." She turned to face him, and found he was much closer than she had thought. All the breath was sucked from her body. He was so big and broad, imposing.

There was an intensity about him that should repel her, but instead it fascinated her.

The air was warm, and she was a little bit sweaty, and that made her wonder if *he* was sweaty, and something about that thought made her want to press her face against his chest and smell his skin.

"Have you ever gone without something?"

She didn't know why she'd asked him that, except that maybe it was the only thing keeping her from actually giving in to her fantasy and pressing her face against his body.

"I don't really think that's any of your business."

"Why not? I just downloaded all of my family issues onto you, and I'm not even sure why. Except that you asked. And I don't think anyone else has ever asked. So… It's just you and me out here."

"And your phone. Which is your link to the outside world on a scale that I can barely understand."

Somehow, that rang false.

"I don't have service," she said. "And anyway, my phone is going back in my pocket." She slipped it into the silky pocket of her black pants.

He looked at her, his dark eyes moving over her body, and she knew he was deliberately taking his time examining her curves. Knew that his gaze was deliberately sexual.

And she didn't feel like she could be trusted with that kind of knowledge, because something deep inside her was dancing around the edge of being bold. That one little piece of her that felt repressed, that had felt bored at the party last night…

That one little piece of her wanted this.

"A few things," he said slowly. And his words were deliberate too.

Without thinking, she sucked her lip between her teeth and bit down on it, then swiped her tongue over the stinging surface to soothe it.

And the intensity in his eyes leaped higher.

She couldn't pretend she didn't know what she'd done. She'd deliberately drawn his focus to her mouth.

Now, she might have done it deliberately, but she didn't know what she wanted out of it.

Well, she did. But she couldn't want *that*. She couldn't. Not when…

Suddenly, he reached out, grabbing her chin between his thumb and forefinger. "I don't know how the boys who run around in your world play, Emerson. But I'm not a man who scrolls through photos and wishes he could touch something. If I want something, I take it. So if I were you… I wouldn't go around teasing."

She stuttered, "I… I… I…" and stumbled backward. She nearly tripped down onto the grass, onto her butt, but he reached out, looping his strong arm around her waist and pulling her upright. The breath whooshed from her lungs, and she found herself pressed hard against his solid body. She put her hand gingerly on his chest. Yeah. He was a little bit sweaty.

And damned if it wasn't sexy.

She racked her brain, trying to come up with something witty to say, something to defuse the situation, but she couldn't think. Her heart was thundering fast, and there was an echoing pulse down in the center of her thighs making it impossible for her to breathe. Impossible for her to think. She felt like she was having an out-of-body experience, or a wild fantasy that was surely happening in her head only, and not in reality.

But his body was hot and hard underneath her hand, and there was a point at which she really couldn't pretend she wasn't touching an actual man.

Because her fingers burned. Because her body burned. Because everything burned.

And she couldn't think of a single word to say, which wasn't like her, but usually she wasn't affected by men.

They liked her. They liked to flirt and talk with her, and since becoming engaged, they'd only liked it even more. Seeing her as a bit of a challenge, and it didn't cost her anything to play into that a little bit. Because she was never tempted to do anything. Because she was never affected. Because it was only ever a conversation and nothing more.

But this felt like more.

The air was thick with *more*, and she couldn't figure out why him, why now.

His lips curved up into a half smile, and suddenly, in a brief flash, she saw it.

Sure, his sculpted face and body were part of it. But he was…an outlaw.

Everything she wasn't.

He was a man who didn't care at all what anyone thought. It was visible in every part of him. In the laconic grace with which he moved, the easy way he smiled, the slow honeyed timbre of his voice.

Yes.

He was a man without a cell phone.

A man who wasn't tied or tethered to anything. Who didn't have comments to respond to at two in the morning that kept him up at night, as he worried about not doing it fast enough, about doing something to damage the very public image she had cultivated—not just for herself—but for her father's entire industry.

A man who didn't care if he fell short of the expectations of a parent, at least he didn't seem like he would.

Looking at him in all his rough glory, the way that he blended into the terrain, she felt like a smooth shiny shell with nothing but a sad, listless urchin curled up inside, who was nothing like the facade that she presented.

He was the real deal.

He was like that mountain behind him. Strong and firm and steady. Unmovable.

It made her want a taste.

A taste of him.

A taste of freedom.

She found herself moving forward, but he took a step back.

"Come on now, princess," he said, grabbing hold of

her left hand and raising it up, so that her ring caught the sunlight. "You don't want to be doing that."

Horror rolled over her and she stepped away.

"I don't… Nothing."

He chuckled. "Something."

"I… My fiancé and I have an understanding," she said. And she made a mental note to actually check with Donovan to see if they did. Because she suspected they might, given that they had never touched each other. And she could hardly imagine that Donovan had been celibate for the past two years.

You have been.

Yeah, she needed to check on the Donovan thing.

"Do you now?"

"Yes," she lied.

"Well, I have an understanding with your father that I'm in his employment. And I would sure hate to take advantage of that."

"I'm a grown woman," she said.

"Yeah, what do you suppose your daddy would think if he found that you were fucking the help?"

Heat washed over her, her scalp prickling.

"I don't keep my father much informed about my sex life," she said.

"The problem is, you and me would be his business. I try to make my sex life no one's business but mine and the lady I'm naked with."

"Me nearly kissing you is not the same as me offering you sex. Your ego betrays you."

"And your blush betrays you, darlin'."

The entire interaction felt fraught and spiky, and Emerson didn't know how to proceed, which was as rare as her feeling at a loss for words. He was right. He worked for her father, and by extension, for the family, for her. But she didn't feel like she had the power here. Didn't feel like she had the control. She was the one with money, with the Maxfield family name, and he was just…a *ranch hand.*

So why did she feel so decidedly at a disadvantage?

"We'd better carry on," she said. "I have things to do."

"Pictures to post."

"But not of you," she said.

He shook his head once. "Not of me."

She got back on her horse, and he did the same. And this time he led the way back down the trail, and she was somewhat relieved. Because she didn't know what she would do if she had to bear the burden of knowing he was watching the back of her the whole way.

She would drive herself crazy thinking about how to hold her shoulders so that she didn't look like she knew that he was staring at her.

But then, maybe he wouldn't stare at her, and that was the thing. She would wonder either way. And she didn't particularly want to wonder.

And when she got back to her office, she tapped her fingers on the desk next to her phone, and did her very best to stop herself from texting Donovan.

Tap. *Don't.* Tap. *Don't.*

And then suddenly she picked up the phone and started a new message.

Are we exclusive?

There were no dots, no movement. She set the phone down and tried to look away. It pinged a few minutes later.

We are engaged.

That's not an answer.

We don't live in the same city.

She took a breath.

Have you slept with someone else?

She wasn't going to wait around with his back-and-forth nonsense. She wasn't interested in him sparing himself repercussions.

We don't live in the same city. So yes, I have.

And if I did?

Whatever you do before the wedding is your business.

She didn't respond, and his next text came in on the heels of the last.

Did you want to talk on the phone?

No.

K.

And that was it. Because they didn't love each other. She hadn't needed to text him, because nothing was going to happen with her and Holden.

And how do you feel about the fact that Donovan had slept with other people?

She wasn't sure.

Except she didn't feel much of anything.

Except now she had a get-out-of-jail-free card, and that was about the only way she could see it. That wasn't normal, was it? It wasn't normal for him to be okay with the fact that she had asked those questions. That she had made it clear she'd thought about sleeping with someone else.

And it wasn't normal for her to not be jealous when Donovan said he *had* slept with someone else.

But she wasn't jealous.

And his admission didn't dredge any deep feelings up to the surface either.

No, her reaction just underlined the fact that something was missing from their arrangement. Which she had known. Neither of them was under the impression they were in a real relationship. They had allowed themselves to be matched, but before this moment she had been sure feelings would grow in time, but they hadn't, and she and Donovan had ignored that.

But she couldn't...

Her father didn't ask much of her. And he gave her endless support. If she disappointed him...

Well, then she would be a failure all around, wouldn't she?

He's not choosing Wren's husband. He isn't choosing Cricket's.

Well, Wren would likely refuse. Emerson couldn't imagine her strong-headed sister giving in to that. And Cricket... Well, nobody could tame Cricket.

Her father hadn't asked them. He'd asked her. And she'd agreed, because that was who she was. She was the one who could be counted on for anything, and it was too late to stop being who she was now.

Texting Donovan had been insane, leaning in toward Holden had been even more insane. And she didn't have time for any of that behavior. She had a campaign to launch and she was going to do it. Because she knew who she was. She was not the kind of person who kissed men she barely knew, not the kind of person who engaged in physical-only flings, not the kind of person who crossed professional boundaries.

The problem was, Holden made her feel very, very *not* like herself. And that was the most concerning thing of all.

Four

Emerson was proving to be deeply problematic.

What he should do was go down to the local bar and find himself a woman to pick up. Because God knew he didn't need to be running around getting hard over his enemy's daughter. He had expected to be disgusted by everything the Maxfield family was. And indeed, when he had stood across from James Maxfield in the man's office while interviewing for this position, it had taken every ounce of Holden's willpower not to fly across the desk and strangle the man to death.

The thing was, death would be too easy an out for a man like him. Holden would rather give James the full experience of degradation in life before he consigned him to burning in hell for all eternity. Holden wanted to maximize the punishment.

Hell could wait.

And hell was no less than he deserved.

Holden had finally gotten what he'd come for.

It had come in the form of nondisclosure agreements he'd found in James's office. He'd paid attention to the code on the door when James had let him in for the interview, and all he'd had to do was wait for a time when the man was out and get back in there.

It fascinated Holden that everything was left unguarded, but it wasn't really a mystery.

This was James's office in his family home. Not a corporate environment. He trusted his family, and why wouldn't he? It was clear that Emerson had nothing but good feelings about her father. And Holden suspected everyone else in the household felt the same.

Except the women James had coerced into bed. Employees. All young. All dependent on him for a paycheck. But he'd sent them off with gag orders and payoffs.

And once Holden figured out exactly how to approach this, James would be finished.

But now there was the matter of Emerson.

Holden hadn't expected the attraction that had flared up immediately the first time he'd seen her not to let up.

And she was always…around. The problem with taking on a job as an opportunity to commit corporate espionage, and to find proof either of monetary malfeasance or of the relationship between James and Holden's sister, was that he had to actually *work* during the day.

That ate up a hell of a lot of his time. It also meant he was in close proximity to Emerson.

And speak of the devil, right as he finished mucking out a stall, she walked in wearing skintight tan breaches that molded to every dimple of her body.

"That's a different sort of riding getup," he said.

"I'm not taking selfies today," she said, a teasing gleam in her blue eyes that made his gut tight.

"Just going on a ride?"

"I needed to clear my head," she said.

She looked at him, seeming vaguely edgy.

"What is it?"

But he knew what it was. It was that attraction that he felt every time she was near. She felt it too, and that made it a damn sight worse.

"Nothing. I just… What is it that you normally do? Are you always a ranch hand? I mean, you must specialize in something, or my father wouldn't have hired you to help with the horses."

"I'm good with horses."

Most everything he'd said about himself since coming to the winery was a lie. But this, at least, was true. He had grown up working other people's ranches.

Now he happened to own one of his own, a good-sized spread, but he still did a portion of the labor. He liked working his own land. It was a gift, after so many years of working other people's.

If there was work to be given over to others, he preferred to farm out his office work, not the ranch work.

He'd found an affinity with animals early on, and that had continued. It had given him something to do, given him something to *be*.

He had been nothing but a poor boy from a poor family. He'd been a cowboy from birth. That connection with animals had gotten him his first job at a ranch, and that line of work had gotten him where he was today.

When one of his employers had died, he'd gifted Holden with a large plot of land. It wasn't his ranch, but totally dilapidated fields a few miles from the ranch he now owned.

He hadn't known what the hell to do with land so undeveloped at first, until he'd gone down to the county offices and found it could be divided. From there, he'd started working with a developer.

Building a subdivision had been an interesting project, because a part of him had hated the idea of turning a perfectly good stretch of land into houses. But then, another part of him had enjoyed the fact that new houses meant more people would experience the land he loved and the town he called home.

Making homes for families felt satisfying.

As a kid who had grown up without one at times, he didn't take for granted the effect four walls could have on someone's life.

And that had been a bargain he'd struck with the developer. That a couple of the homes were his to do with as he chose. They'd been gifted to homeless families going on ten years ago now. And each of the children had been given college scholarships, funded by his corporation now that he was more successful.

He'd done the same ever since, with every development he'd created. It wouldn't save the whole world, but it changed the lives of the individuals involved. And he knew well enough what kind of effect that change could have on a person.

He'd experienced it himself.

Cataloging everything good you've done in the past won't erase what you're doing now.

Maybe not. But he didn't much care. Yes, destroying the Maxfield empire would sweep Emerson right up in his revenge, which was another reason he'd thought it might be more convenient to hate everyone connected with James Maxfield.

He'd managed to steer clear of the youngest daughter, Cricket, who always seemed to be flitting in and out of the place, and he'd seen Wren on many occasions, marching around purposefully, but he hadn't quite figured out exactly what her purpose was. Nor did he want to.

But Emerson… Emerson he couldn't seem to stay away from. Or maybe she couldn't stay away from him. At the end of it all, he didn't know if it mattered which it was.

They kept colliding either way.

"You must be very good with horses," she said.

"I don't know about that. But I was here, available to do the job, so your father gave it to me."

She tilted her head to the side, appraising him like he was a confusing piece of modern art. "Are you married?"

"Hell no," he said. "No desire for that kind of nonsense."

"You think love is nonsense?" she pressed.

"You didn't ask me about love. You asked me about marriage."

"Don't they usually go together?"

"Does it for you? Because you nearly kissed me yesterday, and you're wearing another man's ring."

Great. He'd gone and brought that up. Not a good idea, all things considered. Though, it might make her angry, and if he could get her good and angry, that might be for the best.

Maybe then she would stay away.

"I told you, we're not living near each other right now, so we…have an arrangement."

"So you said. But what does that mean?"

"We are not exclusive."

"Then what the hell is the point of being engaged?

As I understand it, the only reason to put a ring on a woman's finger is to make her yours. Sure and certain. If you were my woman, I certainly wouldn't let another man touch you."

Her cheeks flushed red. "Well, you certainly have a lot of opinions for someone who doesn't see a point to the institution of marriage."

"Isn't the point *possession*?"

"Women aren't seen as cattle anymore. So no."

"I didn't mean a woman being a possession. The husband and wife possess each other. Isn't that the point?"

She snorted. "I think that often the point is dynasty and connections, don't you?"

"Damn, that's cynical, even for me."

She ignored that. "So, you're good with horses, and you don't believe in marriage," she said. "Anything else?"

"Not a thing."

"If you don't believe in marriage, then what do you believe in?"

"Passion," he said. "For as long as it burns hot. But that's it."

She nodded slowly, and then she turned away from him.

"Aren't you going to ride?"

"I… Not right now. I need to… I need to go think."

And then without another word, Emerson Maxfield ran away from him.

The cabin was a shit hole. He really wasn't enjoying staying there. He had worked himself out of places like this. Marginal dwellings that had only woodstoves for heat. But this was the situation. Revenge was a dish best served cold, and apparently his ass had to be kind of cold right along with it.

Not that he didn't know how to build a fire. It seemed tonight he'd have to.

He went outside, into the failing light, wearing nothing but his jeans and a pair of boots, and searched around for an ax.

There was no preprepared firewood. That would've been way too convenient, and Holden had the notion that James Maxfield was an asshole in just about every way. It wasn't just Soraya that James didn't care about. It was everyone. Right down to the people who lived and worked on his property. He didn't much care about the convenience of his employees. It was a good reminder. Of why Holden was here.

Though, Emerson seemed to be under the impression that James cared for *her*. An interesting thing. Because when she had spoken about trying to earn the approval of one of her parents, he had been convinced, of course, that she had meant James's.

But apparently, James was proud of his daughter, and supported her.

Maybe James had used up every ounce of his humanity in his parenting. Though, Holden still had questions about that.

And it was also entirely possible that Emerson knew the truth about how her father behaved. And that she was complicit in covering up his actions in order to protect the brand.

Holden didn't know, and he didn't care. He couldn't concern himself with the fate of anyone involved with James Maxfield.

If you drink water from a poison well, whatever happened, happened.

As far as Holden was concerned, each and every grapevine on this property was soaked through with James Maxfield's poison.

He found an ax and swung it up in the air, splitting the log in front of him with ease. That, at least, did something to get his body warmed up, and quell some of the murder in his blood. He chuckled, positioned another log on top of the large stone sitting before him and swung the ax down.

"Well," came the sound of a soft, feminine voice. "I didn't expect to find you out here. Undressed."

He paused, and turned to see Emerson standing there, wearing a belted black coat, her dark hair loose.

She was wearing high heels.

Nothing covered her legs.

It was cold, and she was standing out in the middle of the muddy ground in front of his cabin, and none of it made much sense.

"What the hell are you doing here?" He looked her up and down. "Dressed like that."

"I could ask you the same question. Why didn't you put a shirt on? It's freezing out here."

"Why didn't *you* put pants on?"

She hesitated, but only for a moment, and then her expression went regal, which he was beginning to recognize meant she was digging deep to find all her stubbornness.

"Because I would be burdened by having to take them off again soon. At least, that's what I hope." Only the faint pink color in her cheeks betrayed the fact that she'd embarrassed herself. Otherwise he'd have thought she was nothing more than an ice queen, throwing out the suggestion of a seduction so cold it might give his dick frostbite.

But that wasn't the truth. No, he could see it in that blush. Underneath all that coolness, Emerson was burning.

And damned if he wasn't on fire himself.

But it made no damn sense to him, that this woman, the princess of Maxfield Vineyards, would come all the way out here, dragging her designer heels in the mud, to seduce him.

He looked behind his shoulder at the tiny cabin, then back at her.

"Really," he said.

The color in her cheeks deepened.

Lust and interest fired through him, and damned if he'd do anything to stop it. Dark, tempting images of taking Emerson into that rough cabin and sullying her on the rock-hard mattress… It was satisfying on so many levels, he couldn't even begin to sort through them all.

His enemy's daughter. Naked and begging for him, in a cabin reserved for workers, people James clearly thought so far beneath his own family that he'd not even given a thought to their basic needs.

Knowing Holden could have her in there, in a hundred different ways, fired his blood in a way nothing but rage had for ages.

Damn, he was hungry for her. In this twisted, intense way he had told himself he wasn't going to indulge.

But she was here.

Maybe with nothing on under that coat. Which meant they were both already half undressed, and it begged the question whether or not they should go ahead and get naked the rest of the way.

A look at her hand. He noticed she didn't have her engagement ring on.

"What the hell kind of game are you playing?" he asked.

"You said that whatever happened between you and a woman in bed was between you and that woman. Well, I'm of the same mind. It's nobody's business but ours what happens here." She bit her lip. "I'm going to be really, really honest with you."

There was something about that statement that burned, because if there was one thing he was never going to be with her, it was honest.

"I don't love my fiancé. I haven't slept with him. Why? Because I'm not that interested in sleeping with him. It's the strangest thing. We've been together for a couple of years, but we don't live near each other. And every time we could have, we just didn't. And the fact that we're not even tempted… Well, that tells you something about the chemistry between us. But this…you. I want to do this with you. It's all I can think about, and trust me when I say that's not me. I don't understand it, I didn't ask for it, or want it, but I can't fight it."

"I'm supposed to be flattered that you're deigning to come down from your shining tower because you can't stop thinking about me?"

"I want you," she said, lifting her chin up. "You asked me earlier if there was anything I had ever wanted that I couldn't have. It's you. I shouldn't have you. But I want you. And if my father found out that I was doing this, he would kill us both. Because my engagement to Donovan matters to him."

"You said you had an arrangement," he stated.

"Oh, Donovan wouldn't care. Donovan knows. I mean, in a vague sense. I texted him to make sure I wasn't just making assumptions. And I found out he already has. Been with someone else, I mean. So, it's not a big deal. But my father… He would never want it being made public. Image is everything to him, and my engagement to Donovan is part of the image right now."

And just like that, he sensed that her relationship with her father was a whole lot more complicated than she let on. But her relationship with James wasn't Holden's problem either way. And neither was whether or not Emerson was a good person, or one who covered up her father's transgressions. None of it mattered.

Nothing really mattered right here but the two of them.

The really fascinating thing was, Emerson didn't know who Holden was. And even if she did, she didn't need anything from him. Not monetarily. It had been a long damn time since he'd appealed to a woman in a strictly physical way. Not that women didn't enjoy him physically. But they also enjoyed what he had—a luxury hotel suite, connections, invitations to coveted parties.

He was standing here with none of that, nothing but a very dilapidated cabin that wasn't even his own.

And she wanted him.

And that, he found, was an incredibly compelling aphrodisiac, a turn-on he hadn't even been aware he'd been missing.

Emerson had *no idea* that he was Holden McCall, the wealthiest developer in the state. All she wanted was a roll in the hay, and why the hell not? Sure, he was supposed to hate her and everything she stood for.

But there was something to be said for a hate screw.

"So let me get this straight," he said. "You haven't even kissed me. You don't even know if I want to kiss you. But you were willing to come down here not even knowing what the payoff would be?"

Her face was frozen, its beauty profound even as she

stared at him with blank blue eyes, her red lips pressed into a thin line. And he realized, this was not a woman who knew how to endure being questioned.

She was a woman used to getting what she wanted. A woman used to commanding the show, that much was clear. It was obvious that Emerson was accustomed to bulldozing down doors, a characteristic that seemed to stand in sharp contrast to the fact that she also held deep concerns over what her parents thought of her and her decisions.

"That should tell you, then," she said, the words stiff. "It should tell you how strong I think the connection is. If it's not as strong for you, that's fine. You're not the one on the verge of getting married, and you're just a man, after all. So you'll get yours either way. This might be *it* for me before I go to the land of boring, banal monogamous sex."

"So you intend to be fully faithful to this man you're marrying? The one you've never been naked with?"

"What's the point of marriage otherwise? You said that yourself. I believe in monogamy. It's just in my particular style of engagement I feel a little less…intense about it than I otherwise might."

He could take this moment to tell her that her father certainly didn't seem to look at marriage that way. But that would be stupid. He didn't have enough information yet to come at James, and when he did, he wasn't going to miss.

"So you just expect that I'll fuck you whether I feel a connection to you or not. Even if I don't feel like it."

She lifted her chin, her imperiousness seeming to intensify. "It's my understanding that men always feel like it."

"Fair enough," he said. "But that's an awfully low bar, don't you think?"

"I don't..."

"I'll tell you what," he said. "I'm going to give you a kiss. And if afterward you can walk away, then you should."

She blinked. "I don't want to."

"See how you feel after the kiss."

He dropped the ax, and it hit the frozen ground with a dull thump.

He already knew.

He already knew that he was going to have a hard time getting his hands off her once they'd been on her. The way that she appealed to him hit a primitive part of him he couldn't explain. A part of him that was something other than civilized.

She took a step toward him, those ridiculous high heels somehow skimming over the top of the dirt and rocks. She was soft and elegant, and he was half dressed and sweaty from chopping wood, his breath a cloud in the cold air.

She reached out and put her hand on his chest. And it took every last ounce of his willpower not to grab her wrist and pin her palm to him. To hold her against him, make her feel the way his heart was beginning to rage out of control.

He couldn't remember the last time he'd wanted a woman like this.

And he didn't know if it was the touch of the forbidden adding to the thrill, or if it was the fact that she wanted his body and nothing else. Because he could do nothing for Emerson Maxfield, not Holden Brown, the man he was pretending to be. The man who had to depend on the good graces of his employer and lived in a cabin on the property. There was nothing he could do for her.

Nothing he could do but make her scream his name, over and over again.

And that was all she wanted.

She was a woman set to marry another man. She didn't even want emotions from him.

She wanted nothing. Nothing but his body.

And he couldn't remember the last time that was the case, if ever. Everyone wanted something from him. Everyone wanted a piece of him.

Even his mother and sister, who he cared for dearly, needed him. They needed his money, they needed his support.

They needed him to engage in a battle to destroy the man who had devastated Soraya.

But this woman standing in front of him truly wanted only this elemental thing, this spark of heat between them to become a blaze. And who was he to deny her?

He let her guide it. He let her be the one to make the next move. Here she was, all bold in that coat, with her hand on his chest, and yet there was a hesitancy to her as well. She didn't have a whole lot of experience seducing men, that much was obvious. And damned if he didn't enjoy the moment where she had to steel herself and find the courage to lean in.

There was something so very enjoyable about a woman playing the vixen when it was clear it wasn't her natural role. But she was doing it. For him. All for the desire she felt for him.

What man wouldn't respond to that?

She licked her lips, and then she pressed her mouth to his.

And that was the end of his control.

He wrapped his arm around her waist and pressed her against him, angling his head and consuming her.

Because the fire that erupted between them wasn't something that could be tamed. Wasn't something that could be controlled. Couldn't be tested or tasted. This was not a cocktail to be sipped. He wanted to drink it all down, and her right along with it.

Needed to. There was no other option.

He felt like a dying man making a last gasp for breath in the arms of this woman he should never have touched.

He didn't let his hands roam over her curves, no matter how much he wanted to. He simply held her, licking his way into the kiss, his tongue sliding against hers as he tasted the most luscious forbidden fruit that had ever been placed in front of him.

But it wasn't enough to have a bite. He wanted her juices to run down his chin. And he was going to have just that.

"Want to walk away?" he asked, his voice rough, his body hard.

"No," she breathed.

And then he lifted her up and carried her into the cabin.

Five

If this moment were to be translated into a headline, it would read: Maxfield Heiress Sacrifices All for an Orgasm.

Assuming, of course, that she would have an orgasm. She'd never had one yet with a man. But if she were going to…it would be with him.

If it were possible, it would be now.

When she had come up to the cabin and seen him standing there chopping wood—of all things—his chest bare, his jeans slung low on his hips, she had known that all good sense and morality were lost. Utterly and completely lost. In a fog of lust that showed no sign of lifting.

There was nothing she could do but give in.

Because she knew, she absolutely *knew*, that whatever this was needed to be explored. That she could not marry Donovan wondering what this thing between herself and Holden was.

Not because she thought there might be something lasting between them—no—she was fairly certain this was one of those moments of insanity that had nothing to do with anything like real life or good sense.

But she needed to know what desire was. Needed to know what sex could be.

For all she knew, this was the key to unlocking it with the man she was going to marry. And that was somewhat important. Maybe Holden was her particular key.

The man who was destined to teach her about her own sexuality.

Whatever the excuse, she was in his arms now, being carried into a modest cabin that was a bit more rundown than she had imagined any building on the property might be.

She had never been in any of the workers' quarters before. She had never had occasion to.

She shivered, with cold or fear she didn't know.

This was like some strange, unexpected, delayed rebellion. Sneaking out of her room in the big house to come and fool around with one of the men who worked for her father. He would be furious if he knew.

And so he would never know.

No one would ever know about this. No one but the two of them.

It would be their dirty secret. And at the moment, she was hoping that it would be very, very dirty. Because she had never had these feelings in her life.

This desire to get naked as quickly as possible. To be as close to someone as possible.

She wanted to get this coat off and rub herself all over his body, and she had never, ever felt that before.

She was a woman who was used to being certain.

She knew why she made the decisions she did, and she made them without overthinking.

She was *confident*.

But this was a part of herself she had never been terribly confident in.

Oh, it had nothing to do with her looks. Men liked her curves. She knew that. She didn't have insecurities when it came to her body.

It was what her body was capable of. What it could feel.

That gave her all kinds of insecurity. Enough that in her previous relationships she had decided to make her own pleasure a nonissue. If ever her college boyfriend had noticed that she hadn't climaxed, he had never said. But he had been young enough, inexperienced enough, that he might not have realized.

She was sure, however, that her last ex had realized.

Occasionally he'd asked her if she was all right. And she had gotten very good at soothing his ego.

It's nice to be close.

It was good for me.

And one night, when he had expressed frustration at her tepid response to his kisses, she had simply shrugged and said, *I'm not very sexual.*

And she had believed it. She had believed each and every one of those excuses. And had justified the times when she had faked it, because of course her inability to feel something wasn't his fault.

But just looking at Holden made a pulse pound between her thighs that was more powerful than any sensation she'd felt during intercourse with a man before.

And with his hands on her like they were right now, with her body cradled in his strong arms…

She could barely breathe. She could barely think.

All she felt was a blinding, white-hot shock of need, and she had never experienced anything like it before in her life.

He set her down on the uneven wood floor. It was cold.

"I was going to build a fire," he said. "Wait right here, I'll be back."

And then he went back outside, leaving her standing in the middle of the cabin, alone and not in his arms, which gave her a moment to pause.

Was she really about to do this?

She didn't have any experience with casual sex. She had experience with sex only in the context of a relationship. And she had never, ever felt anything this intense.

It was the intensity that scared her. Not so much the fact that it was physical only, but the fact that it was so incredibly physical.

She didn't know how this might change her.

Because she absolutely felt like she was on the cusp of being changed. And maybe that was dramatic, but she couldn't rid herself of the sensation. This was somehow significant. It would somehow alter the fabric of who she was. She felt brittle and thin, on the verge of being shattered. And she wasn't entirely sure what was going to put her back together.

It was frightening, that thought. But not frightening enough to make her leave.

He returned a moment later, a stack of wood in his arms.

And she watched as he knelt down before the woodstove, his muscles shifting and bunching in his back as he began to work at lighting a fire.

"I didn't realize the cabins were so...rustic."

"They are a bit. Giving you second thoughts?"

"No," she said quickly.

If he changed his mind now, if he sent her away, she would die. She was sure of it.

He was kneeling down half naked, and he looked so damned hot that he chased away the cold.

"It'll take a bit for the fire to warm the place up," he said. "But I can keep you warm in the meantime."

He stood, brushing the dust off his jeans and making his way over to her.

She had meant to—at some point—take stock of the room. To look around and see what furniture it had, get a sense of the layout. But she found it too hard to look away from him. And when he fixed those eyes on her, she was held captive.

Utterly and completely.

His chest was broad, sprinkled with just the right amount of hair, his muscles cut and well-defined. His pants were low, showing those lines that arrow downward, as if pointing toward the most masculine part of him.

She had never been with a man who had a body like this. It was like having only ever eaten store-bought pie, and suddenly being treated to a homemade extravaganza.

"You are… You're beautiful," she said.

He chuckled. "I think that's my line."

"No. It's definitely mine."

One side of his mouth quirked upward into a grin, and even though the man was a stranger to her, suddenly she felt like he might not be.

Because that smile touched her somewhere inside her chest and made her *feel* when she knew it ought not to. Because this should be about just her body. And not in any way about her heart. But it was far too easy to imagine a world where nothing existed beyond this cabin, beyond this man and the intensity in his eyes, the desire etched into every line of his face.

And that body. Hot *damn*, that body.

Yes, it was very easy to imagine she was a different girl who lived in a different world.

Who could slip away to a secluded cabin and find herself swept up in the arms of a rugged cowboy, and it didn't matter whether or not it was *on brand.* Right now, it didn't.

Right now, it didn't.

This was elemental, something deeper than reality. It was fantasy in all of its bright, brilliant glory. Except it was real. Brought to life with stunning visuals, and it didn't matter whether it should be or not.

It was.

It felt suddenly much bigger than her. And because of that, she felt more connected with her body than she ever had before.

Because this wasn't building inside of her, it surrounded her, encompassed her. She could never have contained so much sensation, so much need. And so it became the world around her.

Until she couldn't remember what it was like to draw breath in a space where his scent didn't fill her lungs, where her need didn't dictate the way she stood, the way she moved.

She put her hands on the tie around her waist.

And he watched.

His attention was rapt, his focus unwavering.

The need between her thighs escalated.

She unknotted the belt and then undid the buttons, let her coat fall to her feet.

She was wearing nothing but a red lace bra and panties and her black high heels.

"Oh, Little Red," he growled. "I do like that color on you."

The hunger in his eyes was so intense she could feel it echoing inside of herself. Could feel her own desire answering back.

No man had ever looked at her like this.

They had wanted her, sure. Had desired her.

But they hadn't wanted to consume her, and she had a feeling that her own personal Big Bad Wolf just might.

She expected him to move to her, but instead he moved away, walking over to the bed that sat in the corner of the humble room. He sat on the edge of the mattress, his thighs splayed, his eyes fixed on her.

"I want you to come on over here," he said.

She began to walk toward him, her heels clicking on the floor, and she didn't need to be given detailed instruction, because she somehow knew what he wanted.

It was strange, and it was impossible, that somehow this man she had barely spent any time with felt known to her in a way that men she'd dated for long periods of time never had.

But he did.

And maybe that was something she had overlooked in all of this.

What she wanted to happen between them might be physical, but there was a spiritual element that couldn't be denied. Something that went deeper than just attraction. Something that spoke to a more desperate need.

His body was both deliciously unknown, and somehow right and familiar all at the same time.

And so were his needs.

She crossed the room and draped an arm over his shoulder, lifting her knee to the edge of the mattress, rocking forward so that the center of her pressed against his hardness. "I'm here," she said.

He wrapped his arm around her waist, pushed his fingertips beneath the waistband of her panties and slid his hands down over her ass. Then he squeezed. Hard. And she gasped.

"I'm going to go out on a limb here and guess that part of the attraction you have to all of this is that it's a little bit rough."

She licked her lips, nodded when no words would come.

She hadn't realized that was what she'd wanted, but when he said it, it made sense. When he touched her like this—possessive and commanding—she knew it was what she needed.

"That suits me just fine, princess, because I'm a man who likes it that way. So you have to tell me right now if you can handle it."

"I can handle whatever you give me," she said, her voice coming out with much more certainty than she felt.

Rough.

The word skated over her skin, painted delicious pictures in her mind and made that place between her legs throb with desire.

Rough. Uncivilized. Untamed.

Right then she wanted that, with a desperation that defied explanation.

She wanted to be marked by this. Changed by it. She wanted to have the evidence of it on her skin as well as on her soul.

Because somehow she felt that tonight, in this bed,

it might be the only chance she'd have to find out what she was.

What she wanted.

What she desired apart from anything else, apart from family and social expectations. Tonight, this, had nothing to do with what anyone else might expect of her.

This was about her.

And on some level she felt like if she didn't have this, the rest of her life would be a slow descent into the madness of wondering.

"If anything goes too far for you, you just say it, you understand?"

"Yes," she said.

"I want to make you scream," he said. "But I want it to be the good kind."

She had never in her life screamed during sex.

The promise, the heat in his eyes, made her suspect she was about to.

That was when he tightened his grip on her and reversed their positions.

He pinned her down on her back, grabbing both wrists with one hand and stretching her arms up over her head. He had his thighs on either side of her hips, the denim rough against her skin. He was large and hard and glorious above her, his face filled with the kind of intensity that thrilled her down to her core.

She rocked her hips upward, desperate for fulfillment. Desperate to be touched by him.

He denied her.

He held her pinned down and began a leisurely tour of her body with his free hand.

He traced her collarbone, the edge of her bra, down the valley between her breasts and to her belly button. Before tracing the edge of her panties. But he didn't touch her anywhere that she burned for him. And she could feel the need for his touch, as if those parts of her were lit up bright with their demand for him. And still, he wouldn't do it.

"I thought you said this was going to be rough."

"Rough's not fun if you're not good and wet first," he said. And then he leaned in, his lips right next to her ear. "And I'm going to make sure you get really, really wet first."

Just those words alone did the job. An arrow of need pierced her center, and she could feel it, molten liquid there in her thighs. And that was when he captured her mouth with his, kissing her deep and long, cupping her breast with one hand and teasing her nipple with his thumb.

She whimpered, arching her hips upward, frustrated when there was nothing there for her to make contact with.

He touched her slowly, thoroughly, first through the lace of her bra, before pushing the flimsy fabric down and exposing her breasts. He touched her bare, his thumbs calloused as they moved over her body.

And then he replaced them with his mouth.

He sucked deep, and she worked her hips against nothing, desperate for some kind of relief that she couldn't find as he tormented her.

She would have said that her breasts weren't sensitive.

But he was proving otherwise.

He scraped his teeth across her sensitive skin. And then he bit down.

She cried out, her orgasm shocking her, filling her cheeks with embarrassed heat as wave after wave of desire pulsed through her core.

But she didn't feel satisfied, because he still hadn't touched her there.

She felt aching and raw, empty when she needed to be filled.

"There's a good girl," he said, and her internal muscles pulsed again.

He tugged her panties down her thighs, stopping at her ankles before pushing her knees wide, eyeing her hungrily as he did.

Then he leaned in, inhaling her scent, pressing a kiss to the tender skin on her leg. "The better to eat you with," he said, looking her in the eye as he lowered his head and dragged his tongue through her slick folds.

She gasped. This was the first time he had touched her there, and it was so... So impossibly dirty. So impossibly intimate.

Then he was done teasing. Done talking. He grabbed her hips and pulled her forward, his grip bruising as he set his full focus and attention on consuming her.

She dug her heels into the bed, tried to brace herself, but she couldn't. She had no control over this, over any of it.

He was driving her toward pleasure at his pace, and it was terrifying and exhilarating all at once.

She climaxed again. Impossibly.

It was then she realized he was no longer holding her in place, but she had left her own wrists up above her head, as if she were still pinned there.

She was panting, gasping for breath, when he moved up her body, his lips pressing against hers.

She could taste her own desire there, and it made her shiver.

"Now I want you to turn over," he said.

She didn't even think of disobeying that commanding voice. She did exactly as she was told.

"Up on your knees, princess," he said.

She obeyed, anticipation making the base of her spine tingle as she waited.

She could hear plastic tearing, knew that he must be getting naked. Getting a condom on.

And when he returned to her, he put one hand on her hip, and she felt the head of his arousal pressed against the entrance to her body.

She bit her lip as he pushed forward, filling her.

He was so big, and this was not a position she was used to.

It hurt a bit as he drove his hips forward, a short curse escaping his lips as he sank in to the hilt.

She lowered her head, and he placed his hand between her shoulder blades, drawing it down her spine, then back up. And she wanted to purr like a very contented cat. Then he grabbed hold of both her hips, pulling out slowly, and slamming back home.

She gasped, arching her back as she met him thrust for punishing thrust. She pressed her face down into the mattress as he entered her, over and over again, the only sounds in the room that of skin meeting skin, harsh breaths and the kinds of feral sounds she had never imagined could come from her.

He grabbed hold of her hair, and moved it to one side, and she felt a slight tug, and then with a pull that shocked her with its intensity, he lifted her head as he held her like that, the tug matching his thrust. She gasped, the pain on her scalp somehow adding to the pleasure she felt between her legs.

And he did it over and over again.

Until she was sobbing. Until she was begging for release.

Then he released his hold on her hair, grabbing both her hips again as he raced her to the end, his hold on her bruising, his thrusts pushing her to the point of pain. Then he leaned forward, growling low and biting her neck as he came hard. And she followed him right over the edge into oblivion.

Six

By the time Emerson went limp in front of him, draped over the mattress like a boneless cat, the fire had begun to warm the space.

Holden was a man who didn't have much in the way of regret in his life—it was impossible when he had been raised with absolutely nothing, and had gotten to a space where he didn't have to worry about his own basic needs, or those of his family. And even now, it was difficult to feel anything but the kind of bone-deep satisfaction that overtook him.

He went into the bathroom and took care of the practicalities, then went back to stoke the fire.

He heard the sound of shifting covers on the bed, and looked over his shoulder to see Emerson lying on her side now, her legs crossed just so, hiding that tempting shadow at the apex of her thighs, her arm draped coquettishly over her breast.

"Enjoying the show?" he asked.

"Yes," she responded, no shame in her voice at all.

"You might return the favor," he said.

She looked down at her own body, as if she only just realized that she was covering a good amount of the tempting bits.

"You're busy," she said. "Making a fire. I would hate to distract."

"You're distracting even as you are."

Maybe even especially as she was, looking timid when he knew how she really was. Wild and uninhibited and the best damn sex he'd ever had in his life.

Hard mattress notwithstanding.

She rolled onto her back then, stretching, raising her arms up above her head, pointing her toes.

He finished with the fire quickly, and returned to the bed.

"I couldn't do it again," she said, her eyes wide.

"Why not?"

"I've never come that many times in a row in my life. Surely it would kill you."

"I'm willing to take the chance," he said.

It surprised him to hear that her response wasn't normal for her. She had seemed more than into it. Though, she had talked about the tepid chemistry between herself and the man she was engaged to.

There was something wrong with that man, because if he couldn't find chemistry with Emerson, Holden doubted he could find it with anyone.

"Well, of course you're willing to take the chance. You're not the one at risk. You only… Once. I already did three times."

"Which means you have the capacity for more," he said. "At least, that's my professional opinion."

"Professional ranch hand opinion? I didn't know that made you an expert on sex."

He chuckled. "I'm an expert on sex because of vast experience in my personal life, not my professional life. Though, I can tell you I've never considered myself a hobbyist when it came to female pleasure. Definitely a professional."

"Well, then I guess I picked a good man to experiment with."

"Is that what this is? An experiment?"

She rolled over so she was halfway on his body, her breast pressed against his chest, her blue eyes suddenly sincere. "I've never had an orgasm with a man before. I have them on my own. But never with… Never with a partner. I've only been with two men. But… They were my boyfriends. So you would think that if it was this easy they would have figured it out. Or I would have figured it out. And I can't for the life of me figure out why we didn't. Myself included."

"Chemistry," he said, brushing her hair back from her face, surprising himself with the tender gesture. But now she was asking him these wide-eyed innocent questions, when she had done things with him only moments ago that were anything but.

"Chemistry," she said. "I thought it might be something like that. Something magical and strange and completely impossible to re-create in a lab setting, sadly."

"We can re-create it right now."

"But what if I can't ever re-create it again? Although, I suppose now I know that it's possible for me to feel this way, I…"

"I didn't know that I was your one-man sexual revolution."

"Well, I didn't want to put that kind of pressure on you."

"I thrive under pressure."

It was easy to forget, right now, that she was the daughter of his enemy. That he was here to destroy her family. That her engagement and the lack of chemistry between herself and her fiancé would be the least of her worries in the next week.

In fact, maybe he could spare her from the marriage. Because the optics for the family would be pretty damned reduced, probably beyond the point of healing. Her marriage to an ad exec was hardly going to fix that.

And anyway, the man would probably be much less interested in marrying into the Maxfield dynasty when it was reduced to more of a one-horse outfit and they didn't have two coins to rub together.

Holden waited for there to be guilt. But he didn't feel it.

Instead, he felt some kind of indefinable sense of satisfaction. Like in the past few moments he had collected another chess piece that had once belonged to his enemy. And Emerson was so much more than a pawn.

But he didn't know how to play this victory. Not yet.

And anyway, she didn't feel much like a victory or a conquest lying here in bed with him when he was still naked. He felt more than a little bit conquered himself.

"This is terrifying," she whispered. "Because I shouldn't be here. And I shouldn't be with you at all. And I think this is the most relaxed and maybe even the happiest I've ever felt in my life." She looked up at him, and a tear tracked down her cheek, and just like that, the guilt hit him right in the chest. "And I know that it can't go beyond tonight. I know it can't. Because you have your life… And I have mine."

"And there's no chance those two things could ever cross," he said, the words coming out a hell of a lot more hostile than he intended.

"I'm not trying to be snobby or anything," she said. "But there's expectations about the kind of man that I'll end up with. And what he'll bring to the family."

"Princess, I don't know why you're talking about marriage."

"Well, that's another problem in and of itself, isn't it? I'm at that point. Where marriage has to be considered."

"You're at that point? What the hell does that mean? Are we in the 1800s?"

"In a family like mine, it matters. We have to… My father doesn't have sons. His daughters have to marry well, marry men who respect and uphold the winery. His sons-in-law are going to gain a certain amount of ownership of the place, and that means…"

"His sons-in-law are getting ownership of the business?"

"Yes," she said. "I mean, I'll retain my share as well, so don't think it's that kind of draconian nonsense. But when we marry, Donovan is going to get a share of the winery. As large as mine. When Wren marries, it will be the same. Then there's Cricket, and her husband will get a share as well, though not as large. And by the time that's all finished, my father will only have a portion. A very small portion."

"How does that math work? Cricket gets less?"

"Well, so far Cricket doesn't have any interest in running the place, and she never has. So yes."

"No wonder your father is so invested in controlling who you marry."

"It's for my protection as well. It's not like he wants me getting involved with fortune hunters."

"You really are from another world," he said, disdain in his voice, even though he didn't mean it to be there. Because it didn't matter. Because it wasn't true—he had money, he had status. And because he didn't care about her. Or her opinion. He didn't care that she was as shallow as the rest of her family, as her father. It didn't concern him and, in fact, was sort of helpful given the fact that he had taken pretty terrible advantage of her, that he'd lied to her to get her into bed.

"I can tell that you think I'm a snob," she said. "I'm not, I promise. I wouldn't get naked with a man I thought was beneath me."

"Well, that's BS. It's a pretty well-documented fact that people find slumming to be titillating, Emerson."

"Well, I don't. You're different. And yes, I find that sexy. You're forbidden, and maybe I find that sexy too, but it's not about you being less than me, or less than other men that I've been with. Somehow, you're more, and I don't know what to do with that. That's why it hurts. Because I don't know if I will ever feel as contented, ever again, as I do right now lying in this cabin, and this is not supposed to be…"

"It's not supposed to be anything you aspire to. How could it be? When your mother thinks that what you have is beneath you as it is."

She swallowed and looked away. "My life's not mine. It's attached to this thing my father built from scratch. This legacy that has meant a life that I'm grateful for, whatever you might think. I don't need to have gone without to understand that what I've been given is extraordinary. I do understand that. But it's an incredible responsibility to bear as well, and I have to be…a steward of it. Whether I want to be or not."

And suddenly, he resented it all. Every last bit. The

lies that stood between them, the way she saw him, and his perceived lack of power in this moment. He growled, reversing their positions so he was over her.

"None of that matters just now," he said.

She looked up at him, and then she touched his face. "No," she agreed. "I don't suppose it does."

He reached down and found her red lace bra, touching the flimsy fabric and then looking back at her. He took hold of her wrists, like he'd done earlier, and, this time, secured them tightly with the lace.

"Right now, you're here," he said. "And I'm the only thing you need to worry about. You're mine right here, and there's nothing outside this room, off of this bed, do you understand?"

Her breath quickened, her breasts rising and falling with the motion. She nodded slowly.

"Good girl," he said. "You have a lot of responsibilities outside, but when you're here, the only thing you have to worry about is pleasing me."

This burned away the words of the last few minutes, somehow making it all feel okay again, even if it shouldn't. As if securing her wrists now might help him hold on to this moment a little tighter. Before he had to worry about the rest, before he had to deal with the fallout and what it would mean for Emerson.

This thing that she cared about so deeply, this dynasty, which she was willing to marry a man she didn't care about at all to secure.

He would free her from it, and in the end, it might be a blessing.

He looked at the way her wrists were tied, and suddenly he didn't want to free her at all.

What he wanted was to keep her.

He got a condom from his wallet and returned to her,

where she lay on the bed, her wrists bound, her thighs spread wide in invitation.

He sheathed himself and gripped her hips, entering her in one smooth stroke. Her climax was instant, and it was hard, squeezing him tight as he pounded into her without mercy.

And he set about proving to her that there was no limit to the number of times she could find her pleasure.

But there was a cost to that game, one that crystallized in his mind after the third time she cried out his name and settled herself against his chest, her wrists still tightly tied.

She was bound to him now.

And she had betrayed a very crucial piece of information.

And the ways it could all come together for him became suddenly clear.

He knew exactly what he was going to do.

Seven

It had been three days since her night in the cabin with Holden. And he was all she could think about. She knew she was being ridiculous. They had another event happening at the winery tonight, and she couldn't afford to be distracted.

There was going to be an engagement party in the large barn, which had been completely and totally made over into an elegant, rustic setting, with vast open windows that made the most of the view, and elegant chandeliers throughout.

Tonight's event wasn't all on her shoulders. Mostly, it was Wren's responsibility, but Emerson was helping, and she had a feeling that in her current state she wasn't helping much.

All she could do was think about Holden. The things he had done to her body. The things he had taught her about her body.

She felt like an idiot. Spinning fantasies about a man, obsessing about him.

She'd never realized she would be into something like bondage, but he had shown her the absolute freedom there could be in giving up control.

She was so used to controlling everything all the time. And for just a few hours in his bed, he had taken the lead. It was like a burden had been lifted from her.

"Are you there, Emerson? It's me, Wren."

Emerson turned to look at her sister, who was fussing with the guest list in front of her.

"I'm here, and I've been here, helping you obsess over details."

"You're here," Wren said. "But you're not *here*."

Emerson looked down at her left hand and cursed. Because there was supposed to be a ring there. She had taken it off before going to Holden's cabin, but she needed to get it back on before tonight. Before she was circulating in a room full of guests.

Tonight's party was different from a brand-related launch. The event was at the heart of the winery itself, and as the manager of the property, Wren was the person taking the lead. When it came to broader brand representation, it was down to Emerson. But Emerson would still be taking discreet photographs of the event to share on social media, as that helped with the broader awareness of the brand.

Their jobs often crossed, as this was a family operation and not a large corporation. But neither of them minded. And in fact, Emerson considered it a good day when she got to spend extra time with her sister. But less so today when Wren was so apparently frazzled.

"What's wrong with you?" Wren asked, and then her

eye fell meaningfully to her left hand. "Did something happen with Donovan?"

"No," Emerson said. "I just forgot to put the ring on."

"That doesn't sound like you. Because you're ever conscious of the fact that a ring like that is a statement."

"I'm well aware of what I'm ever conscious of, *Wren*," she said. "I don't need you to remind me."

"And yet, you forgot something today, so it seems like you need a reminder."

"It's really nothing."

"Except it *is* something. Because if it were nothing, then you wouldn't be acting weird."

"Fine. Don't tell anyone," Emerson said, knowing already that she would regret what she was about to say.

"I like secrets," Wren said, leaning in.

"I had a… I had a one-night stand." Her sister stared at her. Unmoving. "With a man."

Wren huffed a laugh. "Well, I didn't figure you were telling me about the furniture in your bedroom."

"I mean, Donovan and I aren't exclusive, but it didn't feel right to wear his ring while I was…with someone else."

"I had no idea," Wren said, her eyes widening. "I didn't know you were that…"

"Much of a hussy?"

"That *progressive*," she said.

"Well, I'm not. In general. But I was, and am a little thrown off by it. And no one can ever know."

"Solemnly swear."

"You cannot tell Cricket."

"Why would I tell Cricket? She would never be able to look you in the eyes again, and she would absolutely give you away. Not on purpose, mind you."

"No, but it's a secret that she couldn't handle."

"Absolutely."

"Have you met a man that you just…couldn't get out of your head even though he was absolutely unsuitable?"

Wren jolted, her whole body looking like it had been touched by a live wire. "I am very busy with my job."

"Wren."

"Yes. Fine. I do know what it's like to have a sexual obsession with the wrong guy. But I've never…acted on it." The look on her face was so horrified it would have been funny, if Emerson herself hadn't just done the thing that so appalled her sister.

"There's nothing wrong with…being with someone you want, is there? No, I don't really know him, but I knew I wanted him and that seems like a decent reason to sleep with someone, right?"

Wren looked twitchy. "I… Look. Lust and like aren't the same. I get it."

"I like him fine enough," Emerson said. "But we can't ever… *He works for Dad.*"

"Like…in the corporate office?"

"No, like, on the ranch."

"Emersonnnnn."

"What?"

"Are you living out a stable boy fantasy?"

Emerson drew her lip between her teeth and worried it back and forth. "He's not a boy. He's a man. On that you can trust me."

"The question stands."

"Maybe it was sort of that fantasy, I don't know. It was a fantasy, that much I can tell you. But it was supposed to just happen and be done, and I'm obsessing about him instead."

"Who would have ever thought that could happen?" Wren asked in mock surprise.

"In this advanced modern era, I should simply be able to claim my sexuality. Own it! Bring it with me wherever I go. Not…leave it behind in some run-down cabin with the hottest man I've ever seen in my life."

"Those are truly sage words. You should put them on a pretty graphic and post it to your page. Hashtag—girl-boss-of-your-own-sexuality. Put your hair up and screw his brains out!"

Emerson shot her sister a deadly glare. "You know I hate that."

"I also know you never put a toe out of line, and yet here you are, confessing an extremely scandalous transgression."

"This secret goes to your grave with you, or I put you in the ground early, do you understand?"

Wren smirked and seemed to stretch a little taller, as if reminding Emerson she'd outgrown her by two inches when she was thirteen. She and Wren definitely looked like sisters—the same dark hair and blue eyes—but Wren wasn't curvy. She was tall and lean, her hair sleek like her build. She'd honed her more athletic figure with Krav Maga, kickboxing and all other manner of relatively violent exercise.

She claimed it was the only reason she hadn't killed Creed Cooper yet.

She also claimed she liked knowing she *could* kill him if the occasion arose at one of the many different venues where they crossed paths.

Her martial arts skills were yet another reason it was hilarious for Emerson to threaten her sister. She'd be pinned to the ground in one second flat. Though, as the older sibling, she'd done her part to emotionally scar her sister to the point that, when she'd outgrown her, she still believed on some level Emerson could destroy her.

"In all seriousness," Wren said, "it does concern me. I mean, that you're marrying Donovan, and you're clearly more into whoever this other guy is."

"Right. Because I'm going to marry one of the men that work here. That would go over like… What's heavier than a lead balloon?"

"Does it matter?"

"What kind of ridiculous question is that? Of course it matters."

"Dad has never shown the slightest bit of interest in who I'm dating or not dating."

"You're not the oldest. I think… I think he figures he'll get me out of the way first. And it isn't a matter of him showing interest in who I'm dating. He directly told me that Donovan was the sort of man that I should associate with. He set me up with him."

"You're just going to marry who Dad tells you to marry?"

"Would you do differently, Wren? Honestly, I'm asking you."

"I don't think I could marry a man that I wasn't even attracted to."

"If Dad told you a certain man met with his approval, if he pushed you in that direction…you wouldn't try to make it work?"

Wren looked away. "I don't know. I guess I might have to try, but if after two years I still wasn't interested physically…"

"Marriage is a partnership. Our bodies will change. And sex drives and attraction will all change too. We need to have something in common. I mean, it makes way more sense to marry a man I have a whole host of things in common with than it does to marry one who I just want to be naked with."

"I didn't suggest you marry the ranch hand. But perhaps there's some middle ground. A man you like to talk to, and a man you want to sleep with."

"Well, I have yet to find a middle ground that would be suitable for Dad."

Anyway, Emerson didn't think that Holden could be called a middle ground. Not really. He was something so much more than that. Much too much of an extreme to be called something as neutral as middle ground.

"Maybe you should wait until you do."

"Or maybe I should just do what feels best," Emerson said. "I mean, maybe my marriage won't be the best of the best. Maybe I can't have everything. But we are really lucky, you and I. Look at this life." She gestured around the barn. "We have so much. I can make do with whatever I don't have."

Wren looked sad. "I don't know. That seems…tragic to me."

"What about you? You said you wanted a man and you haven't done anything about it."

"That's different."

"So, there's a man you want, and you can't be with him."

"I don't even like him," she said.

Emerson felt bowled over by that statement. Because there was only one man Emerson knew who Wren hated. And the idea that Wren might want him…

Well, no wonder Wren could barely even speak of it. She hated Creed Cooper more than anything else on earth. If the two of them ever touched…well, they would create an explosion of one kind or another, and Emerson didn't know how she hadn't realized that before.

Possibly because she had never before experienced the kind of intense clash she had experienced just a few nights ago with Holden.

"You do understand, then," Emerson said. "That there is a difference between wanting and having. And having for a limited time." She looked down. "Yes, I'm wildly attracted to this guy, and our chemistry is amazing. But it could never be more than that. Though, as someone who has experienced the temporary fun… You know you could."

Wren affected a full-body shudder.

"I really couldn't. I really, really couldn't."

"Suit yourself. But I'm going to go ahead and say that you're not allowed to give me advice anymore, because you live in a big glass house."

"I do not. It's totally different. I'm not marrying someone I shouldn't."

"Well, I'm marrying someone Dad wants me to. I trust Dad. And at the end of the day, I guess that's it. I'm trusting that it's going to be okay because it's what Dad wants me to do, and he's never… He's never steered me wrong. He's never hurt me. All he's ever done is support me."

Her father wanted the best for her. And she knew it. She was just going to have to trust that in the end, like she trusted him.

"I know," Wren said, putting her arm around Emerson. "At least you have some good memories now."

Emerson smiled. "Really good."

"I don't want details," Wren said, patting Emerson's shoulder.

She flashed back to being tied up in bed with Holden. "I am not giving you details. Those are sacred."

"As long as we're on the same page."

Emerson smiled and went back to the checklist she was supposed to be dealing with. “We are on the same page. Which is currently a checklist. Tonight’s party will go off without a hitch.”

“Don’t jinx it,” Wren said, knocking resolutely on one of the wooden tables.

“I’m not going to jinx it. It’s one of your parties. So you know it’s going to be absolutely perfect.”

Eight

The party was going off without a hitch.

Everyone was enjoying themselves, and Emerson was in visual heaven, finding any number of photo opportunities buried in the meticulous decorations that Wren had arranged. With the permission of the couple, she would even share photographs of them, and of the guests. This, at least, served to distract her mildly from the situation with Holden.

Except, there was no *situation*, that was the thing. But it was very difficult for her brain to let go of that truth.

She wanted there to be a situation. But like she had said to Wren earlier, there was really no point in entertaining that idea at all. Marriage was more than just the marriage bed.

And she and Holden might be compatible between the sheets—they were so compatible it made her pulse with desire even thinking about it—but that didn't mean they would be able to make a *relationship*, much less a *marriage*.

They had nothing in common.

You're assuming. You don't actually know that.

Well, it was true. She didn't know, but she could certainly look at the circumstances of his life and make some assumptions.

A passing waiter caught her eye, and she reached out to take hold of a glass of champagne. That was when a couple of things happened all at once. And because they happened so quickly, the reality took her longer to untangle than it might have otherwise.

The first thing she noticed was a man so stunning he took her breath away as he walked into the room.

The second realization was that she knew that man. Even though he looked so different in the sleekly cut black tux he had on his fit body that the name her brain wanted to apply to him couldn't seem to stick.

The third thing that happened was her heart dropping into her feet.

And she didn't even know why.

Because Holden had just walked in wearing a tux.

It might have taken a moment for her brain to link all those details up, but it had now.

She just couldn't figure out what it meant.

That he looked like this. That he was here.

He took a glass of champagne from a tray, and scanned the room. He looked different. But also the same.

Because while he might be clothed in an extremely refined fashion, there was still a ruggedness about him.

Something wild and untamed, even though, on a surface level, he blended in with the people around them.

No, not blended in.

He could never blend in.

He was actually dressed much nicer than anyone else here.

That suit was clearly custom, and it looked horrendously expensive. As did his shoes. As did…everything about him. And could he really be the same man she had happened upon shirtless cutting wood the other day? The same man who had tied her up in his run-down little cabin? The same man who had done desperate, dirty things to her?

And then his eyes collided with hers.

And he smiled.

It made her shiver. It made her ache.

But even so, it was a stranger's smile. It was not the man she knew, and she couldn't make sense of that certainty, even to herself. He walked across the room, acknowledging no one except for her.

And she froze. Like a deer being stalked by a mountain lion. Her heart was pounding in her ears, the sound louder now than the din of chatter going on around her.

"Just the woman I was looking for," he said.

Why did he sound different? He'd been confident in their every interaction. Had never seemed remotely cowed by her position or her money. And maybe that was the real thing she was seeing now.

Not a different man, but one who looked in his element rather than out of it.

"What are you doing here? And where did you get that suit?"

"Would you believe my fairy godmother visited?" The dark humor twisted his lips into a wry smile.

"No," she said, her heart pounding more viciously in her temple.

"Then would you believe that a few of the mice that live in the cabin made the suit for me?"

"Even less likely to believe that. You don't seem like a friend of mice."

"Honey, I'm not really a friend of anyone. And I'm real sorry for what I'm about to do. But if you cooperate with me, things are going to go a whole lot better."

She looked around. As if someone other than him might have answers. Of course, no one offered any if they did. "What do you mean?"

"You see, I haven't been completely honest with you."

"What?"

She couldn't make any sense of this. She looked around the room to see if they were attracting attention, because surely they must be. Because she felt like what was happening between them was shining bright like a beacon on the hill. But somehow they weren't attracting any attention at all.

"Why don't we go outside. I have a meeting with your father in just a few minutes. Unless...unless you are willing to negotiate with me."

"You have a meeting with my father? Negotiate what?"

The thoughts that rolled through her mind sent her into a panic.

He had obviously filmed what had happened between them. He was going to extort money from her family. He was a con man. No *wonder* he didn't want his picture taken.

All those accusations hovered on the edge of her lips, but she couldn't make them. Not here.

"What do you want?" she asked.

He said nothing. The man was a rock in a suit.

No more sophisticated than he'd been in jeans. She'd thought he was different, but he wasn't. This was the real man.

And he was harder, darker than the man she'd imagined he'd been.

Funny how dressing up made that clear.

"What do you want?" she asked again.

She refused to move. She felt like the biggest fool on the planet. How had she trusted this man with her body? He was so clearly not who he said, so clearly…

Of course he hadn't actually wanted her. Of course the only man she wanted was actually just playing a game.

"Revenge," he said. "Nothing more. I'm sorry that you're caught in the middle of it."

"Did you film us?" She looked around, trying to see if people had noticed him yet. They still hadn't. "Did you film us together?"

"No," he said. "I'm not posting anything up on the internet, least of all that."

"Are you going to show my father?"

"No," he said, his lip curling. "This isn't about you, Emerson, whether you believe me or not. It isn't. But what I do next is about you. So I need you to come outside with me."

He turned, without waiting to see if she was with him, and walked back out of the barn. Emerson looked around and then darted after his retreating figure.

When they reached the outdoors, it was dim out, just like the first night they had met. And when he turned to face her, she had the most ridiculous flashback.

He had been in jeans then. With that cowboy hat. And here he was now in a tux. But it was that moment that brought the reality of the situation into focus.

This man was the same man she had been seduced by. Or had she seduced him? It didn't even make sense anymore.

"Tell me what's going on." She looked him up and down. "You clearly aren't actually a ranch hand."

"Your father *did* hire me. Legitimately. So, I guess in total honesty, I do work for your father, and I am a ranch hand."

"What else are you? Are you paparazzi?"

He looked appalled by that. "I'm not a bottom-feeder that makes his living on the misfortunes of others."

"Then what are you? Why are you here?"

"I came here to destroy the winery."

She drew back. The venom in his voice was so intense she could feel the poison sinking down beneath her skin.

He looked her up and down. "But whether or not I do that is up to you now."

"What the hell are you talking about?"

"Your father. Your father had an affair with my sister."

"Your sister? I don't… My father did not have an affair. My father and mother have been married for…more than thirty years. And your sister would have to be…"

"She's younger than you," Holden said. "Younger than you, and incredibly naive about the ways of the world. And your father took advantage of her. When she got pregnant, he tried to pay her to get an abortion, and when she wouldn't, he left. She miscarried, and she's had nothing but health problems since. She's attempted suicide twice and had to be hospitalized. Your father ruined her. Absolutely ruined her."

"No," Emerson said. "It's a mistake. My father would never do that. He would never hurt…"

"I'm not here to argue semantics with you. You can come with me. I'm about to have a meeting with your father, though he doesn't know why. He'll tell you the whole story."

"What does this have to do with me?"

"It didn't have anything to do with you. Until you came to the cabin the other day. I was happy to leave you alone, but you pursued it, and then… And then you told me something very interesting. About the winery. And who'd own it."

Emerson felt like she might pass out. "The man I marry."

"Exactly." He looked at her, those dark eyes blazing. "So you have two choices, really. Let me have that meeting with your father, and you're welcome to attend, where I'll be explaining to him how I've found stacks of NDAs in his employee files. And it doesn't take a genius to figure out why."

"What?"

"Your father has engaged in many, many affairs with workers here on the property. Once I got ahold of the paperwork in his office, I got in touch with some of the women. Most of them wouldn't talk, but enough did. Coercion. And so much of the money for your vineyard comes through all of your celebrity endorsements. Can you imagine the commercial fallout if your father is found to be yet another man who abuses his power? Manipulates women into bed?"

"I don't believe you."

"It doesn't matter whether you believe me or not, Emerson. What matters is that I know I can make other people believe me. And when this is over, you won't be able to give Maxfield wines away with a car wash."

"I don't understand what that gives you," she said,

horror coursing through her veins. She couldn't even entertain the idea of this being true. But the truth of it wasn't the thing, not now. The issue was what he could do.

"Revenge," he said, his voice low and hard.

"Revenge isn't a very lucrative business."

"I don't need the revenge to pay. But… I won't lie to you, I find the idea of revenge and a payout very compelling. The idea of owning a piece of this place instead of simply destroying it. So tell me, how does it work? Your husband getting a stake in the business."

"I get married, and then I just call the lawyers, and they'll do the legal paperwork."

His expression became decisive. "Then you and I are getting married."

"And if I don't?"

"I'll publicize the story. I will make sure to ruin the brand. However, if I marry you, what I'll have is ownership of the brand. And you and I, with our united stakes, will have a hell of a lot of decision-making power."

"But to what end?"

"I want your father to know that I ended up owning part of this. And what I do after that…that will depend on what he's willing to do. But I want to make sure he has to contend with me for as long as I want. Yes, I could ruin the label. But that would destroy everything that you and your sister have worked so hard for, and I'm not necessarily here to hurt you. But gaining a piece of this… Making sure my sister gets something, making sure your father knows that I'm right there… That has value to me."

"What about Donovan?"

"He's not my problem. But it's your call, Emerson.

You can marry Donovan. And inherit the smoldering wreckage that I'll leave behind. Or, you marry me."

"How do I know you're telling the truth?"

"Look up Soraya Jane on your favorite social media site."

"I… Wait. I know who she is. She's… She has millions of followers."

"I know," he said.

"She's your sister."

"Yes."

"And…"

"My name is Holden. Holden McCall. I am not famous on the internet, or really anywhere. But I'm one of the wealthiest developers in the state. With my money, my sister gained some connections, got into modeling. Started traveling."

"She's built an empire online," Emerson said.

"I know," he said. "What she's done is nothing short of incredible. But she's lost herself. Your father devastated her. Destroyed her. And I can't let that stand."

"So I… If I don't marry you…you destroy everything. And the reason for me marrying Donovan doesn't even exist anymore."

"That's the size of it."

"And we have to transfer everything before my father realizes what you're doing."

Emerson had no idea what to do. No idea what to think. Holden could be lying to her about all of this, but if he wasn't, then he was going to destroy the winery, and there was really no way for her to be sure about which one was true until it was too late.

"Well, what do we do, then?"

"I told you, that is up to you."

"Okay. So say we get married. Then what?"

"You were already prepared to marry a man you didn't love, might as well be me."

Except… This was worse than marrying a man she didn't love.

She had trusted Holden with something deep and real. Some part of her that she had never shown to anyone else. She had trusted him enough to let him tie her hands.

To let him inside her body.

And now she had to make a decision about marrying him. On the heels of discovering that she didn't know him at all.

"I'll marry you," she said. "I'll marry you."

Nine

The roar of victory in Holden's blood hadn't quieted, not even by the time they boarded his private plane. They'd left the party and were now taking off from the regional airport, bound for Las Vegas, and he was amused by the fact that they both just so happened to be dressed for a wedding, though they hadn't planned it.

"Twenty-four-hour wedding chapels and no waiting period," he said, lifting a glass of champagne, and then extending his hand and offering it to her.

The plane was small, but nicely appointed, and fairly quiet.

He wasn't extraordinarily attached to a great many of the creature comforts that had come with his wealth. But being able to go where he wanted, when he wanted, and without a plane full of people was certainly his favorite.

"You have your own plane," she said, taking the

glass of champagne and downing it quickly. "You are private-plane rich."

She didn't look impressed so much as pissed.

"Yep," he said.

She shook her head, incredulous. "I… I don't even know what to say to that."

"I didn't ask you to say anything."

"No. You asked me to marry you."

"I believe I *demanded* that you marry me or I'd ruin your family."

"My mistake," she said, her tone acerbic. "How could I be so silly?"

"You may not believe me, but I told you, I didn't intend to involve you in this."

"I just conveniently involved myself?"

"If it helps, I found it an inconvenience at first."

"Why? You felt *guilty*? In the middle of your quest to take down my family and our fortune? Yes, that must've been inconvenient for you."

"I didn't want to drag you into it," he said. "Because I'm not your father. And I sure as hell wasn't going to extract revenge by using you for sex. The sex was separate. I only realized the possibilities when you told me about how your husband would be given an ownership stake in the vineyard."

"Right," she said. "Of course. Because I was an idiot who thought that since you had been inside me, I could maybe have a casual conversation with you."

"I'm sorry, but the information was too good for me to let go. And in the end, your family gets off easier."

"Except that you might do something drastic and destroy the winery with your control of the share."

"I was absolutely going to do that, but now I can own

a piece of it instead. And that benefits me. I also have his daughter, right with me."

"Oh, are you going to hold a gun to my head for dramatics?"

"No gun," he said. "In fact, we're on a private plane, and you're drinking champagne. You're not in any danger from me, and I didn't force you to come with me."

"But you did," she said, her voice thick.

"I offered you two choices."

"I didn't like either of them."

"Welcome to life, princess. You not liking your options isn't the same as you not having any."

She ignored that statement. "This is *not* my life."

"It is now." He appraised her for a long moment, the elegant line of her profile. She was staring out the window, doing her very best not to look at him. "The Big Bad Wolf was always going to try and eat you. You know how the fairy tale goes."

"Say whatever you need to say to make yourself feel better," she said. "You're not a wolf. You're just a dick."

"And your father?"

That seemed to kill her desire to banter with him. "I don't know if I believe you."

"But you believe me just enough to be on a plane with me going to Las Vegas to get married, because if I'm right, if I'm telling the truth..."

"It ruins everything. And I don't think I trust anyone quite so much that I would take that chance. Not even my father. I don't trust you at all, but what choice do I have? Because you're right. I was willing to marry a man that I didn't love to support my family. To support the empire. The dynasty. So why the hell wouldn't I do it now?"

"Oh, but you hate me, don't you?"

"I do," she said. "I really do."

He could sense that there was more she wanted to say, but that she wouldn't. And they were silent for the next hour, until the plane touched down in Nevada.

"Did you want an Elvis impersonator?" he asked, when they arrived on the Strip, at the little white wedding chapel he'd reserved before they landed.

"And me without my phone," she said.

"Did you want to take pictures and post them?"

She narrowed her eyes. "I wanted to beat you over the head with it."

"That doesn't answer my question about Elvis."

"Yeah, that would be good. If we don't have an Elvis impersonator, the entire wedding will be ruined."

"Don't tease me, because I will get the Elvis impersonator."

"Get him," she said, making a broad gesture. "Please. Because otherwise this would be *absurd*."

The edge of hysteria in her voice suggested she felt it was already absurd, but he chose to take what she said as gospel.

And he checked the box on the ridiculous paperwork, requesting Elvis, because she thought he was kidding, and she was going to learn very quickly that he was not a man to be trifled with. Even when it came to things like this.

They waited until their names were called.

And sadly, the only impersonator who was available past ten thirty on a Saturday night seemed to be Elvis from the mid-1970s.

"Do you want me to sing 'Burning Love' or 'Can't Help Falling in Love' at the end of the ceremony?" he asked in all seriousness.

"Pick your favorite," Emerson replied, her face stony.

And Holden knew she had been certain that this level of farce would extinguish the thing that burned between them. Because she hated him now, and he could see the truth of that in her eyes.

But he was happy to accept her challenge. Happy to stand there exchanging vows with an Elvis impersonator as officiant, and a woman in a feathered leotard as witness, because it didn't change the fact that he wanted her.

Desperately.

That all he could think about was when this was finished, he was going to take her up to a lavish suite and have her fifty different ways.

And she might not think she wanted it, but she would.

She might think that she could burn it all out with her anger, but she couldn't. He knew it.

He knew it because he was consumed by it.

He should feel only rage. Should feel only the need for revenge.

But he didn't.

And she wouldn't either.

"You may kiss the bride," Elvis said.

She looked at him with a warning in her eyes, but that warning quickly became a challenge.

She would learn pretty quickly that he didn't back down from a challenge.

He cupped her chin with his hand, and kissed her, hard and fast, but just that light, quick brush of their mouths left them both breathing hard.

And as soon as they separated, the music began to play and Elvis started singing about how he just couldn't help falling in love.

Well, Holden could sure as hell help falling in love.

But he couldn't keep himself from wanting Emerson. That was a whole different situation.

They signed the paperwork quickly, and as soon as they were in the car that had been waiting for them, he handed her his phone. "Call your lawyer."

"It's almost midnight," she said.

"He'll take a call from you, you know it. We need to get everything set into motion so we have it all signed tomorrow morning."

"*She* will take a call from me," she said pointedly. But then she did as he asked. "Hi, Julia. It's Emerson. I just got married." He could hear a voice saying indiscriminate words on the other end. "Thank you. I need to make sure that I transfer the shares of the company into my husband's name. As soon as possible." She looked over at him. "Where are we staying?"

She recited all of the necessary information back to Julia at his direction, including the information about him, before getting off the phone.

"She'll have everything faxed to us by morning."

"And she won't tip off your father?"

"No," she said. "She's the family lawyer, but she must know... She's going to realize that I eloped. And she's going to realize that I'm trying to bypass my father. That I want my husband to have the ownership shares he—I—is entitled to. She won't allow my father to interfere."

"She's a friend of yours, then."

"We became friends, yes. People who aren't liars make friends."

"I'm wounded."

"I didn't think you could wound granite."

"Why did you comply with what I asked you to do so easily?"

Suddenly, her voice sounded very small and tired. "Because. It makes no sense to come here, to marry you, if I don't follow through with the rest. You'll ruin my family if you don't get what you asked for. I'm giving it to you. Protesting now is like tying my own self to the railroad tracks, and damsel in distress isn't my style." She looked at him, her blue eyes certain. "I made my bed. I'll lie in it."

They pulled up to the front of a glitzy casino hotel that was far from his taste in anything.

But what he did like about Las Vegas was the sexual excess. Those who created the lavish hotel rooms here understood exactly why a man was willing to pay a lot of money for a hotel room. And it involved elaborate showers, roomy bathtubs and beds that could accommodate all manner of athletics.

The decor didn't matter to him at all with those other things taken into consideration.

They got out of the car, and he tipped the valet.

"Your secretary called ahead, Mr. McCall," the man said. "You're all checked in and ready to go straight upstairs. A code has been texted to your phone."

Holden put his arm around her, and the two of them began to walk to an elevator. "I hope you don't think… I… We're going to a hotel room and…" Emerson said.

"Do you think you're going to share a space with me tonight and keep your hands off me?"

They got inside the elevator, and the doors closed. "I hate you," she said, shoving at his chest.

"And you want me," he said. "And that might make you hate me even more, but it doesn't make it not true."

"I want to…"

"Go ahead," he said. "Whatever you want."

"I'm going to tear that tux right off your body," she said, her voice low and feral. "Absolutely destroy it."

"Only if I can return the favor," he said, arousal coursing through him.

"You might not be all that confident when I have the most fragile part of you in my hand."

He didn't know why, but that turned him on. "I'll take my chances."

"I don't understand what this is," she said. "I should be…disgusted by you."

"It's too late. You already got dirty with me, honey. You might as well just embrace it. Because you know how good it is between us. And you wanted me when I was nothing other than a ranch hand. Why wouldn't you want me when you know that I'm a rich man with a vengeful streak a mile wide?"

"You forced me into this."

"I rescued you from that boring bowl of oatmeal you called a fiancé. At least you hate me. You didn't feel anything for him."

Her hackles were up by the time they got to the suite door, and he entered his code. The door opened and revealed the lavish room that had all the amenities he wanted out of such a place.

"This is tacky," she said, throwing her purse down on the couch.

"And?"

"Warm," she said.

She reached behind her body and grabbed hold of her zipper, pulling down the tab and letting her dress fall to the floor.

"I figured you were going to make me work for it."

"Your ego doesn't deserve that. Then you'd get to call it a seduction. I want to fuck you, I can't help myself. But I'm not sure you should be particularly flattered by that. I hate myself for it."

"Feel free to indulge your self-loathing, particularly if at some point it involves you getting that pretty lipstick all over me."

"I'm sure it will. Because I'm here with you. And there's not much I can do about my choices now. We're married. And a stake in the vineyard is close to being transferred into your name. I've already had sex with you. I got myself into this. I might as well have an orgasm."

"We can certainly do better than one orgasm," he said.

She looked good enough to eat, standing there in some very bridal underwear, all white and lacy, and unintentionally perfect for the moment, still wearing the red high heels she'd had on with her dress.

He liked her like this.

But he liked her naked even better.

She walked over to where he stood, grabbed hold of his tie and made good on her promise.

She wrenched the knot loose, then tore at his shirt, sending buttons scattering across the floor. "I hope that was expensive," she said, moving her hand over his bare chest.

"It was," he said. "Very, very expensive. But sadly for you, expensive doesn't mean anything to me. I could buy ten more and not notice the expense."

He could see the moment when realization washed over her. About who had the power. She was so very comfortable with her financial status and she'd had an idea about his, and what that meant, and even though she'd seen the plane, seen him in the tux, the reality of who he'd been all along was just now hitting her.

"And to think," she said, "I was very worried about taking advantage of you that night we were together."

"That says more about you and the way you view people without money than it does about me, sweetheart."

"Not because of that. You work for my father. By extension, for me, since I own part of the winery. And I was afraid that I might be taking advantage of you. But here you were, so willing to blackmail me."

"Absolutely. Life's a bastard, and so am I. That's just the way of things."

"Here I thought she was a bitch. Which I've always found handy, I have to say." She pushed his shirt off his shoulders, and he shed it the rest of the way onto the floor, and then she unhooked his belt, pulling it through the loops.

He grinned. "Did you want to use that?"

"What?"

"You know, you could tie me down if you wanted," he said. "If it would make you feel better. Make you feel like you have some control."

Something flared in her eyes, but he couldn't quite read it. "Why would I want that? That wouldn't give me more control. It would just mean I was doing most of the work." She lifted her wrists up in supplication, her eyes never leaving his. "You can tie my wrists, and I'll still have the control."

He put the tip of the leather through the buckle, and looped it over her wrists, pulling the end tight before he looped it through the buckle again, her wrists held fast together. Then, those blue eyes never leaving his, she sank down onto her knees in front of him.

Ten

She had lost her mind, or something. Her heart was pounding so hard, a mixture of arousal, rage and shame pouring over her.

She should have told him no. She should have told him he was never touching her again. But something about her anger only made her want to play these games with him even more, and she didn't know what that said about her.

But he was challenging her, with everything from his marriage proposal to the Elvis at the chapel. This room itself was a challenge, and then the offer to let her tie him up.

All of it was seeing if he could make her or break her, and she refused to break. Because she was Emerson Maxfield, and she excelled at everything she did. And if this was the way she was going to save her family's dynasty, then she was going to save it on her knees in front of Holden McCall.

"You think I'm just going to give you what you want?" he asked, stroking himself through his pants. She could see the aggressive outline of his arousal beneath the dark fabric, and her internal muscles pulsed.

"Yes," she said. "Because I don't think you're strong enough to resist me."

"You might be right about that," he said. "Because I don't do resisting. I spent too much of my life wanting, and that's not something that I allow. I don't want anymore. I have."

He unhooked the closure on his pants, slid the zipper down slowly and then freed himself.

He wrapped his hand around the base, holding himself steady for her. She arched up on her knees and took him into her mouth, keeping her eyes on his the entire time.

With her hands bound as they were, she allowed him to guide her, her hair wrapped around his fist as he dictated her movements.

It was a game.

She could get out of the restraints if she wanted to. Could leave him standing there, hard and aching. But she was submitting to this fiction that she was trapped, because somehow, given the marriage—which she truly was trapped in—this felt like power.

This choice.

Feeling him begin to tremble as she took him in deep, feeling his power fracture as she licked him, tasted him.

She was the one bound, but he couldn't have walked away from her now if he wanted to, and she knew it.

They both did.

He held all the power outside this room, outside this moment. But she'd claimed her own here, and she was going to relish every second.

She teased him. Tormented him.

"Stand up," he said, the words scraping his throat raw.

She looked up at him, keeping her expression serene. "Are you not enjoying yourself?"

"Stand up," he commanded. "I want you to walk to the bed."

She stood slowly, her hands still held in that position of chosen obedience. Then with her eyes never leaving his, she walked slowly toward the bedroom. She didn't turn away from him until she had to, and even then, she could feel his gaze burning into her. Lighting a fire inside of her.

Whatever this was, it was bigger than them both.

Because he hated her father, and whether or not the reasons that he hated James Maxfield were strictly true or not, the fact was he did.

And she didn't get the impression that he was excited to find himself sexually obsessed with her. But he was.

She actually believed that what he wanted from her in terms of the winery was separate from him wanting her body, because this kind of intensity couldn't be faked.

And most important, it wasn't only on his side.

That had humiliated her at first.

The realization that she had been utterly captivated by this man, even while he was engaged in a charade.

But the fact of the matter was, he was just as enthralled with her.

They were both tangled in it.

Whether they wanted to be or not.

She climbed onto the bed, positioning herself on her back, her arms held straight down in front of her, covering her breasts, covering that space between her thighs. And she held that pose when he walked in.

Hunger lit his gaze and affirmed what she already knew to be true in her heart. He wanted her.

He hated it.

There was something so deliciously wicked about the contrast.

About this control she had over him even now.

A spark flamed inside her stomach.

He doesn't approve of this, or of you. But he can't help himself.

She arched her hips upward unconsciously, seeking some kind of satisfaction.

It was so much more arousing than it had any right to be. This moment of triumph.

Because it was private. Because it was secret.

Emerson lived for appearances.

She had been prepared to marry a man for those appearances.

And yet, this moment with Holden was about nothing more than the desire between two people. That he resented their connection? That only made it all feel stronger, hotter.

He removed his clothes completely as he approached the bed.

She looked down at her own body, realizing she was still wearing her bra and panties, her high heels.

"You like me like this," she whispered.

"I like you any way I can get you," he said, his voice low and filled with gravel.

"You like this, don't you? You had so much commentary on me wanting to slum it with a ranch hand. I think you like something about having a rich girl. Though, now I don't know why."

"Is there any man on earth who doesn't fantasize about corrupting the daughter of his enemy?"

"Did you corrupt me? I must've missed the memo."

"If I haven't yet, honey, then it's going to be a long night." He scooted her up the mattress, and lifted her arms, looping them back over her head, around one of the posts on the bed frame. Her hands parted, the leather from the belt stretching tight over the furniture, holding her fast. "At my mercy," he said.

He took his time with her then.

Took her high heels off her feet slowly, kissing her ankle, her calf, the inside of her thigh. Then he teased the edges of her underwear before pulling them down slowly, kissing her more intimately. He traveled upward, to her breasts, teasing her through the lace before removing the bra and casting it to the floor. And then he stood back, as if admiring his hard work.

"As fun as this is," he said, "I want your hands on me."

She could take her own hands out of the belt, but she refused. Refused to break the fiction that had built between the two of them.

So she waited. Waited as he slowly, painstakingly undid the belt and made a show of releasing her wrists. Her entire body pulsed with need for him. And thankfully, it was Vegas, so there were condoms on the bedside table.

He took care of the necessities, quickly, and then joined her on the bed, pinning her down on the mattress.

She smiled up at him, lifting her hand and tracing the line of his jaw with her fingertip. "Let's go for a ride," she whispered.

He growled, gripped her hips and held her steady as he entered her in one smooth stroke.

She gasped at the welcome invasion, arching against

his body as he tortured them both mercilessly, drove them both higher than she thought she could stand.

And when she looked into his eyes, she saw the man she had been with that first night, not a rich stranger.

Holden.

His last name didn't matter. It didn't matter where he was from. What was real was *this*.

And she knew it, because their desire hadn't changed, even if their circumstances had. If anything, their desire had sharpened, grown in intensity.

And she believed with her whole soul that what they'd shared in his bed had never been about manipulating her.

Because the intensity was beyond them. Beyond sex in a normal sense, so much deeper. So much more terrifying.

She took advantage of her freedom. In every sense of the word.

The freedom of her hands to explore every ridge of muscle on his back, down his spine, to his sculpted ass.

And the freedom of being in this moment. A moment that had nothing to do with anything except need.

This…this benefited no one. In fact, it was a short road off a cliff, but that hadn't stopped either of them.

They couldn't stop.

He lowered his head, growling again as he thrust into her one last time, his entire body shaking with his release.

And she followed him over the edge.

She let out a hoarse cry, digging her fingernails into his skin as she crested that wave of desire over and over again.

She didn't think it would end.

She thought she might die.

She thought she might not mind, if this was heaven, between the sheets with him.

And when her orgasm passed, she knew she was going to have to deal with the fact that he was her husband.

With the reality of what her father would think.

With Holden, her father's enemy, owning a share in the winery.

But those realizations made her head pound and her heart ache.

And she would rather focus on the places where her body burned with pleasure.

Tomorrow would come soon enough, and there would be documents to fax and sign, and they would have to fly back to Oregon.

But that was all for later.

And Emerson had no desire to check her phone. No desire to have any contact with the outside world.

No desire to take a picture to document anything.

Because none of this could be contained in a pithy post. None of it could even be summed up in something half so coherent as words.

The only communication they needed was between their bodies.

Tomorrow would require words. Explanations. Probably recriminations.

But tonight, they had this.

And so Emerson shut the world out, and turned to him.

Eleven

By the time he and his new wife were on a plane back to Oregon, Emerson was looking sullen.

"It's possible he'll know what happened by the time we get there," she said.

"But you're confident there's nothing he can do to stop it?"

She looked at him, prickles of irritation radiating off her. A sharp contrast to the willing woman who had been in his bed last night.

"Why do you care? It works out for you either way."

"True. But it doesn't work out particularly well for you."

"And you care about that?"

"I married you."

"Yeah, I still don't really get that. What exactly do you think is going to happen now?"

"We'll have a marriage. Why not?"

"You told me you didn't believe in marriage."

"I also told you I was a ranch hand."

"Have you been married before?" She frowned.

"No. Would it matter if I had?"

"In a practical sense, obviously nothing is a deal breaker, since I'm already married to you, for the winery. So no. But yes. Actually, it does."

"Never been married. No kids."

"Dammit," she said. "It didn't even occur to me that you might have children."

"Well, I don't."

"Thank God."

"Do you want to have some?"

The idea should horrify him. But for some reason, the image of Emerson getting round with his baby didn't horrify him at all. In fact, the side effect of bringing her into his plans pleased him in ways he couldn't quite articulate.

The idea of simply ruining James Maxfield had been risky. Because there was every chance that no matter how hard Holden tried there would be no serious blowback for the man who had harmed Holden's sister the way that he had.

Wealthy men tended to be tougher targets than young women. Particularly young women who traded on the image of their beauty.

Not that Holden wasn't up to the task of trying to ruin the man.

Holden was powerful in his own right, and he was ruthless with it.

But there was something deeply satisfying about owning a piece of his enemy's legacy. And not only that, he got James's precious daughter in the bargain.

This felt right.

"I can't believe that you're suggesting we..."

"You wanted children, right?"

"I... Yes."

"So, it's not such an outrageous thought."

"You think we're going to stay married?"

"You didn't sign a prenuptial agreement, Emerson. You leave me, I still get half of your shares of the vineyard."

"You didn't sign one either. I have the impression half of what's yours comes out to an awful lot of money."

"Money is just money. I'll make more. I don't have anything I care about half as much as you care about the vineyard. About the whole label."

"Well, why don't we wait to discuss children until I decide how much I hate you."

"You hate me so much you climbed on me at least five times last night."

"Yes, and in the cold light of day that seems less exciting than it did last night. The chemistry between us doesn't have anything to do with...our marriage."

"It has everything to do with it," he said, his tone far darker and more intense than he'd intended it to be.

"What? You manufactured this chemistry so we could..."

"No. The marriage made sense because of our chemistry. I was hardly going to let you walk away from me and marry another man, Emerson. Let him get his hands on your body when he has had all this time? He's had the last two years and he did nothing? He doesn't deserve you. And your father doesn't get to use you as a pawn."

"My father..."

"He's not a good man. Whether you believe me or not, it's true. But I imagine that when we impart the happy news to him today… You can make that decision for yourself."

"Thanks. But I don't need your permission to make my own decisions about my father or anything else."

But the look on her face was something close to haunted, and if he were a man prone to guilt, he might feel it now. They landed not long after, and his truck was there, still where he'd left it.

When they paused in front of it, she gave it a withering stare. "This thing is quite the performance."

It was a pretty beat-up truck. But it was genuinely his.

"It's mine," he said.

"From when?"

"Well, I got it when I was about…eighteen. So going on fifteen years ago."

"I don't even know how old you are. I mean, I do now, because I can do math. But really, I don't know anything about you, Holden."

"Well, I'll be happy to give you the rundown after we meet with your father."

"Well, looking forward to all that."

She was still wearing her dress from last night. He had found a replacement shirt in the hotel shop before they'd left, and it was too tight on his shoulders and not snug enough in the waist. When they arrived at the winery and entered the family's estate together, he could only imagine the picture they made.

Him in part of a tux, and her in last night's gown.

"Is my father in his study yet?" she questioned one of the first members of the household staff who walked by.

"Yes," the woman said, looking between Emerson and him. "Shall I see if he's receiving visitors?"

"He doesn't really have a choice," Holden said. "He'll make time to see us."

He took Emerson's hand and led her through the house, their footsteps loud on the marble floors. And he realized as they approached the office, what a pretentious show this whole place was.

James Maxfield wasn't that different from Holden. A man from humble beginnings hell-bent on forging a different path. But the difference between James and Holden was that Holden hadn't forgotten where he'd come from. He hadn't forgotten what it was to be powerless, and he would never make anyone else feel that kind of desperation.

James seemed to enjoy his position and all the power that came with it.

You don't enjoy it? Is that why you're standing here getting ready to walk through that door with his daughter and make him squirm? Is that why you forced Emerson to marry you?

He pushed those thoughts aside. And walked into the office without knocking, still holding tightly to Emerson.

Her father looked up, looked at him and then at Emerson. "What the hell is this?" he asked.

"I..."

"A hostile takeover," Holden said. "You ruined my sister's life. And now I'm here to make yours very, very difficult. And only by your daughter's good grace am I leaving you with anything other than a smoldering pile of wreckage. Believe me when I say it's not for your sake. But for the innocent people in your family who don't deserve to lose everything just because of your sins."

"Which sins are those?"

"My sister. Soraya Jane."

The silence in the room was palpable. Finally, James spoke.

"What is it you intend to do?"

"You need to guard your office better. I know you think this house isn't a corporation so you don't need high security, but you're such a damned narcissist you didn't realize you'd hired someone who was after the secrets you keep in your home. And now I have them. And thanks to Emerson, I now have a stake in this winery too. You can contest the marriage and my ownership, but it won't end well for you. It might not be my first choice now, but I'm still willing to detonate everything if it suits me."

James Maxfield's expression remained neutral, and his focus turned to his daughter.

"Emerson," her father said, "you agreed to this? You are allowing him to blackmail us?"

"What choice did I have?" she asked, a thread of desperation in her voice. "I trust you, Dad. I do. But he planned to destroy us. Whether his accusations are true or not, that was his intent. He gave me no time, and he didn't give me a lot of options. This marriage was the only way I could salvage what we've built, because he was ready to wage a campaign against you, against our family, at any cost. He was going to come at us personally and professionally. I couldn't take any chances. I couldn't. I did what I had to do. I did what you would have done, I'm sure. I did what needed doing."

"You were supposed to marry Donovan," James said, his tone icy.

"I know," Emerson said. "But what was I supposed to do when the situation changed? This man…"

"Have you slept with him?"

Emerson drew back, clearly shocked that her father had asked her that question. "I don't understand what that has to do with anything."

"It certainly compromises the purity of your claims," James returned. "You say you've been blackmailed into this arrangement, but if you're in a relationship with him…"

"Did you sleep with his sister?" she asked. "All those… All those other women in the files. Did you… Did you cheat on Mom?"

"Emerson, there are things you don't need to know about, and things you don't understand. My relationship with your mother works, even if it's not traditional."

"You *did*." She lowered her voice to a near whisper. "His sister. She's younger than me."

"Emerson…"

Holden took a step toward James's desk. "Men like you always think it won't come back on you. You think you can take advantage of women who are young, who are desperate, and no one will come for you. But I am here for you. This empire of yours? It serves me now. Your daughter? She's mine too. And if you push me, I swear I will see it all ruined and everyone will know what you are. How many people do you think will come here for a wedding, or parties, then? What of the brand worldwide? Who wants to think about sexual harassment, coercion and the destruction of a woman young enough to be your daughter when they have a sip of your merlot?"

Silence fell, tense and hard between them.

"The brand is everything," James said finally. "I've done everything I can to foster that family brand, as has your mother. What we do in private is between us."

"And the gag order you had my sister sign, and all

those other women? Soraya has been institutionalized because of all of this. Because of the fallout. And she might have signed papers, but I did not. And now I don't need to tell the world about your transgressions to have control over what you've built. And believe me, in the years to come, I will make your life hell." Holden leaned forward, placing his palms on the desk. "Emerson was your pawn. You were going to use her as a wife to the man you wanted as part of this empire. But Emerson is with me now. She's no longer yours."

"*Emerson* is right here," Emerson said, her voice vibrating with emotion. "And frankly, I'm disgusted by the both of you. I don't belong to either of you. Dad, I did what I had to do to save the vineyard. I did it because I trusted you. I trusted that Holden's accusations were false. But you did all of this, didn't you?"

"It was an affair," James said. "It looks to me like you are having one of your own, so it's a bit rich for you to stand in judgment of me."

"I hadn't made vows to Donovan. And I never claimed to love him. He also knows..."

"Your mother knows," James said. "The terms of a marriage are not things you discuss with your children. You clearly have the same view of relationships that I do, and here you are lecturing me."

"It's not the same," she said. "And as for you," she said, turning to Holden. "I married you because it was the lesser of two evils. But that doesn't make me yours. You lied to me. You made me believe you were someone you weren't. You're no different from him."

Emerson stormed out of the room, and left Holden standing there with James.

"She makes your victory ring hollow," James said.

"Even if she divorces me, part of the winery is still

mine. We didn't have a prenuptial agreement drafted between us, something I'm sure you were intending to take care of when she married that soft boy from the East Coast."

"What exactly are you going to do now?"

"I haven't decided yet. And the beauty of this is I have time. You can consider me the sword of Damocles hanging over your head. And one day, you know the thread will break. The question is when."

"And what do you intend to do to Emerson?"

"I've done it already. She's married to me. She's mine."

Those words burned with conviction, no matter her protests before storming out. And he didn't know why he felt the truth of those words deeper than anything else.

He had married her. It was done as far as he was concerned.

He went out of the office, and saw Emerson standing there, her hands planted firmly on the balustrade, overlooking the entry below.

"Let's talk," he said.

She turned to face him. "I don't want to talk. You should go talk with my father some more. The two of you seemed to be enjoying that dialogue."

"*Enjoy* is a strong word."

"You betrayed me," she said.

"I don't know you, Emerson. You don't know me. We hadn't ever made promises to each other. I didn't betray you. Your *father* betrayed you."

She looked stricken by that, and she said nothing.

"I want you to come live with me."

"Why would I do that?"

"Because we're married. Because it's not fake."

"Does that mean you love me?" she asked, her tone scathing.

"No. But there's a lot of mileage between love and fake. And you know it."

"I live here. I work here. I can't leave."

"Handily, I have bought a property on the adjacent mountain. You won't have to leave. I do have another ranch in Jackson Creek, and I'd like to visit there from time to time. I do a bit of traveling. But there's no reason we can't be based here, in Gold Valley."

"You'll have to forgive me. I'm not understanding the part of your maniacal plan where we try to pretend we're a happy family."

"The vineyard is more yours now than it was before. I have no issue deferring to you on a great many things."

"You're not just going to…let it get run into the ground?"

"If I wanted to do that, I wouldn't have to own a piece. I own part of your father's legacy. And that appeases me.

"So," he concluded, "shall we go?"

Twelve

Emerson looked around the marble halls of the Maxfield estate, and for the very first time in all her life, she didn't feel like she was home.

The man in the office behind her was a stranger.

The man in front of her was her husband, whether or not he was a stranger.

And his words kept echoing in her head.

I didn't betray you. Your father betrayed you.

"Let's go," she said. Before she could think the words through.

She found herself bundled back up into his truck, still wearing the dress she had been wearing at yesterday's party. His house was a quick drive away from the estate, a modern feat of design built into the hillside, all windows to make the most of the view.

"Tell me about your sister," she said, standing in the drive with him, feeling decidedly flat and more than a bit defeated.

"She's my half sister," Holden said, taking long strides toward the front entry. He entered a code, opened the door and ushered her into a fully furnished living area.

"I had everything taken care of already," he said. "It's ready for us."

Ready for us.

She didn't know why she found that comforting. She shouldn't. She was unaccountably wounded by his betrayal, had been forced into this marriage. And yet, she wanted him. She couldn't explain it.

And her old life didn't feel right anymore, because it was even more of a lie than this one.

"My mother never had much luck with love," Holden said, his voice rough. "I had to take care of her. Because the men she was with didn't. They would either abuse her outright or manipulate her, and she wasn't very strong. Soraya came along when I was eight. About the cutest thing I'd ever seen. And a hell of a lot of trouble. I had to get her ready, had to make sure her hair was brushed for school. All of that. But I did it. I worked, and I took care of them, and once I got money, I made sure they had whatever they wanted." He looked away from her, a muscle jumping in his jaw. "It was after Soraya had money that she met your father. I don't think it takes a genius to realize she's got daddy issues. And he played each and every one of them. She got pregnant. He tried to get her to terminate. She wouldn't. She lost the baby anyway. And she lost her mind right along with it."

Hearing those words again, now knowing that they were true…they hit her differently.

She sat down on the couch, her stomach cramping with horror.

"You must love her a lot," she said. "To do all of this for her."

She thought about her father, and how she had been willing to marry a stranger for him. And then how she had married Holden to protect the winery, to protect her family, her father. And now she wasn't entirely convinced she shouldn't have just let Holden do what he wanted.

He frowned. "I did what had to be done. Like I always do. I take care of them."

"Because you love them," she said.

"Because no one else takes care of them." He shook his head. "My family wasn't loving. They still aren't. My mother is one of the most cantankerous people on the face of the planet, but you do what you do. You keep people going. When they're your responsibility, there's no other choice."

"Oh," she said. She took a deep, shuddering breath. "You see, I love my father. I love my mother. That's why her disapproval hurts. That's why his betrayal… I didn't know that he was like this. That he could have done those things to someone like your sister. It hurts me to know it. You're right. He is the one who betrayed me. And I will never be able to go into the estate again and look at it, at him, the same way. I'll never be able to look at him the same. It's just all broken, and I don't think it can ever be put back together."

"We'll see," he said. "I never came here to put anything back together. Because I knew it was all broken beyond the fixing of it. I came here to break *him*, because he broke Soraya. And I don't think she's going to be fixed either." He came to stand in front of Emerson, his hands shoved into his pockets, his expression grim. "And I'm sorry that you're caught up in the middle of this, because I don't have any stake in breaking you. But here's what I know about broken things. They can't be put back together exactly as they were. I think you can make something new out of them, though."

"Are you giving me life advice? Really? The man who blackmailed me into marriage?" He was still so absurdly beautiful, so ridiculously gorgeous and compelling to her. It was wrong. But she didn't know how to fix it. How to change it. Like anything else in her life. And really, right at the moment, it was only one of the deeply messed up things in her reality.

That she felt bonded to him even as the bonds that connected her to her family were shattered.

"You can take it or not," he said. "That doesn't change the fact that it's true. Whether or not I exposed him, your father is a predator. This is who he is. You could have lived your life without knowing the truth, but I don't see how that's comforting."

It wasn't. It made a shiver race down her spine, made her feel cold all over. "I just… I trusted him. I trusted him so much that I was willing to marry a man he chose for me. I would have done anything he asked me to do. He built a life for me, and he gave me a wonderful childhood, and he made me the woman that I am. For better or for worse. He did a whole host of wonderful things for me, and I don't know how to reconcile that with what else I now know about him."

"All *I* know is your father is a fool. Because the way you believe in him… I've never believed in anyone that way. Anyone or anything. And the way my sister believed in him… He didn't deserve that, from either of you. And if just one person believed in me the way that either of you believed in him, the way that I think your mother believes in him, your sisters… I wouldn't have done anything to mess that up."

Something quiet and sad bloomed inside of her. And she realized that the sadness wasn't for losing her faith in her father. Not even a little.

"I did," she said.

"What?"

"I did. Believe in you like that. Holden Brown. That ranch hand I met not so long ago. I don't know what you think about me, or women like me. But it mattered to me that I slept with you. That I let you into my body. I've only been with two other men. For me, sex is an intimate thing. And I've never shared it with someone outside of a relationship. But there was something about you. I trusted you. I believed what you told me about who you were. And I believed in what my body told me about what was between us. And now what we shared has kind of turned into this weird and awful thing, and I just… I don't think I'll ever trust myself again. Between my father and you…"

"I didn't lie to you." His voice was almost furious in its harshness. "Not about wanting you. Nothing that happened between you and me in bed was a lie. Not last night, and not the first night. I swear to you, I did not seduce you to get revenge on your father. Quite the opposite. I told myself when I came here that I would never touch you. You were forbidden to me, Emerson, because I didn't want to do the same thing your father had done. Because I didn't want to lie to you or take advantage of you in any way. When I first met you in that vineyard, I told myself I was disgusted by you. Because you had his blood in your veins. But no matter how much I told myself that, I couldn't make it true.

You're not your father. And that's how I feel. This thing between us is separate, and real."

"But the marriage is for revenge."

"Yes. But I wouldn't have taken the wedding *night* if I didn't want you."

"Can I believe in you?"

She didn't know where that question came from, all vulnerable and sad, and she wasn't entirely sure that she liked the fact that she'd asked it. But she needed to grab on to something. In this world where nothing made sense, in this moment when she felt rootless, because not even her father was who she thought he was, and she didn't know how she was going to face having that conversation with Wren, or with Cricket. Didn't know what she was going to say to her mother, because no matter how difficult their own relationship was, this gave Emerson intense sympathy for her mother.

Not to mention her sympathy for the young woman her father had harmed. And the other women who were like her. How many had there been just like Soraya? It made Emerson hurt to wonder.

She had no solid ground to stand on, and she was desperate to find purchase.

If Holden was telling the truth, if the chemistry between them was as real to him as it was to her, then she could believe in that if nothing else. And she needed to believe in it. Desperately.

"If I… If I go all in on this marriage, Holden, on this thing between us, if we work together to make the vineyard…ours—Wren and Cricket included—promise me that you'll be honest with me. That you will be faithful to me. Because right now, I'll pledge myself to you, because I don't know what the hell else to believe in. I'm angry with you, but if you're telling me the truth about wanting me, and you also told me the truth about my father, then you are the most real and honest thing in my life right now, and I will… I'll bet on that. But only if you promise me right now that you won't lie to me."

"I promise," he said, his eyes like two chips of obsidian, dark and fathomless. Hard.

And in her world that had proven to be built on a shifting sand foundation, his hardness was something steady. Something real.

She needed something real.

She stood up from her position on the couch, her legs wobbling when she closed the distance between them. "Then take me to bed. Because the only thing that feels good right now is you and me."

"I notice you didn't say it's the only thing that makes sense," he said, his voice rough. He cupped her cheek, rubbing his thumb over her cheekbone.

"Because it doesn't make sense. I should hate you. But I can't. Maybe it's just because I don't have the energy right now. Because I'm too sad. But this…whatever we have, it feels *real*. And I'm not sure what else is."

"This *is* real," he said, taking her hand and putting it on his chest. His heart was raging out of control, and she felt a surge of power roll through her.

It was real. Whatever else wasn't, the attraction between them couldn't be denied.

He carried her to the bed, and they said vows to each other's bodies. And somehow, it felt right. Somehow, in the midst of all that she had lost, her desire for Holden felt like the one right thing she had done.

Marrying him. Making this real.

Tonight, there were no restraints, no verbal demands. Just their bodies. Unspoken promises that she was going to hold in her heart forever.

And as the hours passed, a feeling welled up in her chest that terrified her more than anything else.

It wasn't hate. Not even close.

But she refused to give it a name. Not yet. Not now.

She would have a whole lot of time to sort out what she felt for this man.

She'd have the rest of her life.

Thirteen

The day he put Maxfield Vineyards as one of the assets on his corporate holdings was sadistically satisfying. He was going to make a special new label of wine as well. Soraya deserved to be indelibly part of the Maxfield legacy.

Because James Maxfield was indelibly part of Soraya's. And Holden's entire philosophy on the situation was that James didn't deserve to walk away from her without being marked by the experience.

Holden was now a man in possession of a very powerful method through which to dole out if not traditional revenge, then a steady dose of justice.

He was also a man in possession of a wife.

That was very strange indeed. But he counted his marriage to Emerson among the benefits of this arrangement.

Her words kept coming back to him. Echoing inside of him. All day, and every night when he reached for her.

Can I believe in you?

He found that he wanted her to believe in him, and he couldn't quite figure out why. Why should it matter that he not sweep Emerson into a web of destruction?

Why had he decided to go about marrying her in the first place when he could have simply wiped James Maxfield off the map?

But no. He didn't want to question himself.

Marrying her was a more sophisticated power play. And at the end of the day, he liked it better.

He had possession of the man's daughter. He had a stake in the man's company.

The sword of Damocles.

After all, ruination could be accomplished only once, but this was a method of torture that could continue on for a very long time.

His sense of satisfaction wasn't just because of Emerson.

He wasn't so soft that he would change direction because of a woman he'd slept with a few times.

Though, every night that he had her, he felt more and more connected to her.

He had taken great pleasure a few days ago when she broke the news to her fiancé.

The other man had been upset, but not about Emerson being with another man, rather about the fact that he was losing his stake in the Maxfield dynasty. In Holden's estimation that meant the man didn't deserve Emerson at all. Of course, he didn't care what anyone deserved, not in this scenario. *He* didn't deserve Emerson either, but he wanted her. That was all that mattered to him.

It was more than her ex-fiancé felt for her.

There was one person he had yet to call, though.

Soraya. She deserved to know everything that had happened.

He was one of her very few approved contacts. She was allowed to speak to him over the phone.

They had done some very careful and clever things to protect Soraya from contact with the outside world. He, his mother and Soraya's therapists were careful not to cut her off completely, but her social media use was monitored.

They had learned that with people like her, who had built an empire and a web of connections in the digital world, they had to be very careful about cutting them off entirely, or they felt like they had been cast into darkness.

But then, a good amount of their depression often came from that public world.

It was a balance. She was actually on her accounts less now than she had been when she'd first been hospitalized.

He called, and it didn't take long for someone to answer.

"This is Holden McCall. I'm calling for Soraya."

"Your sister is just finishing an art class. She should be with you in a moment."

In art class. He would have never picked something like that for her, but then, her sense of fashion was art in and of itself, he supposed. The way she framed her life and the scenes she found herself in. It was why she was so popular online. That she made her life into art. It pleased him to know she had found another way to express that. One that was maybe about her more than it was about the broader world.

"Holden?" Her voice sounded less frantic, more relaxed than he was used to.

"Yes," he said. "It's me."

"I haven't heard from you in a while." She sounded a bit petulant, childlike and accusing. Which, frankly, was the closest to her old self he'd heard her sound in quite some time.

"I know. I'm sorry. I've been busy. But I have something to tell you. And I hope this won't upset you. I think it might make you happy."

"What is happy?" She said it a bit sharply, and he wondered if she was being funny. It was almost impossible to tell with her anymore.

He ignored that question, and the way it landed inside of him. The way that it hollowed him out.

"I got married," he said.

"Holden," she said, sounding genuinely pleased. "I'm so glad. Did you fall in love? Love is wonderful. When it isn't terrible."

He swallowed hard. "No. I've married James Maxfield's daughter."

She gasped, the sound sharp in his ear, stabbing him with regret. "Why?"

"Well, that's the interesting part," he said. "I now own some of Maxfield Vineyards. And, Soraya, I'm going to make a wine and name it after you. Because he shouldn't be able to forget you, or what he did to you."

There was silence. For a long moment. "And I'm the one that's locked up because I'm crazy."

"What?"

"Did you hear yourself? You sound… You married somebody you don't love."

"It's not about love. It's about justice. He didn't deserve to get away with what he did to you."

"But he has," she said. "He has because he doesn't care."

"And I've made him care. His daughter knows what kind of man he is now. He's lost a controlling share in his own winery. He's also lost an alliance that he was hoping to build by marrying Emerson off to someone else."

"And the cost of those victories is your happiness. Because you aren't with a woman you love."

"I was never going to fall in love," he said. "It's not in me."

"Yeah, that's what I said too. Money was the only thing I loved. Until it wasn't." There was another long stretch of silence.

"I thought you would be happy. I'm getting a piece of this for you."

"I don't… I don't want it."

"You don't…"

"You have to do what you have to do," she said.

"I guess so." He didn't know what to say to that, and for the first time since he'd set out on this course, he questioned himself.

"Holden, where is my baby? They won't answer me."

Rage and grief seized up in his chest. She had sounded better, but she wasn't. "Sweetheart," he said. "You lost the baby. Remember?"

The silence was shattering. "I guess I did. I'm sorry. That's silly. It doesn't seem real. I don't seem real sometimes."

And he knew then, that no matter what she said, whether or not she accepted this gift he'd won for her, he didn't regret it. Didn't regret doing this for his sister, who slid in and out of terrible grief so often, and then had to relive her loss over and over again. At least this time she had accepted his response without having a breakdown. But talking about Maxfield cut her every time, he knew.

"Take care of yourself," he said.

"I will," she said.

And he was just thankful that there was someone there to take care of her, because whatever she said, he worried she wouldn't do it for herself.

And he was resolved then that what he'd done was right.

It had nothing to do with Emerson, or his feelings for her.

James deserved everything that he got and more.

Holden refused to feel guilt about any of it.

Very little had been said between herself and Wren about her elopement. And Emerson knew she needed to talk to her sister. Both of her sisters. But it was difficult to work up the courage to do it.

Because explaining it to them required sharing secrets about their father, secrets she knew would devastate them. She also knew devastating them would further her husband's goals.

Because she and Holden currently had the majority ownership in the vineyard. And with her sisters, they could take absolute control, which she knew was what Holden wanted ultimately.

Frankly, it all made her very anxious.

But anxious or not, talking with her sisters was why she had invited them to have lunch with her down in Gold Valley.

She walked into Bellissima, and the hostess greeted her, recognizing her instantly, and offering her the usual table.

There wasn't much in the way of incredibly fancy dining in Gold Valley, but her family had a good relationship with the restaurants, since they often supplied wine to them, and while they weren't places that required reservations or anything like that, a Maxfield could always count on having the best table in the house.

She sat at her table with a view, morosely perusing the menu while her mouth felt like it was full of sawdust. That was when Cricket and Wren arrived.

"You're actually taking a lunch break," Wren said. "Something must be wrong."

"We need to talk," Emerson said. "I thought it might be best to do it over a basket of bread."

She pushed the basket to the center of the table, like a very tasty peace offering.

Wren eyeballed it. "Things must be terrible if you're suggesting we eat carbs in the middle of the day."

"I eat carbs whenever I want," Cricket said, sitting down first, Wren following her younger sister's lead.

"I haven't really talked to you guys since—"

"Since you defied father and eloped with some guy that none of us even know?" Wren asked.

"Yeah, since that."

"Is he the guy?" Wren asked.

"*What* guy?" Cricket asked.

"She cheated on Donovan, had a one-night stand with some guy that I now assume is the guy she married. And the reason she disappeared from my party the other night."

"You did *what*?" Cricket asked.

"I'm sorry, now you're going to be more shocked about my one-night stand and about my random marriage?"

Cricket blinked. "Well. Yes."

"Yes. It is the same guy."

"Wow," Wren said. "I didn't take you for a romantic, Emerson. But I guess I was wrong."

"No," Emerson said. "I'm not a romantic."

But somehow, the words seemed wrong. Especially with the way her feelings were jumbled up inside of her.

"Then what happened?"

"That's what I need to talk to you about," she said. "It is not a good story. And I didn't want to talk to either of you about it at the winery. But I'm not sure bringing you into a public space to discuss it was the best choice either."

"You do have your own house now," Cricket pointed out.

"Yes. And Holden is there. And… Anyway. It'll all become clear in a second."

Before the waitress could even bring menus to her sisters, Emerson spilled out everything. About their father. About Holden's sister. And about the ultimatum that had led to her marriage.

"You just went along with it?" Wren asked.

"There was no *just* about it," Emerson responded. "I didn't know what he would do to the winery if I didn't comply. And I wasn't sure about Dad's piece in it until… until I talked to him. Holden and I. Dad didn't deny any of it. He says that him and Mom have an understanding, and of course it's something he wouldn't talk about with any of us. But I don't even know if that's true. And my only option is going to Mom and potentially hurting her if I want to find out that truth. So here's what I know so far. That Dad hurt someone. Someone younger than me, someone my new husband loves very much."

"But he's only your husband because he wants to get revenge," Cricket pointed out.

"I… I think that's complicated too. I hope it is."

"You're not in love with him, are you?" Wren asked.

She decided to dodge that question and continue on

with the discussion. "I love Dad. And I don't want to believe any of this, but I have to because…it's true."

Cricket looked down. "I wish that I could say I'm surprised. But it's different, being me. I mean, I feel like I see the outside of things. You're both so deep on the inside. Dad loves you, and he pays all kinds of attention to you. I'm kind of forgotten. Along with Mom. And when you're looking at him from a greater distance, I think the cracks show a lot more clearly."

"*I'm* shocked," Wren said sadly. "I've thrown my whole life into this vineyard. Into supporting him. And I… I can't believe that the man who encouraged me, treated me the way he did, could do that to someone else. To many women, it sounds like."

"People and feelings are very complicated," Emerson said slowly. "Nothing has shown me that more than my relationship with Holden."

"You do love him," Wren said.

Did she? Did she love a man who wanted to ruin her family?

"I don't know," Emerson said. "I feel something for him. Because you know what, you're right. I would never have just let him blackmail me into marriage if on some level I didn't… I… It's a real marriage." She felt her face getting hot, which was silly, because she didn't have any hang-ups about that sort of thing normally. "But I'm a little afraid that I'm confusing…well, that part of our relationship being good with actual love."

"I am not the person to consult about that kind of thing," Cricket said, taking a piece of bread out of the basket at the center of the table and biting into it fiercely.

"Don't look at me," Wren said. "We've already had the discussion about my own shameful issues."

Cricket looked at Wren questioningly, but didn't say anything.

"Well, the entire point of this lunch wasn't just to talk about me. Or my feelings. Or Dad. It's to discuss what we are going to do. Because the three of us can band together, and we can make all the controlling decisions for the winery. We supersede my husband even. We can protect the label, keep his actions in check and make our own mark. You're right, Cricket," Emerson said. "You have been on the outside looking in for too long. And you deserve better."

"I don't actually want to do anything at the winery," Cricket said. "I got a job."

"You did?"

"Yes. At Sugar Cup."

"Making coffee?"

"Yes," Cricket said proudly. "I want to do something different. Different from the whole Maxfield thing. But I'm with you, in terms of banding together for decision-making. I'll be a silent partner, and I'll support you."

"I'm in," Wren said. "Although, you realize that your husband has the ace up his sleeve. He could just decide to ruin us anyway."

"Yes, he could," Emerson said. "But now he owns a piece of the winery, and I think ownership means more to him than that."

"And he has you," Wren pointed out.

"I know," Emerson said. "But what can I do about it?"

"You do love him," Cricket said, her eyes getting wide. "I never thought you were sentimental enough."

"To fall in love? I have a heart, Cricket."

"Yes, but you were going to marry when you didn't love your fiancé. It's so patently obvious that you don't have any feelings for Donovan at all, and you were just going to marry him anyway. So, I assumed it didn't matter to you. Not really, and now you've gone and fallen in love with this guy… Someone who puts in danger the very thing you care about most. The thing you were willing to marry that bowl of oatmeal for."

"He wasn't a bowl of oatmeal," Emerson said.

"You're right," Wren said. "He wasn't. Because at least a person might want to eat a bowl of oatmeal, even if it's plain. You'd never want to eat him."

"Oh, for God's sake."

"Well," Wren said. "It's true."

"What matters is that the three of us are on the same page. No matter what happens. We are stronger together."

"Right," Wren and Cricket agreed.

"I felt like the rug was pulled out from under me when I found out about Dad. The winery didn't feel like it would ever seem like home again. I felt rootless, drifting. But we are a team. *We* are the Maxfield label. We are the Maxfield name. Just as much as he is."

"Agreed," Wren said.

"Agreed," said Cricket.

And their agreement made Emerson feel some sense of affirmation. Some sense of who she was.

She didn't have the relationship with her father she'd thought she had. She didn't have the father she'd thought she had.

Her relationship with Holden was…

Well, she was still trying to figure it out. But her relationship with Wren and Cricket was real. And it was strong. Strong enough to weather this, any of it.

And eventually she would have to talk to her mother. And maybe she would find something there that surprised her too. Because if there was one thing she was learning, it was that it didn't matter how things appeared. What mattered was the truth.

Really, as the person who controlled the brand of an entire label using pictures on the internet, she should have known better from the start. But somehow, she had thought that because she was so good at manipulating those images, that she might be immune to falling for them.

Right at this moment she believed in two things: her sisters, and the sexual heat between herself and Holden. Those seemed to be the only things that made any sense. The only things that had any kind of authenticity to them.

And maybe how you feel about him.

Well. Maybe.

But the problem was she couldn't be sure if he felt the same. And just at the moment she was too afraid to take a chance at being hurt. Because she was already raw and wounded, and she didn't know if she could stand anything more.

But she had her sisters. And she would rest in that for now.

Fourteen

The weeks that followed were strange. They were serene in some ways, which Emerson really hadn't expected. Her life had changed, and she was surprised how positive she found the change.

Oh, losing her respect for her father wasn't overly positive. But working more closely with her sisters was. She and Wren had always been close, but both of them had always found it a bit of a challenge to connect with Cricket, but it seemed easier now.

The three of them were a team. It wasn't Wren and Emerson on Team Maxfield, with Cricket hanging out on the sidelines.

It was a feat to launch a new sort of wine on the heels of the select label, which they had only just released. But the only demand Holden had made of the company so far was that they release a line of wines under his sister's name.

Actually, Emerson thought it was brilliant. Soraya had such a presence online—even if she wasn't in the public at the moment—and her image was synonymous with youth. Soraya's reputation gave Emerson several ideas for how to market wines geared toward the youthful jet-set crowd who loved to post photographs of their every move.

One of the first things Emerson had done was consult a graphic designer about making labels that were eminently postable, along with coming up with a few snappy names for the unique blends they would use. And of course, they would need for the price point to be right. They would start with three—Tempranillo Tantrum, Chardonyay and No Way Rosé.

Cricket rolled her eyes at the whole thing, feeling out of step with other people her age, as she had no desire to post on any kind of social media site, and found those puns ridiculous. Wren, while not a big enthusiast herself, at least understood the branding campaign. Emerson was ridiculously pleased. And together the three of them had enjoyed doing the work.

Cricket, true to her word, had not overly involved herself, given that she was in training down at the coffee shop. Emerson couldn't quite understand why her sister wanted to work there, but she could understand why Cricket felt the need to gain some independence.

Being a Maxfield was difficult.

But it was also interesting, building something that wasn't for her father's approval. Sure, Holden's approval was involved on some level, but…this was different from any other work she'd done.

She was doing this as much for herself as for him, and he trusted that she would do a good job. She knew she would.

It felt…good.

The prototype labels, along with the charms she had chosen to drape elegantly over the narrow neck of each bottle, came back from production relatively quickly, and she was so excited to show Holden she could hardly contain herself.

She wasn't sure why she was so excited to show him, only that she was.

It wasn't as if she wanted his approval, the way she had with her father. It was more that she wanted to share what she had created. The way she felt she needed to please him. This was more of an excitement sort of feeling.

She wanted to please Holden in a totally different way. Wanted to make him… Happy.

She wondered what would make a man like him happy. If he *could* be happy.

And suddenly, she was beset by the burning desire to try.

He was a strange man, her husband, filled with dark intensity, but she knew that part of that intensity was an intense capacity to love.

The things that he had done for his sister…

All of her life, really. And for his mother.

It wasn't just this, though it was a large gesture, but everything.

He had protected his mother from her endless array of boyfriends. He had made sure Soraya had gotten off to school okay every day. He had bought his mother and sister houses the moment he had begun making money.

She had done research on him, somewhat covertly, in the past weeks. And she had seen that he had donated large amounts of money, homes, to a great many people in need.

He hid all of that generosity underneath a gruff, hard exterior. Knowing what she knew now, she continually came back to that moment when he had refused to say his plan for revenge was born out of love for his sister. As if admitting to something like love would be disastrous for him.

She saw the top of his cowboy hat through the window of the tasting room, where she was waiting with the Soraya-branded wines.

He walked in, and her heart squeezed tight.

"I have three complete products to show you. And I hope you're going to like them."

She held up the first bottle—the Tempranillo Tantrum—with a little silver porcupine charm dangling from the top. "Because porcupines are grumpy," she said.

"Are they?"

"Well, do you want to hassle one and find out how grumpy they are? Because I don't."

"Very nice," he said, brushing his fingers over the gold foil on the label.

"People will want to take pictures of it. Even if they don't buy it, they're going to post and share it."

He looked at the others, one with a rose-gold unicorn charm, the next with a platinum fox. And above each of the names was *Soraya*.

"She'll love this," he said, his voice suddenly soft.

"How is she doing?"

"Last I spoke to her? I don't know. A little bit better. She didn't seem as confused."

"Do they know why she misremembers sometimes?" He had told her about how his sister often didn't remember she'd had a fairly late-term miscarriage. That sometimes she would call him scared, looking for a baby that she didn't have.

It broke Emerson's heart. Knowing everything Soraya had gone through. And she supposed there were plenty of young women who could have gone through something like that and not ended up in such a difficult position, but Soraya wasn't one of them. And the fact that Emerson's father had chosen someone so vulnerable, and upon learning how vulnerable she was, had ignored the distress she was in…

If Emerson had been on the fence about whether or not her father was redeemable…the more she knew about the state Holden's sister had been left in, the less she thought so.

"Her brain is protecting her from the trauma. Though, it's doing a pretty bad job," he said. "Every time she has to hear the truth again…it hurts her all over."

"Well, I hope this makes her happy," she said, gesturing to the wine. "And that it makes her feel like… she is part of this. Because she's part of the family now. Because of you. My sisters and I… We care about what happens to her. People do care."

"You've done an amazing job with this," he said, the sincerity in his voice shocking her. "I could never have figured out how to make this wine something she specifically would like so much, but this… She's going to love it." He touched one of the little charms. "She'll think those are just perfect."

"I'm glad. I'd like to meet her. Someday. When she is feeling well enough for something like that."

"I'm sure we can arrange it."

After that encounter, she kept turning her feelings over and over inside of her.

She was changing. What she wanted was changing.

She was beginning to like her life with Holden. More than like it. There was no denying the chemistry they shared. That what happened between them at night was singular. Like nothing else she had ever experienced. But it was moments like that one—the little moments that happened during the day—that surprised her.

She liked him.

And if she were really honest with herself, she more than liked him.

She needed…

She needed to somehow show him that she wanted more.

Of course, she didn't know what more there was, considering the fact that they were already married.

She was still thinking about what she wanted, what she could do, when she saw Wren later that day.

"Have you ever been in love?"

Wren looked at her, jerking her head abruptly to the side. "No," she said. "Don't you think you would have known if I'd ever been in love?"

"I don't know. We don't really talk about that kind of stuff. We talk about work. You don't know if I've ever been in love."

"Well, other than Holden? You haven't been. You've had boyfriends, but you haven't been in love."

"I didn't tell you I was in love with Holden."

"But you are," Wren said. "Which is why I assume you're asking me about love now."

"Yes," Emerson said. "Okay. I am. I'm in love with Holden, and I need to figure out a way to tell him. Because how do you tell a man that you want more than marriage?"

"You tell him that you love him."

"It doesn't feel like enough. Anyone can say anything anytime they want. That doesn't make it real. But I want him to see that the way I feel has changed."

"Well, I don't know. Except... Men don't really use words so much as..."

"Sex. Well, our sex life has been good. Very good."

"Glad to hear it," Wren said. "But what might be missing from that?"

Emerson thought about that. "Our wedding night was a bit unconventional." Tearing tuxedos and getting tied up with leather belts might not be everyone's idea of a honeymoon. Though, Emerson didn't really have any complaints.

There had been anger between them that night. Anger that had burned into passion. And since then, they'd had sex in all manner of different ways, because she couldn't be bored when she shared a bed with someone she was so compatible with, and for whatever reason she felt no inhibition when she was with him. But they hadn't had a real wedding night.

Not really.

One where they gave themselves to each other after saying their vows.

That was it. She needed to make a vow to him. With her body, and then with her words.

"I might need to make a trip to town," she said.

"For?"

"Very bridal lingerie."

"I would be happy to knock off work early and help you in your pursuit."

"We really do make a great team."

When she and Wren returned that evening, Emerson was triumphant in her purchases, and more than ready to greet her husband.

Now she just had to hope he would understand what she was saying to him.

And she had to hope he would want the same thing she did.

When Holden got back to the house that night, it was dark.

That was strange, because Emerson usually got home before he did. He was discovering his new work at the winery to be fulfilling, but he also spent a good amount of time dealing with work for his own company, and that made for long days.

He looked down at the floor, and saw a few crimson spots, and for a moment, he knew panic. His throat tightened.

Except… It wasn't blood. It was rose petals.

There was a trail of them, leading from the living room to the stairwell, and up the stairs. He followed the path, down the dimly lit hall, and into the master bedroom that he shared with Emerson.

The rose petals led up to the bed, and there, perched on the mattress, was his wife.

His throat went dry, all the blood in his body rushing south. She was wearing… It was like a bridal gown, but made entirely of see-through lace that gave peeks at her glorious body underneath. The straps were thin, the neckline plunging down between her breasts, which were spilling out over the top of the diaphanous fabric.

She looked like temptation in the most glorious form he'd ever seen.

"What's all this?"

"I… I went to town for a few things today."

"I see that."

"It's kind of a belated wedding gift," she said. "A belated wedding night."

"We had a wedding night. I remember it very clearly."

"Not like this. Not..." She reached next to her, and pulled out a large velvet box. "And we're missing something."

She opened it up, and inside was a thick band of metal next to a slimmer one.

"They're wedding bands," she said. "One for you and one for me."

"What brought this on?"

He didn't really know what to say. He didn't know what to think about this at all.

The past few weeks had been good between the two of them, that couldn't be denied. But he felt like she was proposing to him, and that was an idea he could barely wrap his mind around.

"I want to wear your ring," she said. "And I guess... I bought the rings. But this ring is mine," she said, pulling out the man's ring. "And I want you to wear it. This ring is yours. I want to wear it." She took out the slim band and placed it on her finger, and then held the thicker one out for him.

"I've never been one for jewelry."

"You've never been one for marriage either, but here we are. I know we had a strange start, but this has... It's been a good partnership so far, hasn't it?"

The work she had done on his sister's wine had been incredible, it was true. The care she had put into it had surprised him. It hadn't simply been a generic nod to Soraya. Emerson had made something that somehow managed to capture his sister's whole personality, and he knew Emerson well enough to know that she had done it by researching who Soraya was. And when Emerson asked him about his sister, he knew that she cared. Their own mother didn't even care that much.

But she seemed to bleed with her caring, with her regret that Soraya had been hurt. And now Emerson wanted rings. Wanted to join herself to him in a serious way.

And why not? She's your wife. She should be wearing your ring.

"Thanks," he said, taking the ring and putting it on quickly.

Her shoulders sagged a little, and he wondered if she had wanted this to go differently, but he was wearing the ring, so it must be okay. She let out a shaking breath. "Holden, with this ring, I take you as my husband. To have and to hold. For better or for worse. For richer or poorer. Until death separates us."

Those vows sent a shiver down his spine.

"We took those vows already."

"I took those vows with you because I had to. Because I felt like I didn't have another choice. I'm saying them now because I choose to. Because I want to. And because I mean them. If all of this, the winery, everything, goes away, I still want to be partners with you. In our lives. Not just in business. I want this to be about more than my father, more than your sister. I want it to be about us. And so that's my promise to you with my words. And I want to make that official with my body."

There were little ties at the center of the dress she was wearing, and she began to undo the first one, the fabric parting between her breasts. Then she undid the next one, and the next, until it opened, revealing the tiny pair of panties she had on underneath. She slipped the dress from her shoulders and then she began to undress him.

It was slow, unhurried. She'd torn the clothes from his body before. She had allowed him to tie her hands. She had surrendered herself to him in challenging and intense ways that had twisted the idea of submission on its head, because when her hands were tied, he was the one that was powerless.

But this was different. And he felt…

Owned.

By that soft, sweet touch, by the brush of her fingertips against him as she pushed his shirt up over his head. By the way her nimble fingers attacked his belt buckle, removing his jeans.

And somehow, *he* was the naked one then, and she was still wearing those panties. There was something generous about what she was doing now. And he didn't know why that word came to the front of his mind.

But she was giving.

Giving from a deep place inside of her that was more than just a physical gift. Without asking for anything in return. She lay back on the bed, lifting her hips slightly and pushing her panties down, revealing that tempting triangle at the apex of her thighs, revealing her whole body to him.

He growled, covering her, covering her mouth with his own, kissing her deep and hard.

And she opened to him. Pliant and willing.

Giving.

Had anyone ever given to him before?

He'd had nothing like this ever. That was the truth.

Everyone in his life had taken from him from the very beginning. But not her. And she had no reason to give to him. And if this were the same as all their other sexual encounters, he could have put it off to chemistry.

Because everybody was a little bit wild when there was sexual attraction involved, but this was more.

Sex didn't require vows.

It didn't require rings.

And it didn't feel like this.

This was more.

It touched him deeper, in so many places deep inside, all the way to his soul.

And he didn't know what to say, or feel, so he just kissed her. Because he knew how to do that. Knew how to touch her and make her wet. Knew how to make her come.

He knew how to find his pleasure in her.

But he didn't know how to find the bottom of this deep, aching need that existed inside of him.

He settled himself between her thighs, thrust into her, and she cried out against his mouth. Then her gaze met his, and she touched him, her fingertips skimming over his cheekbone.

"I love you." The words were like an arrow straight through his chest.

"Emerson..."

She clung to him, grasping his face, her legs wrapped around his. "I love you," she said, rocking up into him, taking him deeper.

And he would have pulled away, done something to escape the clawing panic, but his desire for her was too intense.

Love.

Had anyone ever said those words to him? He didn't think so. He should let go of her, he should stop. But he was powerless against the driving need to stay joined to her. It wasn't even about release. It was about something else, something he couldn't name or define.

Can't you?

He ignored that voice. He ignored that burning sensation in his chest, and he tried to block out the words she'd said. But she said them over and over again, and something in him was so hungry for them, he didn't know how to deny himself.

He looked down, and his eyes met hers, and he was sure she could see straight inside of him, and that what she saw there would be woefully empty compared to what he saw in hers.

He growled, lowering his head and chasing the pleasure building inside of him, thrusting harder, faster, trying to build up a pace that would make him forget.

Who he was.

What she'd said.

What he wanted.

What he couldn't have.

But when her pleasure crested, his own followed close behind, and he made the mistake of looking at her again. Of watching as pleasure overtook her.

He had wanted her from the beginning.

It had never mattered what he could get by marrying her.

It had always been about her. Always.

Because he had seen her, and he could not have her, from the very first.

He had told himself he should hate her because she had Maxfield blood in her veins. Then he had told himself that he needed her, and that was why it had to be marriage.

But he was selfish, down to his core.

And he had manipulated, used and blackmailed her. He was no different than her father, and now here she was, professing her love. And he was a man who didn't even know what that was.

All this giving. All this generosity from her. And he didn't deserve it. Couldn't begin to.

And he deserved it from her least of all.

Because he had nothing to give back.

He shuddered, his release taking him, stealing his thoughts, making it impossible for him to feel anything but pleasure. No regrets. No guilt. Just the bliss of being joined to her. And when it was over, she looked at him, and she whispered one more time, "I love you."

And that was when he pulled away.

Fifteen

She had known it was a mistake, but she hadn't been able to hold it back. The declaration of love. Because she did love him. It was true. With all of herself. And while she had been determined to show him, with her body, with the vows she had made and with the rings she had bought, it wasn't enough.

She had thought the words by themselves wouldn't be enough, but the actions without the words didn't mean anything either. Not to her. Not when there was this big shift inside her, as real and deep as anything ever had been. She had wanted for so long to do enough that she would be worthy. And she felt like some things had crystallized inside of her. Because all of those things she craved, that approval, it was surface. It was like a brand. The way that her father saw brand. That as long as the outside looked good, as long as all the external things were getting done, that was all that mattered.

But it wasn't.

Because what she felt, who she was in her deepest parts, those were the things that mattered. And she didn't have to perform or be good to be loved. She, as a person, was enough all on her own. And that was what Holden had become to her. And that was what she wanted. For her life, for her marriage. Not something as shallow as approval for a performance. A brand was meaningless if there was no substance behind it. A beautiful bottle of wine didn't matter if what was inside was nothing more than grape juice.

A marriage was useless if love and commitment weren't at the center.

It was those deep things, those deep connections, and she hadn't had them, not in all her life. Not really. She was beginning to forge them with her sisters, and she needed them from Holden.

And if that meant risking disapproval, risking everything, then she would. She had. And she could see that her declaration definitely hadn't been the most welcome.

Since she'd told him she loved him, everything about him was shut down, shut off. She knew him well enough to recognize that.

"I don't know what you expect me to say."

"Traditionally, people like to hear 'I love you too.' But I'm suspecting I'm not going to get that. So, here's the deal. You don't have to say anything. I just… I wanted you to know how I felt. How serious I am. How much my feelings have changed since I first met you."

"Why?"

"Because," she said. "Because you…you came into my life and you turned it upside down. You uncovered so many things that were hidden in the dark for so long.

And yes, some of that uncovering has been painful. But more than that, you made me realize what I really wanted from life. I thought that as long as everything looked okay, it would be okay. But you destroyed that. You destroyed the illusions all around me, including the ones I had built for myself. Meeting you, feeling that attraction for you, it cut through all this…bullshit. I thought I could marry a man I didn't even feel a temptation to sleep with. And then I met you. I felt more for you in those few minutes in the vineyard that night we met than I had felt for Donovan in the two years we'd been together. I couldn't imagine not being with you. It was like an obsession, and then we were together, and you made me want things, made me do things that I never would have thought I would do. But *those* were all the real parts of me. All that I am.

"I thought that if I put enough makeup on, and smiled wide enough, and put enough filters on the pictures, that I could be the person I needed to be, but it's not who I am. Who I am is the woman I am when I'm with you. In your arms. In your bed. The things you make me feel, the things you make me want. That's real. And it's amazing, because none of this is about optics, it's not about pleasing anyone, it's just about me and you. It's so wonderful. To have found this. To have found you."

"You didn't find me, honey. I found you. I came here to get revenge on your father. This isn't fate. It was calculated through and through."

"It started that way," she said. "I know it did. And I would never call it fate. Because I don't believe that it was divine design that your sister was injured the way that she was. But what I do believe is that there has to be a way to make something good out of something broken, because if there isn't, then I don't know what future you and I could possibly have."

"There are things that make sense in this world," he said. "Emotion isn't one of them. Money is. What we can do with the vineyard, that makes sense. We can build that together. We don't need any of the other stuff."

"The other stuff," she said, "is only everything. It's only love. It took me until right now to realize that. It's the missing piece. It's what I've been looking for all this time. It really is. And I… I love you. I love you down to my bones. It's real. It's not about a hashtag or a brand. It's about what I feel. And how it goes beyond rational and reasonable. How it goes beyond what should be possible. I love you. I love you and it's changed the way that I see myself."

"Are you sure you're not just looking for approval from somewhere else? You lost the relationship with your father, and now…"

"You're not my father. And I'm not confused. Don't try to tell me that I am."

"I don't do love," he said, his voice hard as stone.

"Somehow I knew you would say that. You're so desperate to make me believe that, aren't you? Mostly because I think you're so desperate to make yourself believe it. You won't even admit that you did all of this because you love your sister."

"Because you are thinking about happy families, and you're thinking about people who share their lives. That's never been what I've had with my mother and sister. I take care of them. And when I say that, I'm telling you the truth. It's not… It's not give-and-take."

"You loving them," she said, "and them being selfish with that love has nothing to do with who you are.

Or what you're capable of. Why can't we have something other than that? Something other than me trying to earn approval and you trying to rescue? Can't we love each other? Give to each other? That's what I want. I think our bodies knew what was right all along. I know why you were here, and what you weren't supposed to want. And I know what I was supposed to do. But I think we were always supposed to be with each other. I do. From the deepest part of my body. I believe that."

"Bodies don't know anything," he said. "They just know they want sex. That's not love. And it's not anything worth tearing yourself apart over."

"But I… I don't have another choice. I'm torn apart by this. By us. By what we could be."

"There isn't an us. There is you and me. And we're married, and I'm willing to make that work. But you have to be realistic about what that means to a man like me."

"No," Emerson said. "I refuse to be realistic. Nothing in my life has ever been better because I was realistic. The things that have been good happened because I stepped out of my comfort zone. I don't want to be trapped in a one-sided relationship. To always be trying to earn my place. I've done that. I've lived it. I don't want to do it anymore."

"Fair enough," he said. "Then we don't have to do this."

"No," she said. "I want our marriage. I want…"

"You want me to love you, and I can't. I'm sorry. But I can't, I won't. And I…" He reached out, his callused fingertips skimming her cheek. "Honey, I appreciate you saying I'm not like your father, but it's pretty clear that I am. I'm not going to make you sign a nondisclosure agreement or anything like that. I'm going to ask one thing of you. Keep the Soraya wine going for my sister. But otherwise, my share of the winery goes to you."

"What?"

"I'm giving it back. I'm giving it to you. Because it's yours, it's not mine."

"You would rather…do all of that than try to love me?"

"I never meant to hurt you," he said. "That was never my goal, whether you believe it or not. I don't have strong enough feelings about you to want to hurt you."

And those words were like an arrow through her heart, piercing deeper than any other cruelty that could have come out of his mouth.

It would've been better, in fact, if he had said that he hated her. If he had threatened to destroy the winery again. If her ultimatum had made him fly into a rage. But it didn't. Instead, he was cold, closed off and utterly impassive. Instead, he looked like a man who truly didn't care, and she would've taken hatred over that any day, because it would have meant that at least he felt something. But she didn't get that. Instead, she got a blank wall of nothing.

She couldn't fight this. Couldn't push back against nothing. If he didn't want to fight, then there was nothing for her to do.

"So that's it," she said. "You came in here like a thunderstorm, ready to destroy everything in your path, and now you're just…letting me go?"

"Your father is handled. The control of the winery is with you and your sisters. I don't have any reason to destroy you."

"I don't think that you're being chivalrous. I think you're being a coward."

"Cowards don't change their lives, don't make something of themselves the way I did. Cowards don't go out seeking justice for their sisters."

"Cowards *do* run when someone demands something that scares them, though. And that's what you're doing. Make no mistake. You can pretend you're a man without fear. You're hard in some ways, and I know it. But all that hardness is just to protect yourself. I wish I knew why. I wish I knew what I could do."

"It won't last," he said. "Whatever you think you want to give me, it won't last."

"Why do you think that?"

"I've never actually seen anyone want to do something that wasn't ultimately about serving themselves. Why would you be any different?"

"It's not me that's different. It's the feelings."

"But you have to be able to put your trust in feelings in order to believe in something like that, and I don't. I believe in the things you can see, in the things you can buy."

"I believe in us," she said, pressing her hand against her chest.

"You believe wrong, darlin'."

Pain welled up inside of her. "You're not the Big Bad Wolf after all," she said. "At least he had the courage to eat Red Riding Hood all up. You don't even have the courage to do that."

"You should be grateful."

"You don't get to break my heart and tell me I should be grateful because you didn't do it a certain way. The end result is the same. And I hope that someday you realize you broke your own heart too. I hope that someday you look back on this and realize we had love, and you were afraid to take it. And I hope you ask yourself why it was so much easier for you to cross a state because of rage than it was for you to cross a room and tell someone you love them."

She started to collect her clothes, doing her very best to move with dignity, to keep her shoulders from shaking, to keep herself from dissolving. And she waited. As she collected her clothes. Waited for her big, gruff cowboy to sweep her up in his arms and stop her from leaving. But he didn't. He let her gather her clothes. And he let her walk out the bedroom door. Let her walk out of the house. Let her walk out of his life. And as Emerson stood out in front of the place she had called home with a man she had come to love, she found herself yet again unsure of what her life was.

Except… Unlike when the revelations about her father had upended everything, this time she had a clear idea of who *she* was.

Holden had changed her. Had made her realize the depth of her capacity for pleasure. For desire. For love. Had given her an appreciation of depth.

An understanding of what she could feel if she dug deep, instead of clinging to the perfection of the surface.

And whatever happened, she would walk away from this experience changed. Would walk away from this wanting more, wanting better.

He wouldn't, though.

And of all the things that broke her heart in this moment, that truth was the one that cut deepest.

Emerson knew she couldn't avoid having a conversation with her mother any longer. There were several reasons for that. The first being that she'd had to move back home. The second being that she had an offer to make her father. But she needed to talk to her mom about it first.

Emerson took a deep breath, and walked into the sitting room, where she knew she would find her mother at this time of day.

She always took tea in the sitting room with a book in the afternoon.

"Hi," she said. "Can we talk?"

"Of course," her mom said, straightening and setting her book down. "I didn't expect to see you here today."

"Well. I'm kind of…back here. Because I hit a rough patch in my marriage. You know, by which I mean my husband doesn't want to be married to me anymore."

"That is a surprise."

"Is it? I married him quickly, and really not for the best reasons."

"It seemed like you cared for him quite a bit."

"I did. But the feeling wasn't mutual. So there's not much I can do about that in any case."

"We all make choices. Although, I thought you had finally found your spine with this one."

Emerson frowned. "My spine?"

"Emerson, you have to understand, the reason I've always resisted your involvement in the winery is because I didn't want your father to own you."

"What are you talking about?"

"I know you know. The way that he is. It's not a surprise to me, I've known it for years. He's never been faithful to me. But that's beside the point. The real issue is the way that he uses people."

"You've known. All along?"

"Yes. And when I had you girls the biggest issue was that if I left, he would make sure that I never saw you again. That wasn't a risk I could take. And I won't lie to you, I feared poverty more than I should have. I didn't want to go back to it. And so I made some decisions that I regret now. Especially as I watched you grow up. And I watched the way he was able to find closeness with you and with Wren. When I wasn't able to."

"I just… No matter what I did, you never seemed like you thought I did enough. Or like I had done it right."

"And I'm sorry about that. I made mistakes. In pushing you, I pushed you away, and I think I pushed you toward your father. Which I didn't mean to do. I was afraid, always, and I wanted you to be able to stand on your own feet because I had ended up hobbling myself. I was dependent on his money. I didn't know how to do anything separate from this place, separate from him that could keep me from sinking back into the poverty that I was raised in. I was trapped in many ways by my own greed. I gave up so much for this. For him." Her eyes clouded over. "That's another part of the problem. When I chose your father over… When I chose your father, it was such a deep, controversial thing, it caused so much pain, to myself included, in many ways, and I'm too stubborn and stiff-necked to take back that kind of thing."

"I don't understand."

She ran a hand over her lined brow, pushing her dark hair off her face. "I was in love with someone else. There was a misunderstanding between us, and we broke up. Then your father began to show an interest, because of a rivalry he had with my former beau. I figured that I would use that. And it all went too far. This is the life I made for myself. And what I really wanted, to try and atone for my sins, was to make sure you girls had it different. But then he was pushing you to marry… So when you came back from Las Vegas married to Holden, what I hoped was that you had found something more."

Emerson was silent for a long moment, trying to process all this information. And suddenly, she saw everything so clearly through her mother's eyes. Her fears, the reason she had pushed Emerson the way she had. The way she had disapproved of Emerson pouring everything into the winery.

"I do love Holden," Emerson said. "But he…he says he doesn't love me."

"That's what happened with the man I loved. And I got angry, and I went off on my own. Then I went to someone else. I've always regretted it. Because I've never loved your father the way that I loved him. Then it was too late. I held on to pride, I didn't want to lower myself to beg him to be with me, but now I wish I had. I wish I had exhausted everything in the name of love. Rather than giving so much to stubbornness and spite. To financial security. Without love, these sorts of places just feel like a mausoleum. A crypt for dead dreams." She smiled sadly, looking around the vast, beautiful room that seemed suddenly so much darker. "I have you girls. And I've never regretted that. I have regretted our lack of closeness, Emerson, and I know that it's my fault."

"It's mine too," Emerson said. "We've never really talked before, not like this."

"There wasn't much I could tell you. Not with the way you felt about your father. And… You have to understand, while I wanted to protect you, I also didn't want to shatter your love for him. Because no matter what else he has done, he does love his daughters. He's a flawed man, make no mistake. But what he feels for you is real."

"I don't know that I'm in a place where that can matter much to me."

"No, I don't suppose you are. And I don't blame you."

"I want to buy Dad out of the winery," Emerson said. "When Holden left, he returned his stake to me. I want to buy Dad out. I want to run the winery with Wren and Cricket. And there will be a place here for you, Mom. But not for him."

"He's never going to agree to that."

"If he doesn't, I'll expose him myself. Because I won't sit by and allow the abuse of women and of his power to continue. He has two choices. He can leave of his own accord, or I'll burn this place to the ground around me, but I won't let injustice go on."

"I didn't have to worry about you after all," her mother said. "You have more of a spine than I've ever had."

"Well, now I do. For this. But when it comes to Holden..."

"Your pride won't keep you warm at night. And you can't trade one man for another, believe me, I've tried. If you don't put it all on the line, you'll regret it. You'll have to sit by while he marries someone else, has children with her. And everything will fester inside of you until it turns into something dark and ugly. Don't let that be you. Don't make the mistakes that I did."

"Mom... Who..."

"It doesn't matter now. It's been so long. He probably doesn't remember me anyway."

"I doubt that."

"All right, he remembers me," she said. "But not fondly."

"I love him," Emerson said. "I love him, and I don't know what I'm going to do without him. Which is silly, because I've lived twenty-nine years without him. You would think that I would be just fine."

"When you fall in love like that, you give away a piece of yourself," her mom said. "And that person always has it. It doesn't matter how long you had them for. When it's real, that's how it is."

"Well, I don't know what I'm supposed to do."

"Hope that he gave you a piece of him. Hope that whatever he says, he loves you just the way you love him. And then do more than hope. You're strong enough to come in here and stand up to your father. To do what's right for other people. Do what's right for you too."

Emerson nodded slowly. "Okay." She looked around, and suddenly laughter bubbled up inside of her.

"What?"

"It's just… A few weeks ago, at the launch for the select label, I was thinking how bored I was. Looking forward to my boring future. My boring marriage. I would almost pay to be bored again, because at least I wasn't heartbroken."

"Oh, trust me," her mom said. "As painful as it is, love is what gets you through the years. Even if you don't have it anymore. You once did. Your heart remembers that it exists in the world, and then suddenly the world looks a whole lot more hopeful. Because when you can believe that two people from completely different places can come together and find something that goes beyond explanation, something that goes beyond what you can see with your eyes…that's the thing that gives you hope in your darkest hour. Whatever happens with him…"

"Yeah," Emerson said softly. "I know."

She did. Because he was the reason she was standing here connecting with her mother now. He was the reason she was deciding to take this action against her father.

And she wouldn't be the reason they didn't end up together. She wouldn't give up too soon.

She didn't care how it looked. She would go down swinging.

Optics be damned.

Sixteen

Holden wasn't a man given to questioning himself. He acted with decisiveness, and he did what had to be done. But his last conversation with Emerson kept replaying itself in his head over and over again. And worse, it echoed in his chest, made a terrible, painful tearing sensation around his heart every time he tried to breathe. It felt like... He didn't the hell know. Because he had never felt anything like it before. He felt like he had cut off an essential part of himself and left it behind and it had nothing to do with revenge.

He was at the facility where his sister lived, visiting her today, because it seemed like an important thing to do. He owed her an apology.

He walked through the manicured grounds and up to the front desk. "I'm here to see Soraya Jane."

The facility was more like high-end apartments, and his sister had her rooms on the second floor, overlooking the ocean. When he walked in, she was sitting there on the end of the bed, her hair loose.

"Good to see you," he said.

"Holden."

She smiled, but she didn't hug him.

They weren't like that.

"I came to see you because I owe you an apology."

"An apology? That doesn't sound like you."

"I know. It doesn't."

"What happened?"

"I did some thinking and I realized that what I did might have hurt you more than it helped you. And I'm sorry."

"You've never hurt me," she said. "Everything you do is just trying to take care of me. And nobody else does that."

He looked at his sister, so brittle and raw, and he realized that her issues went back further than James Maxfield. She was wounded in a thousand ways, by a life that had been more hard knocks than not. And she was right. No one had taken care of her but him. And he had been the oldest, so no one had taken care of him at all.

And the one time that Soraya had tried to reach out, the one time she had tried to love, she had been punished for it.

No wonder it had broken her the way it had.

"I abandoned my revenge plot. Emerson and I are going to divorce."

"You don't look happy," she said.

"I'm not," he said. "I hurt someone I didn't mean to hurt."

"Are you talking about me or her?"

He was quiet for a moment. "I didn't mean to hurt either of you."

"Did you really just marry her to get back at her father?"

"No. Not only that. I mean, that's not why I married her."

"You look miserable."

"I am, but I'm not sure what that has to do with anything."

"It has to do with love. This is how love is. It's miserable. It makes you crazy. And I can say that."

"You're not crazy," he said, fiercely. "Don't say that about yourself, don't think it."

"Look where I am."

"It's not a failure. And it doesn't… Soraya, there's no shame in having a problem. There's no shame in getting help."

"Fine. Well, what's your excuse then? I got help and you ruined your life."

"I'm not in love."

"You're not? Because you have that horrible look about you. You know, like someone who just had their heart utterly ripped out of their chest."

He was quiet for a moment, and he took a breath. He listened to his heart beat steadily in his ears. "My heart is still there," he said.

"Sure. But not your *heart* heart. The one that feels things. Do you love her?"

"I don't know how to love people. How would we know what real, healthy love looks like? I believe that you loved James Maxfield, but look where it got you. Weird… We are busted up and broken from the past, how are we supposed to figure out what's real?"

"If it feels real, it is real. I don't think there's anything all that difficult to understand about love. When you feel like everything good about you lives inside another person, and they're wandering around with the best of you in their chest, you just want to be with them all the time. And you're so afraid of losing them, because if you do, you're going to lose everything interesting and bright about you too."

He thought of Emerson, of the way she looked at him. And he didn't know if what Soraya said was true. If he felt like the best of him was anywhere at all. But what he knew for sure was that Emerson made him want to be better. She made him want something other than money or success. Something deep and indefinable that he couldn't quite grasp.

"She said she loved me," he said, his voice scraped raw, the admission unexpected.

"And you left her?"

"I forced her to marry me. I couldn't..."

"She loves you. She's obviously not being forced into anything."

"I took advantage..."

"You know, if you're going to go worrying about taking advantage of women, it might be helpful if you believe them when they tell you what they want. You deciding that you know better than she does what's in her heart is not enlightened. It's just more of some man telling a woman what she ought to be. And what's acceptable for her to like and want."

"I..." He hadn't quite expected that from his sister.

"She loves you. If she loves you, why won't you be with her?"

"I..."

He thought about what Emerson had said. When she called him a coward.

"Because I'm afraid I don't know how to be in love," he said finally.

It was the one true thing he'd said on the matter. He hadn't meant to lie, he hadn't known that he had. But it was clear as day to him now.

"Look at how we were raised. I don't know a damn thing about love."

"You're the only one who ever did," Soraya said. "Look what you've done for me. Look at where I am. It's not because of me."

"No," he said. "It's because of me. I got you started on all the modeling stuff, and you went to the party where you met James…"

"That's not what I meant. I meant the reason that I'm taken care of now, the reason that I've always been taken care of, is because of you. The reason Mom has been taken care of… That's you. All those families you gave money to, houses to. And I know I've been selfish. Being here, I've had a lot of time to think. And I know that sometimes I'm not…lucid. But sometimes I am, and when I am, I think a lot about how much you gave. And no one gave it back to you. And I don't think it's that you don't know how to love, Holden. I think it's that you don't know what it's like when someone loves you back. And you don't know what to do with it."

He just sat and stared, because he had never thought of himself the way that his sister seemed to. But she made him sound…well, kind of like not a bad guy. Maybe even like someone who cared quite a bit.

"I don't blame you for protecting yourself. But this isn't protecting yourself. It's hurting yourself."

"You might be right," he said, his voice rough. "You know, you might be right."

"Do you love her?"

He thought about the way Emerson had looked in the moments before he had rejected her. Beautiful and bare. His wife in every way.

"Yes," he said, his voice rough. "I do."

"Then none of it matters. Not who her father is, not being afraid. Just that you love her."

"Look what it did to you to be in love," he said. "Don't you think I'm right to be afraid of it?"

"Oh," she said. "You're definitely right to be afraid of it. It's terrifying. And it has the power to destroy everything in its path. But the alternative is this. This kind of gray existence. The one that I'm in. The one that you're in. So maybe it won't work out. But what if it did?"

And suddenly, he was filled with a sense of determination. With a sense of absolute certainty. There was no what-if. Because he could make it turn out with his actions. He was a man who had—as Emerson had pointed out—crossed the state for revenge.

He could sure as hell do the work required to make love last. It was a risk. A damn sight bigger risk than being angry.

But he was willing to take it.

"Thank you," he said to his sister.

"Thank you too," she said. "For everything. Even the revenge."

"Emerson is making a wine label for you," he said. "It's pretty brilliant."

Soraya smiled. "She is?"

"Yes."

"Well, I can't wait until I can come and celebrate with the both of you."

"Neither can I."

And now all that was left was for him to go and make sure he had Emerson, so the two of them could be together for the launch of the wine label, and for the rest of forever.

Emerson was standing on the balcony to her bedroom, looking out over the vineyard.

It was hers now, she supposed. Hers and Wren's and Cricket's. The deal with her father had been struck, and her mother had made the decision to stay there at the winery, and let James go off into retirement. The move would cause waves; there was no avoiding it. Her parents' separation, and her father removing himself from the label.

But Emerson had been the public face of Maxfield for so long that it would be a smooth enough transition.

The moonlight was casting a glow across the great fields, and Emerson sighed, taking in the simple beauty of it.

Everything still hurt, the loss of Holden still hurt. But she could already see that her mother was right. Love was miraculous, and believing in the miraculous, having experienced it, enhanced the beauty in the world, even as it hurt.

And then, out in the rows, she was sure that she saw movement.

She held her breath, and there in the moonlight she saw the silhouette of a cowboy.

Not just a cowboy. *Her* cowboy.

For a moment, she thought about not going down. She thought about staying up in her room. But she couldn't. She had to go to him.

Even if it was foolish.

She stole out and padded down the stairs, out the front door of the estate and straight out to the vines.

"What are you doing here?"

"I know I'm not on the guest list," he said.

"No," she said. "You're not. In fact, you were supposed to have ridden off into the sunset."

"Sorry about that. But the sun has set."

"Holden…"

"I was wondering if you needed a ranch hand."

"What?"

"The winery is yours. I want it to stay yours. Yours and your sisters'. I certainly don't deserve a piece of it. And I just thought… The one time I had it right with you was when I worked here. When it was you and me, and not all this manipulation. So I thought maybe I would just offer me."

"Just you?"

"Yeah," he said. "Just me."

"I mean, you still have your property development money, I assume."

"Yeah," he said. "But… I also love you. And I was sort of hoping that you still love me."

She blinked hard, her heart about to race out of her chest. "Yes," she said. "I love you still. I do. And all I need is you. Not anything else."

"I feel the same way," he said. "You. Just the way you are. It quit being about revenge, and when it quit being about revenge, I didn't have an excuse to stay anymore, and it scared the hell out of me. Because I never thought that I would be the kind of man that wanted forever. And wanting it scared me. And I don't like being scared."

"None of us do. But I'm so glad that you came here, though," she said. "Because if you hadn't… I thought as long as everything looked good, then it was close enough to being good. I had no idea that it could be like this."

"And if I had never met you, then I would never

have had anything but money and anger. And believe me, compared to this, compared to you, that's nothing."

"You showed me my heart," she said. "You showed me what I really wanted."

"And you showed me mine. I was wrong," he said. "When I said things couldn't be fixed. They can be. When I told my sister that I came here to get revenge, she wasn't happy. It's not what she needed from me. She needed love. Support. Revenge just destroys, love is what builds. I want to love you and build a life with you. Forever."

"So do I." She threw herself into his arms, wrapped her own around his neck and kissed him. "So do I."

Emerson Maxfield knew without a shadow of a doubt, as her strong, handsome husband held her in his arms, that she was never going to be bored with her life again.

Because she knew now that it wasn't a party, a launch, a successful campaign that was going to bring happiness or decide who she was.

No, that came from inside of her.

And it was enough.

Who she was loved Holden McCall. And whatever came their way, it didn't scare her. Because they would face it together.

She remembered that feeling she'd had, adrift, like she had nowhere to go, like her whole life had been untethered.

But she had found who she was, she had found her heart, in him.

And she knew that she would never have to question where she belonged again. Because it was wherever he was.

Forever.

* * * * *

[illegible]

[illegible]

[illegible]

[illegible]

[illegible]

[illegible]

[illegible]

[illegible]

[illegible]

[illegible]

[illegible]

HOT HOLIDAY RANCHER

CATHERINE MANN

To my children, the best gift all year round!

One

Esme Perry had basked in the sun on a private beach in the South of France. She'd surfed with the best of them in California, Hawaii and Australia. But not even the threat of heatstroke or sharks had concerned her as much as the rush of water rolling down the country Texas back road toward her low-slung Porsche.

Rain sheeting against her windshield, Esme shifted into Reverse, willing her pulse to slow. *Be calm. Take deep breaths.* A quick three-point turn should have her ready to race out of harm's way. It would be a tight maneuver since the road was narrow, bracketed by a ditch on one side and sycamore trees on the other. It was tough enough to make such a maneuver during the daytime, but after dark? In the middle of a storm?

Not that she had a choice but to move. Flash floods were dangerous, especially in the country.

But her V-8 engine could outrace just about anything. Perhaps the Porsche wasn't the best choice for dirt roads, but she'd been excited about her early Christmas gift to herself.

Two points into Esme's three-point turn, the wave of rainwater slammed into the side of her vehicle. Her stomach clenched. She struggled to control the steering wheel as her car slid along the mud-slicked road. The Porsche's back end fishtailed. Her foot slipped off the clutch, her spiky heel wedging under the brake. The heel snapped. But she didn't have time to mourn the demise of her favorite leopard-print pumps. The Porsche lurched, then spun out, whipping the wheel from her clenched grip.

Her heart rose into her throat with panic as she battled what felt like g-forces slamming her against the door. Worse yet, she couldn't see due to vertigo and the rush of water over her candy apple–red hood. Was she close to the side of the road? How deep was the ditch? Where were the trees?

And, oh God, were those headlights or lampposts?

She braced. Struggled not to close her eyes. And prayed.

The spinning stopped, her car halting with a jolt. But not a crash. She exhaled a shaky breath, her ears ringing so loudly it almost drowned out the rain pounding the roof and a Christmas carol flowing from the speaker.

"Silent Night"?

Hardly.

But she was all right, in one piece, as was her car.

With luck, she could still reach her destination before bedtime. She would have arrived earlier, but an accident on the interstate from Houston to Royal had delayed her arrival. At least she was close enough to her destination to walk. According to her GPS, the front gate to Jesse Stevens's ranch should be less than a mile away.

She pressed the clutch, threw the car into Neutral and pressed the ignition.

The engine turned over. Then spluttered out.

She tried again and…

Nothing. Not even a catch.

She'd bought the stick-shift model, a purist when it came to her sports cars. She liked the control of a manual transmission, a talent she'd learned when teaching herself to drive on one of her father's older trucks on their Houston ranch. She'd been determined to perfect the skill, to win his approval.

Not much had changed on that front, since she was here to please her dad, to bolster his image with the charter branch of the Texas Cattleman's Club here in Royal, in hopes that he could be president of the new Houston branch.

Her PR plan would start with a surprise visit to Royal's own Jesse Stevens, an influential player at the TCC. If she could ever get there.

She bit back a curse, weighing her options. The odds of a tow truck showing up out here in this weather were slim. Should she wait to see if the car started and risk getting hit by another wave? Or start walking? In her broken shoes. In the rain. And mud. Sighing in resignation, she angled to get her umbrella.

Bracing, she opened the door, and rain sheeted inside. She wedged her umbrella through the opening, although it was fast becoming a moot point. Even her Prada trench was losing the fight against the deluge. Frigid water lapped around her ankles, soaking the hem of her slacks as she leaned into the wind, shivering. Still, she was determined to forge ahead, one step at a time.

She couldn't bear the thought of telling her father she needed to postpone the promotion trip. He'd put his trust in her, and even knowing a thirty-four-year-old woman shouldn't care this much what her father thought, she couldn't deny she was still trying to win his approval, to be something other than the often-forgotten middle child.

In college, she'd found her niche with an aptitude for public relations. It was her chance to shine. When her father had taken note of her success after graduation, he'd hired her as PR executive for the family business, Perry Holdings.

And if ever Sterling Perry had needed a promotional face-lift, it was now, when the new Houston Texas Cattleman's Club was cranking up. Fledgling organizations hated nothing more than a scandal.

And her father's good name had taken quite a few blows, first with an arrest on charges of orchestrating a Ponzi scheme that nearly caused a collapse of one of his investment funds.

No sooner had her father gotten out from under the weight of the fraud rumors than he was under suspicion for the murder of a Perry Holdings assistant. And, as if her father wasn't already stressed enough, just last week a Currin Oil executive named Willem Inwood had been arrested under suspicion of being behind the Ponzi scheme. He wasn't talking yet, but already people were coming forward saying he was the one who'd started those nasty rumors.

Now, even though his innocence had been proven on the murder charge and Ponzi issue, he still needed a serious image makeover if he expected to win the club's leadership spot.

And she intended to give him that fresh start, with some help from Jesse Stevens. Wrestling her bedraggled umbrella, she trudged ahead another couple of steps.

Were those lights flickering ahead? Hope and wariness jockeyed inside her. She was so very cold and soggy. But this also wasn't Houston, with her high-rise condo secured by round-the-clock guards.

She pulled one hand from the umbrella and reached inside her coat to her cross-body bag, fumbling for her can of Mace.

The lights drew closer, grew stronger, until the glow focused into two beams. High off the ground. A truck. The driver's-side door swung wide and a large, looming figure jumped out, ducking into the rain while holding his Stetson in place.

She gripped her Mace harder. She'd taken self-defense classes in college, but she was seriously off-balance with one broken heel and the other spiked into the mud.

"Ma'am, what are you doing out here tonight? Are you waiting for a tow truck?"

That voice. It couldn't be… But her ears told her it was. After all, she'd spent countless hours watching videos of Jesse Stevens giving interviews, memorized them, in fact, to decide the best tactic for approaching him. She tilted her head to catch sight of his face below the brim to confirm.

And she gasped.

No picture could do him justice. Even with the Stetson covering his blond hair, he bore the look of a cowboy Viking. An image she found difficult to let go of once it came to life in her mind.

Spluttering on a mouthful of rain, she tucked her Mace can back into her purse, no longer needing protection.

She should have suspected the truck could belong to Jesse Stevens. She was near his ranch, after all. But still, weren't the odds higher it would be one of his employees rather than him at this hour, in the rain?

Yet there was no doubting who this man was, even in the dark with just his headlights slicing through the night. She'd done her research on the man and his spread well before this excursion to meet him, persuade him.

But she wasn't ready to let him know who she was. Not just yet. She swallowed hard. "My car won't start, and the cell reception is garbage out here in the middle of nowhere."

"Speaking as the landlord of the Middle of Nowhere, I've never had any trouble with mine." Rain dripped from the brim of his hat as he towered over her. "You should check with your provider."

Was that irony or irritation coating his words?

Not good if she'd already made him angry. This would be over before it started.

She longed for higher heels to make her taller, closer to his eye level. "I'll be sure to look into my provider as soon as I find dry clothes. If you could just help me call for a tow, I'll get my suitcase so I can change. I'm freezing to death."

It was cold for Texas, even in December.

"Your car's not going anywhere tonight, ma'am. And there's no way either of us should risk walking back over to your vehicle to retrieve your luggage. The ground could give way at any time."

Her foot slipped. She looked quickly at him. "It's just my broken shoe."

Then her other foot shot out from under her. She lurched to the side, her umbrella whipping away in the wind. Her arms pinwheeled as she lost her balance, tumbling toward the rushing swell of water alongside the dirt road.

Strong hands clasped her waist and stopped her fall. Before she could catch her breath, he'd hauled her against his chest. His warm breath fanned her cheek.

"Are you all right?"

Other than goose bumps that had nothing to do with the cold because she was in the arms of a Viking cowboy? "I'm fine." Her words came out husky. "Thank you."

"What are you doing out here this time of night in such crummy weather?" Thunder rolled in the distance.

She braced her palms on his impossibly broad shoulders and looked straight into Jesse Stevens's emerald green eyes. "I'm looking for you."

Jesse Stevens held the drenched woman against him, her willowy body enticing even through her soaked raincoat and his hastily-tossed-on jacket. He'd been making a last check of the horses, concerned about the thunder spooking them, when he'd seen the car lights. He'd been surprised, not expecting anyone until tomorrow. Not that he was complaining.

The matchmaker he'd hired had outdone herself in sending this candidate.

He wondered which of the three contenders this was—the single mom, the veterinarian or the Miss Texas pageant runner-up. This woman certainly could be the latter, and that might explain the high heels and flashy car choice. The height seemed to be right, based on the stats in her profile. Although it was difficult to tell much in the dark. He was definitely curious to learn more about the husky-voiced siren. All the more reason to resist the temptation to hold on for an extra second or two.

Stepping back, he still cupped her elbow. Just to make sure she didn't lose her balance, of course. "Are you okay? You weren't hurt when your car spun out, were you?"

She nodded, pulling one foot, then the other, out of the mud. "I'm fine, thank you. I truly didn't expect the weather to get this bad."

Given her slick trench and Porsche, she had more of a city-girl vibe that he had doubts would hold up out here. But the matchmaker would have told her about him and his rural lifestyle. He'd sure filled out a checklist of his criteria for the kind of woman he was looking for.

"Ma'am, the road is at risk of giving way further. You need to get to safety. My truck can take an alternate path that's not accessible to the public."

"Let's go, then." She started forward, her purse

tucked tight to her side, but her foot sank deeper into the mud, stopping her progress. Sighing, she cursed under her breath. Like a sailor, no less.

An unexpected surprise. She had grit to go along with all of that glam. He could still feel the imprint of her against him.

She glanced up at him, her eyelashes spiky wet, her ponytail slick and sleek down the front of her coat. "The heels aren't holding up well out here."

"Then I'll carry you." He wasn't sure where the invitation came from, but now that he'd said it, the idea had taken root. An appealing option, and with each passing second, an increasingly necessary one.

"Whoa, wait." She held up a manicured hand, with two chipped nails and another broken. "That's a bit extreme."

"Ma'am..." He smiled. "The longer we talk, the worse the roads will be. And I don't know about you, but I'm cold even though I have on boots."

Indecision flickered across her face. But then she shivered and her hand lowered. She nodded quickly, her teeth chattering.

All the invitation he needed.

He scooped her up into his arms, tucking her against him as he made tracks toward his truck. With a squeak of surprise, she looped her arms around his neck, a light scent of something floral and exotic riding the humid air to tempt his nose. Her body fit against him, the curve of her breast pressed to him.

So much for feeling cold. Heat fired through his veins. But he needed to learn more about her. His days of sowing wild oats were in the past. He was ready to settle down, build a family, and he wasn't waiting around for chance to bring him the woman he needed.

He'd contacted a selective, high-priced matchmaker to assist him in the search. His days were packed with running his ranch. His only social life involved the occasional event at the Texas Cattleman's Club and he already knew every one of the members. He wanted a wife, children—heirs. He didn't believe in grand romance or love. But he was a firm advocate of the benefits of a winning partnership.

Yes, he more than wanted a wife. He *needed* a wife and he was prepared to offer that spouse his full partnership in return. A win-win for them both.

Once he found the right candidate.

Stopping by the passenger side of his dual-cab truck, he set the woman on her feet carefully, ensuring the ground beneath her was safe before he let go. The rain was coming down in buckets.

He opened the door for her, offering a hand as she stepped on the running board. Damn, those dainty shoes of hers were mighty mangled. She hadn't been prepared. The clasp of her cold fingers in his hand reminded him of how badly this stormy evening could have turned out for her.

And it still could if he didn't get his butt in gear and drive back to the house. He braced a hand on the hood as he jogged around to the driver's side. Once behind the wheel, he slammed his door closed against the wall of rain being blown inside.

At least the heater was still blasting, since he'd never turned the vehicle off. He swept aside his Stetson, flinging it to the back seat beside a horse blanket and a thermos.

"I'm so glad you came along," she said, her teeth still chattering. She kicked off her broken shoes and wriggled her toes under the blast of warm air circling at the floorboard.

"And I'm glad I saw you out there." He started to ask her name, but the rain picked up pace on the roof. It could wait. "I hate to think what could have happened to you if those waters swept your car away."

As she'd said right away, she knew who he was. So he didn't have to worry about reassuring her she was safe to come with him.

"You were right to question the wisdom of my driving into this storm," she conceded. "I was so eager to get here, I just kept thinking I could outpace the weather."

She shook her head, laughing softly. The husky melody of her chuckle filled the truck cab, stroking his senses. That matchmaker sure had a knack.

He cleared his throat. "And the weather still might win if we don't get moving."

Jesse eased the four-wheel-drive vehicle out of Park and accelerated carefully. The tires spun, then caught, the truck surging forward, toward the dim twinkling of Christmas lights strung along the split-rail fence. The storm smudged the glow until it was just a smear of green, red and white.

"I'm sorry to inconvenience you so late," she said. "I certainly intended to arrive earlier." The truck jostled along a rut in the road and she braced a hand against the door.

"You'd have had better luck with a utility vehicle instead of that sports car of yours."

"It would appear so." She squeezed excess water from her ponytail, her wet hair clearly blond now in the glow of the dash.

But he wasn't any closer to identifying which of the matchmaker's candidates she might be.

"I'm Jesse Stevens, as you already seem to know. And you are?"

"Esme Perry. Nice to meet you, Jesse."

He looked over sharply in surprise at her name. She was not one of the three women the matchmaker had provided. Surely he couldn't have forgotten a recommended candidate. Perhaps he'd missed an email from the matchmaker?

Except… Wait… Alarms sounded in the back of his mind. There were plenty of Perrys in Texas. But one branch in particular was heavy-duty on the radar of the Royal branch of the Texas Cattleman's Club. "Perry, as in…"

"Yes, my father is Sterling Perry. We're very excited about the new branch of the Texas Cattleman's Club opening in Houston. My father sent me here to talk to you. To do a little recon," she said with a sassy smile.

Disappointment churned. She hadn't been sent by the matchmaker. He focused on the path ahead, a back road on higher ground to his home.

"A spy in our midst," he said dryly. Granted, one helluva sexy Mata Hari.

"Not anything so nefarious." She tugged at the belt of her trench coat. "I'm just here to see how you run things at the Royal branch."

"Or to curry favor for your dad."

She straightened in the seat, clearly bristling at the criticism of her father. But it wasn't any secret that Sterling Perry had a sketchy past and a quest for power.

A quest that was currently playing out in a battle with Ryder Currin as they vied for control of the new Houston branch, to be opened in a historic building site, a former luxury boutique hotel. Ryder Currin was a self-made man. Whereas Esme's family was led by the old-money, charming, larger-than-life patriarch Sterling Perry, who continued to grow the Perry fortune in banking, real estate and property development.

Jesse's impression of the man? All show but little substance.

Was this woman like her dad? It seemed so, judging by her car and her clothes and her defense of her father.

He pulled up to his ranch home. More lights glimmered in the trees lining the driveway, and a wreath glowed on the front door of his white two-story house. A sprawling place he'd had built with hopes of one day having a family of his own. His parents were dead. He only had one sister, and while he loved her, she had her own life.

Now he was ready to build a future for himself.

Keeping his eyes off the woman beside him, he steered off the path and onto the driveway, circling around back. More twinkling lights marked the way. He'd arranged for decorations outdoors to make his place more welcoming, but hadn't gotten around to the indoors. His life definitely needed a woman's touch.

He activated the garage door opener, steered into the six-bay garage, and turned off the truck as the automatic door closed behind them. "You can stay at my place until morning…or until the weather blows over."

"I appreciate the offer. Clearly, I'm in no position to turn you down." She gestured to her bare feet and soggy clothes.

"Call it club loyalty. It would be irresponsible of me to send you back out into this weather." He draped a hand over the steering wheel and allowed himself an unrestrained look at the bombshell beside him. "But I don't talk about club business in my off-hours, so I won't be discussing your father or the Houston chapter."

"Fair enough. I just have one question, nothing about the Texas Cattleman's Club." She tipped her head to one side, her raincoat parting to reveal the curve of her breasts in the soaked silk shirt. "Who did you think I was?"

Two

Toying with her seat belt and not in any hurry to leave the truck just yet, Esme waited for Jesse's answer, more curious than she would have liked to admit about what mystery woman he was expecting. Even knowing that cowboys weren't her type, she couldn't deny the appeal of those piercing green eyes.

He cocked an eyebrow as he reached for his Stetson. "I certainly didn't think you were one of the infamous Perry family."

She bristled at the censure in his voice. *"Infamous?"* she repeated, the bubble of romance officially burst. She unbuckled her seat belt and reached for the door handle. "That's rather harsh, don't you think?"

"I didn't mean to offend," he said as his boots hit the pristine cement floor of his six-car garage with a solid thud. "Your father was investigated on fraud charges and the murder of a Perry Holdings assistant not too long ago."

Vincent Hamm had gone missing, the assistant presumed to have quit and moved to the British Virgin Islands to spend his life surfing, based on a text he'd sent his boss. But then his body had been discovered with a bullet wound to the chest, his skull bashed, making identification difficult. But DNA tests had confirmed the man's identity.

Esme slammed the door, the sound reverberating in the dimly lit space. Her damp and muddy feet slipped ever so slightly as she charged forward alongside a speedboat, her toes still so icy cold, her mangled shoes dangling from her hand. An SUV, a motorcycle and a pair of four-wheelers filled the rest of the space. The man sure liked his toys.

Or maybe his family did?

She glanced at his left hand as he tapped the security code at the door leading into the house. No ring. But then, there was still the mystery woman.

Esme pulled her focus back to her reason for being here. To clean up her father's image among the Texas Cattleman's Club members here in Royal.

"My father was cleared of fraud *and* the murder of Vincent Hamm." All hell had broken loose when the body was found at the site of the new Texas Cattleman's Club, where her father's construction company was doing the renovations. The murderer still hadn't been found. "As I recall, you were under suspicion, too, after leaving an angry message on Hamm's voice mail."

"Valid point." He waved her inside with a broad

hand, his square jaw flexing. "Lucky for me, I have an airtight alibi."

While he turned on the lights, she flung her damp hair over her shoulders and unbuttoned her trench coat. "Clearly there's something more you want to say?"

Texas landscapes lined the walls of the corridor, one end leading to a washroom and the other leading into the house. He eyed her for a moment, sizing her up before nodding tightly. "Your father has led a cutthroat life in the business world. Sterling Perry may not be guilty of this, but the man he has been made it easier to believe it could be him."

She couldn't deny the truth in that. But that was still her daddy Jesse was talking about. "You certainly know how to win friends and influence people."

Sighing, he swept off his hat. "Ma'am, you're clearly tired. I'll make you something to drink—decaf coffee? Tea? Hot chocolate?"

She was exhausted. But she had a narrow window of time. If she kept bristling this way, she would lose the chance to plead her father's case to be the president of the Houston branch of the club. It was tough enough already with all the politics back home, given the other contender for the position was his longtime rival, Ryder Currin, who her father felt had unjustly gotten an oil-rich piece of land that should have stayed in the family. It didn't seem to matter to Sterling that he already had more money than royalty and that Ryder had made the bulk of his fortune through savvy investments.

Although they had to get along these days since Ryder was seeing her sister Angela, that didn't change the fact that her dad wanted the position. And Angela would have to live with that, because Esme intended to make this happen for her father.

"Hot chocolate, please, if it's not too much trouble." It sounded like something that would take longer to make. Give her more time to collect herself. Mold herself into the perfect influencer. "And no worries. I'm thick-skinned like my father."

A fib. She actually was the most sensitive of her siblings, but that would smooth things over for now.

As the sensitive sibling, she'd learned early how to play family peacekeeper. To de-escalate tension and defuse situations—even though her heart often thudded loudly in her chest and panic rose in her blood.

With footfalls uncharacteristically silent for such a tall, broad-chested man, he moved into the laundry room. Light flickered on, and Esme peered inside the well-kept pale yellow room with green plant accents. He pulled clothes out of a basket on top of the dryer, then strode with cowboy swagger back to her. He motioned down the hallway. Sconces on the wall provided a warm light as they made their way to the massive kitchen. He placed the neatly folded clothes on the island.

With a surveying glance, she took in the open, sprawling layout. White granite countertops provided a sleek contrast to the dark wood cabinets. Open shelves displayed simple white dishes and mugs. A countertop overlooked a large bay window that, despite the night storm raging outside, offered an enviable view of the large barn and fence. Unlike the interior of the house, the barn and fence sported twinkling Christmas lights.

A thick but unfinished sandwich took up the majority

of a white plate on the countertop. He must have been eating there when he'd spotted her car outside.

Jesse's rough-cut smile lit up his green eyes. "Good, I'm glad to hear you're tough. If we're going to be trapped here together until the road's cleared, it will be easier if we get along."

Trapped? Now, that sounded promising.

"True enough." She slid off her trench coat.

The room went silent as his eyes flickered with awareness, taking in her damp blouse and slacks. Her chilled skin warmed at his gaze.

Then he looked away, clearing his throat as he picked up a remote control off the island and thumbed on the sound system. Holiday tunes played softly, jazz renditions. That surprised her. She would have expected him to pick country music.

Rubbing the back of his neck, he walked over to the double wooden doors of his pantry. Intricately carved, the wood depicted a rearing horse on a landscape. It was a touch of personality in this state-of-the-art kitchen that was otherwise pretty much devoid of personality. He removed a bag of marshmallows and a mason jar filled with hot chocolate mix and set them on the counter. He pulled out milk from the fridge.

"Well, then, Esme, let's agree not to talk about your father." He spun a pan in his hand, setting it down on the front right burner.

Not discussing her dad was rather counterproductive to her reason for braving the storm to see him. But she wasn't going to argue with him. She would work her way back to the subject when the opportunity arose.

"Fair enough." And while she waited, she couldn't resist asking, "Let's start with who you were expecting."

"Actually, three someones." The milk simmered on the gas stove.

He reached up to the open shelves, selecting an oversize mug. His hands were calloused and capable, telling a story. He didn't just own this massive spread. He worked it.

Surprise lit through her. "Three people you didn't know and wouldn't recognize?"

So...mystery *women*. What was this man up to?

Jesse had maneuvered to a well-stocked bar next to the stainless steel fridge. She noticed a sole picture beside it—of a girl in her twenties who shared his intense green eyes. A sibling perhaps? It was the first—and only—sign of personal effects she'd spotted since entering his ranch house/mansion. A private man, then.

He held up a bottle of peppermint schnapps and quirked an inquiring eyebrow. She nodded and he set the bottle on the counter beside the rest of the ingredients.

"In my defense, Esme, it was dark when I found you and you were—*are* drenched. Speaking of which, you should change before you catch a cold. Your hot chocolate will be ready soon." He stood toe to toe, the spicy and damp scent of him teasing her senses. He passed over the stack of clothes—sweats, a tee and socks—his calloused knuckles brushing hers. "I'll tell you all about the three mystery women when you get back."

Her hands still tingling from the light touch, she sure

hoped her father appreciated her efforts here. Because she suspected focus on her task was going to be tough to come by with Jesse Stevens.

She wasn't even one day into this promotional excursion and already she'd made a mess of things. One that not even the longest, steamiest of showers could make right.

Esme was no stranger to luxury, but she still appreciated the plush robe and heated floors in the guest bathroom he led her to.

An all-Texas bathroom for sure, with a touch of modern rustic charm in the form of the polished horns on the wall opposite the luxurious Jacuzzi. But there was also a large tinted window that offered a view of the Christmas lights lining the fence. The only other lights came from a bunkhouse in the distance.

Under this roof, she was alone. With Jesse Stevens.

Exhaling hard, she plucked one of the lotions from the basket on the counter. She opened the top and inhaled the delicious scent of peppermint, which reminded her of that spiked cocoa waiting for her. Along with the man.

Smoothing the lotion onto her legs, she found her thoughts drifting back to Jesse. His broad shoulders. His blond hair spiked and mussed. Her skin tingled from more than the minty cream.

She'd never doubted her professionalism. Her cool head. And while she worked for the family company, she'd allowed this to become too personal. This wasn't even about the business. This was about her father's quest to be the president of a club. Which many would have thought meant she was doing a favor, not a job.

Many would be wrong. This was more than a favor. She was trying to earn her dad's approval. Even knowing that shouldn't matter so much to her, an adult woman, she couldn't dodge the truth.

She risked a glance in the mirror. With her hair wet and snarled, she was a mess. A far cry from how she'd started the morning with a spa day. Even her manicure hadn't survived, one nail broken and two others chipped.

It was almost comical, really, as if all her professional facade had been wiped away. Her slacks were ruined. Her silk blouse very likely unsalvageable, too.

All that was left of the real her were her champagne-colored satin underwear and her diamond stud earrings.

At least she had something to wear other than the robe. She stepped into the baggy sweatpants, then the Texas A&M pullover, the fabric warm and tantalizing against her bare skin. She tugged on the athletic socks, bunching them around her ankles. A far cry from the heels she'd slipped on this morning with such relish. But as least she was warm. And clean.

She left the steam-filled bathroom and returned to her suite. Swiping her phone from the coffee table, she dropped down into the desk chair next to the fireplace. Stones flanked the fireplace, giving the guest suite the feel of a swanky cabin. Her toes sank into the plush rug as she FaceTimed her sister.

Of all of her siblings, Angela Perry worried the most. And judging by the four texts Esme had received while she was showering, her sister was imagining every worst-case scenario.

She propped the phone against a leather-bound book on the desk to free her hands to brush through the rat's nest that had replaced her hair.

Within a few rings, her sister's blond hair and rounded face came into view. Angela sat on the ground in front of the new gas fireplace she'd just had installed, flames flickering. Orchestral carols played softly in the background.

"Well, hello there." Angela stared back at her, her blue eyes flaring in surprise. "You look…not like yourself. No offense meant."

"None taken." Running the brush through a knot in her hair, Esme laughed lightly. Her sister had never been a clotheshorse, preferring an understated style. A love of fashion had been at least one thing Esme could share with Melinda, since Angela and her twin had just about everything else in common.

They even lived in the same condominium building—an upscale thirty-two-floor limestone high-rise with wraparound windows and expansive views. The twins had even chosen the same layout, Angela on the fifteenth floor and Melinda on the twenty-fourth.

"Well, this has been quite a day. Or night, rather."

Angela tossed a scrap of Christmas wrapping paper into the fire behind her, then reached for another roll. "Definitely not the image of my glamorous sister."

"Stranger things have happened." But heat still stung her cheeks. One of the ways Esme gained her confidence—and kept her sensitive soul in check—was through a careful curation of makeup, hair and luxurious clothes. The oversize sweats she was wearing rattled her. Threw her off-balance.

Though, if she were being honest, not any more than her sexy host.

Her sister's thin fingers moved deftly over a small stack of jewelry boxes with elegant silver script reading "Diamonds in the Rough." Esme guessed the packages were for her and Melinda, not that she could see inside. Most likely Melinda's contained something to celebrate her baby on the way. The pregnancy had been a surprise to Melinda and her new husband, Slade, but a welcome one. And pregnancy hadn't slowed down her sister's philanthropic works one bit.

To her right, Angela had a bin filled with gold and red foil paper with intricate bows. Designer-level gift-wrapping supplies. A small stack of already-wrapped presents glistened in the fire glow. Esme always told her sister they could afford to pay someone to wrap the gifts for them, but Angela insisted she enjoyed doing it herself, making each one a work of art.

And Christmas was all the more special since Angela had reunited with her former fiancé, Ryder Currin.

Angela ripped clear tape off to secure the golden foil on one of the smaller jewelry boxes. "I'm glad you called. I was starting to get worried. Weather reports are looking terrible in Royal."

Esme thought of the soaked, muddy clothes she had carefully placed in a bag next to the bathtub. She winced a little. "The reports are accurate."

"But you're okay?" her sister asked, genuine worry in her voice.

She nodded, enjoying the soft sounds of violins surging through "Ave Maria."

"I got caught in a flash flood, but lucky for me, I was close to Stevens's ranch. He saw my headlights and came to my rescue."

"Sounds like a close call. I can't imagine your low-slung car held up well in those conditions."

"You can get the judgy tone out of your voice. I know you weren't a fan of my purchase." Esme worked the last of the tangles from her hair, smoothing the brush down the length until she was satisfied that all the knots were out. At least she'd managed to restore some semblance of order in her life.

"It's your money to do with as you please," her sister said as she reached toward a stack of unwrapped presents. Picking up a handsome brass shaving kit, she started sizing up the necessary material to wrap it.

"Well, you can rest easy. My next purchase will come with four-wheel drive." Sporty four-wheel drive.

Angela set down the paper and peered into the screen, her blue eyes fixed but still kind. The look of an older sister. "I just care about you."

"I know." It was tough to discard the defensiveness sometimes, feeling like an outsider with her sisters' twin bond. "And thank you for caring."

Her sister nodded, continuing her methodical wrapping. Without looking up from lining up the edge of the paper with machinelike precision, she said, "So, what's the progress with Jesse Stevens?"

"I've barely had time to shower, much less make progress."

"Shower?" She raised a blond eyebrow. "At Jesse Stevens's house? You're there now?"

"Yes, and no need to sound scandalized. I was drenched. I needed to change." She glanced down at her clothes. When was the last time she'd worn sweats? High school maybe. Or middle school. As rarely as she could manage. "But enough about me. How was your date with Ryder last night?"

Her sister had been engaged to none other than their father's longtime nemesis Ryder Currin, who also happened to be in the running to head the Houston branch of the Texas Cattleman's Club. Angela and Ryder had broken up, but were now back together again with Sterling Perry's blessing. Esme would wager money a re-engagement wasn't too far off.

She just hoped Ryder was really right for her sister. He'd been married twice before—divorced from the first wife and widowed by the second. He had one child from each of those marriages, plus an adopted daughter. All adults. Such a complicated blended family.

Angela deserved to have a man love her unconditionally.

"I never thought he and I would have another chance, but things are good, really good."

Her blue eyes turned wistful and the smile that warmed her face drew a pang of guilt from Esme over her doubts and concerns.

"I wish I could have been there for us to talk all about it in person over lunch."

Angela nodded, her smile still present but soft. "That would have been fun, but I understand."

Her sister leaned back to the pile of gifts—a cashmere scarf, leather-bound books, artisanal reclaimed-wood trays. The silver strands in her chunky gray sweater glimmered.

Christmas was coming at the end of the month and Esme hadn't even begun her shopping. She wished she had her sister's love for organization and gift-giving. Maybe then she would feel more connected to the holiday. "If only I'd waited to leave..."

"Dad appreciates what you're doing for him. This is important."

Was it, though? More important than being with her sister? She'd tried to convince her dad that this could wait a couple of days, but he'd insisted. And she hadn't stood up to him. She'd even had the weather as an excuse and she hadn't taken it.

"Well, I'll be back in Houston before you know it. We can have brunch and chat over mimosas."

"That would great. Just let me know when you're finished there and I'll line it up with Melinda, too. We'll definitely need to make it brunch and not breakfast, since Melinda still gets morning sickness." She chewed her fingernail thoughtfully, then added, "Perhaps we could include Tatiana, as well, if you don't mind."

Esme bit her lip to keep from blurting how she wanted to do things on her own with Angela, without their sister, much less Angela's bestie, Tatiana Havery.

Tatiana, a vice president at Perry Holdings who specialized in real estate, had been going through a tough time ever since it came out that Willem Inwood was her estranged half brother. And now that he'd been arrested last week? It would be petty to exclude her.

"Mimosa brunch with you, Melinda and Tatiana.

Count on it. Maybe we should invite Ryder's two daughters. I could get to know my future nieces better." She chuckled at the irony of that, since Ryder's daughters were both adults. There was an age gap between Ryder and Angela, but since her sister didn't mind, then who was Esme to judge?

"Okay, then. I will." Angela fluffed her golden-blond hair, surveying the mess of ribbon and foil paper strips around her. "All right, sis, I need to clean up this mess. Thank you for checking in. Please stay in touch."

"I will, just as soon as I have something to report." Esme waved before signing off.

Sighing, she swept her hair into a loose topknot. Casual glam, she told herself.

Time to face her sexy host and try not to wonder if a kiss from him would taste of peppermint schnapps.

Jesse stared out the kitchen window at the water pooling outside, covering the driveway. As the storm continued to rage, he was glad he'd reached Esme when he did.

No denying it, the woman who'd crashed into his life this evening had made quite an impression. He thought about the way her wet clothes clung to her, outlined her shapely body.

Not that she was his type. Too city. Too polished for a ranch lifestyle. Not that it mattered. He had three potential matches coming to the ranch.

Still, his thoughts drifted to the way her wet hair fell in waves. No. He couldn't deny being intrigued by the woman who was currently cleaning herself up in his shower as the rain pelted down.

In the oversize mug, he stirred the hot chocolate. The mug in his hand had been a gift from his little sister. She'd made it in a pottery class, rightly guessing that something homemade would mean more to him. He could buy anything he wanted.

His sister had a knack. The pottery was expertly crafted. She'd called it part of her robin's-egg collection.

He wasn't an overly sentimental man, and even though he and his sister weren't close, this mug represented his last link to family. To something grounding.

After giving the hot chocolate a final stir, he popped the top of the peppermint schnapps, deciding Esme should be the judge of her alcohol level. He didn't want to pour too much. Who knew what her alcohol tolerance was? And he wasn't one to take advantage. He prided himself on being a man of honor.

And he needed to stay focused on his search for a bride, someone who wanted to share this lifestyle with him and build a family.

He turned back to the kitchen and poured himself a cup of coffee with a shot of whiskey in it. Then settled onto a barstool at the kitchen island where his half-eaten sandwich still waited. Fried steak between two thick slices of Texas toast. He took another bite and washed it down with his spiked coffee, the taste firing through his veins on this damn long day.

As he continued to eat his sandwich to the rhythm of rain and thunder, he reflected on the events of the last hour. Now he regretted calling Esme's family "infamous." The word had a crueler inflection than he had meant. Especially since Esme's father was no longer a suspect in the murder. He understood too well what it felt like to be wrongly accused.

Tearing into another bite of his sandwich, he went over the events of the murder investigation in his mind.

He'd been shocked when he was questioned by keen Houston detective Zoe Warren. All because of an argument he'd had with Vincent Hamm. Someone he'd thought he could count on. His kid sister just graduated with an MBA from one of the top programs in the country. Not only was she his sister and he had a strong sense of family, but his sister was also brilliant, with a sharp mind for business. Jesse had asked Vincent to help get his sister in at Perry Holdings. But Vincent refused to even set up an interview for Janet.

Jesse took another sip of his coffee, still trying to understand why, despite all the favors Jesse had done for him, Vincent wouldn't lift a finger to help.

Rage had filled him. He'd believed the worst of his friend. That a big-city job with a fancy salary at Perry Holdings had gone to Vincent's head. That he'd forgotten who he was. Jesse had responded with anger.

And then, a few weeks after their strange encounter, Vincent Hamm was dead. And not just dead—murdered.

A brief angry voice mail from Jesse to Vincent had turned up in the authorities' investigation. A handful of words. Crazy. But Jesse, ever a rule follower and ever meticulous, had a solid alibi. He'd been three hours away at a cattle auction. His location south of Houston was certifiable, easily tracked through his purchase records and through his hotel visit. Nearly all his time was accounted for. There was no feasible way he could have been the murderer. As a law-abiding man, he'd voluntarily submitted to a lie detector test, which he'd passed. He wanted Vincent's actual killer to be found. Sooner rather than later.

He thumped the edge of his own mug, heat transferring ever so slightly from the ceramic to his fingertips.

Jesse's attention returned to the present as he heard the creak of the guest suite door and soft footfalls on the hardwood floor. Then there she was. Esme Perry.

He stood slowly. Damn.

The mug was no longer the only thing throwing heat in the kitchen.

Esme walked deeper into the kitchen, looking too damn sexy in his Texas A&M sweats. Even wearing his athletic socks bunched down around her ankles, she somehow made it all work into an elegant ensemble right down to her diamond stud earrings.

"Well, Miss Esme, you are definitely unmistakable now," he said, nudging her mug and the bottle of schnapps toward her.

"It's nice to be dry again." She gestured to her wet hair. "At least somewhat." She poured some of the liquor into the mug, stirred thoughtfully. Almost absently.

She lifted the mug to her lips, and he found himself unable to look away, imagining how soft they would be.

"I'm glad to help." He waited for her to sit before reclaiming his place on the barstool. "Did you reach home to let them know you're okay?"

"I did. Just now. I called my sister Angela. We were talking about plans to meet for brunch." Her delicate nose scrunched with worry. "We haven't had much time to talk lately since she got back together with Ryder."

Everyone in Royal had been blown away at the news when Angela and Ryder had gotten engaged. A Perry and a Currin? Unimaginable. Then they had broken things off, and now were apparently a couple again.

Jesse shook his head. He wanted something more stable in his life. "You and she are close?"

She hesitated for a telling moment. "Angela and Melinda are twins. Then I have a brother, Roarke. We all love one another."

He'd heard the gossip that Roarke was rumored to be Ryder Currin's biological son, rumors so strong they'd taken a DNA test. A test that proved Roarke truly was a Perry. Still, the whole ordeal must have put a strain on their family. "That's not the same as being close."

"The twins are close, and our brother has always gone his own way. He's happy, though, working at Perry Holdings in Houston in a newly formed ethics department. He still does part-time work offering legal, too."

"He sounds like quite the crusading attorney for the underdog. I imagine you're proud of him."

"I am. It wasn't easy for him to find his own path. He and Dad butt heads because our father expected Roarke to go into the family business. But that's enough of our family drama." She shrugged, her hair rippling over her shoulder in a blond waterfall. "So you have siblings?"

Her eyes flickered to the photograph tucked on the marble countertop.

Esme was observant. He'd give her that.

"I have a sister. She's all the family I have left, actually. I thought I was going to lose her not too long ago. Her appendix ruptured and she had to have emergency surgery."

Hospital runs and the smell of antiseptic filled his memory. The bargaining and praying for his sister's life he'd done were still a visceral memory in his stomach.

"I'm so sorry. Is she all right now?"

"She is." He looked at the mug in Esme's hand, thankful for his sister's recovery.

"Thank goodness. Still, that had to have been a scary time for you."

"It was."

Rain continued to fall outside, filling the pause with controlled chaos.

She looked into her mug, swirling the hot chocolate around without meeting his gaze. "Actually, you weren't wrong. My sisters have a special bond. My brother, well, his earlier move to Dallas wasn't all that surprising. Now that he's back, that seems to be changing some. Regardless, I'm still stuck somewhere in the middle. But that's all right. Not everyone has the same relationship."

"You don't sound like it's okay."

She raised an eyebrow in surprise, then took another sip of the hot chocolate as she leaned on the granite countertop. She spread her fingers out wide as if soaking in the cool texture. "About those three someones… I'm dying to know more."

"Dates."

Her eyes went wide, and she inched back. "All three? At the same time?"

"Whoa. It's not what you're thinking." He held up his hands defensively, chuckling. "I signed up for a dating service, a matchmaker. She's lined up a trio of candidates. They were each supposed to come out here individually to meet with me, to see my ranching lifestyle and decide if it's off-putting. It's not for everyone."

Her gaze flickering away at the mention of ranching not being for all, she wriggled her toes in his overlarge socks. "A matchmaker. Seriously?"

"Plenty of people sign up for online services. I opted for the matchmaker because of lack of time." Absolutely the truth. And he found a certain sort of…practicality about having an expert match him with someone with similar interests. It saved time rather than meeting scores of women socially and trusting fate to somehow work out his future.

Her forehead furrowing in confusion, Esme leaned slightly forward. "Why do you want to have a girlfriend if you don't even have time to look for one?"

Well, that was easy enough to answer. "I don't want a girlfriend. I want a wife."

Three

"A wife?" Esme repeated, certain she couldn't have heard him correctly. Hot cocoa cradled in her hand, she studied him through narrowed eyes, but couldn't read if he was serious or not. Which could have something to do with how she kept looking at his impossibly broad shoulders. "You're punking me, aren't you?"

"Not at all." He set his coffee cup aside. "I'm looking for a wife."

A flash of disappointment rippled through her. Silly really, since the last thing she wanted was a rancher. "A wife. Not simply a date. That's just... Well, I'm surprised you're already thinking that far down the road about someone you haven't even met."

He crossed his arms over his chest. "Your shock is a little insulting."

"But you're a man." Her eyes were drawn to his arms

before she could stop herself. His muscular arms. Arms that had carried her so effortlessly.

"And that comment is decidedly sexist." His green eyes flashed with heat.

She grabbed her mug quickly. She should probably hush before she alienated him altogether. "I apologize. I only meant it's a leap from first date to the altar."

"Apology accepted." He reached for the refrigerator door, his flannel shirt pulling taut along his muscular chest. "Whipped cream?"

"What?" she asked, startled, her gaze shooting back up to his face.

"For your hot chocolate." He held out a can, pointing in her direction.

Her mind traveled sexy pathways, imagining things they could do with that sweet treat.

"Uh, sure." She reached for the can, spraying a swirl inside her mug, when she really wanted to fill her mouth with the stuff and quench at least one hunger. "Of course, there's no reason in the world why you shouldn't find love."

"I didn't say anything about love," he said in the most logical of voices. "Just marriage."

Again, he'd surprised her. This man wasn't at all what she'd expected from reading about him online before her trip to Royal. "Marriage but no love?"

The thought of that chilled her with memories of her parents' loveless marriage. Too many nights, her mother had cried herself to sleep over her husband's staying late at the office yet again. Esme wanted more for herself than that and felt sorry for anyone willing to settle for less.

"Why not? I have my life in order—this house, the ranch." He ticked off points one finger at a time. "The timing is right for the next step. A wife. Then kids."

He'd laid out the events as matter-of-factly as he'd laid out the ingredients to make her hot chocolate. He'd described the process of creating a family as if he was listing the week's upcoming groceries.

She raised an eyebrow. "Do these three mystery women know they're expected to pop out children right away?"

Esme imagined what his dream woman was like. What she wanted. What would make her forsake the idea of love.

Not that Esme had had a lot of luck in that department. Still, she wasn't giving up on finding love—when the time was right, with the man who was right.

She gulped down more hot cocoa and struggled not to wince as it burned her tongue.

"We all filled out extensive questionnaires. Our wishes for the future are in line."

Well, now, that wasn't subtle at all. "And I'm in the way."

Esme blinked a sting of jealousy. She'd only just met Jesse. And while he was sure one sexy cowboy with his slightly tousled blond hair, she knew better than to assume they were anything more than two very opposite people stuck together riding out a rainstorm.

With precise, athletic footfalls, he made his way over to the window and looked outside into the tempest.

"In this storm, I seriously doubt any of them will be showing up." He turned to her and his gaze held on her upper lip, and she realized she had a hint of whipped cream clinging there.

Jesse returned to her, offering her a napkin. She took it, dabbing her mouth slowly. His eyes flamed hotter and she wondered what it would have been like to let him kiss her upper lip, to taste him in return.

She swallowed hard to will away the sensation. "How do they feel about being a part of this edition of *Catch a Bachelor: Rancher Style*?"

He shot her an amused glance, easing back a step. "This isn't a reality show."

"Of course not." She rolled her eyes, struggling for levity. "No cameras."

He cocked an eyebrow. "And they're coming at different times so they don't cross paths."

"How very…civil." And cold. "How do your brides-to-be feel about this emotionless transaction?"

"To be fair, they know about the process. No one's being deceived."

He leaned against the island, an arm's length away. Esme's eyes drifted to his shiny engraved belt buckle. Snapping her attention back to their conversation, she considered the less robotic aspects of such an arrangement. All likes and dislikes already sorted. Everyone knowing the rules of the game. Everyone understanding expectations, too. No mystery. Nothing as quirky as fate intervening.

That was something, at least. "Glad to hear it."

A slow, disarming grin spread across his face. "Are you interested in joining the process?"

"Whoa, nuh-uh." She held up her hands in protest.

"I'm in no hurry to fill a nursery, and I've had enough of ranch living."

He tipped his head to the side, studying her, amusement in his eyes replaced by curiosity. "Yet you grew up on a ranch."

Her childhood home on the outskirts of Houston was a sprawling mansion, almost castle-like, surrounded by pastures, elegant barns. The spread was a huge, billion-dollar cattle-and-horse operation started by her maternal grandfather, then passed on to her parents. And even with all of that, Esme had still moved into the city the first chance she had.

"Exactly. No more ranching for me." And that was all the reminder she needed for why she should keep her distance from this man and stay focused on her reason for being here. "Thank you for the hot cocoa and the clothes and the rescue. I should turn in for the night."

She rinsed her mug and made fast tracks for the guest suite before she was tempted to stay in the kitchen. To listen to the warm timbre of his voice.

To imagine the taste of whiskey from his coffee on his tongue if he kissed her.

Sleep had been a difficult commodity for Jesse, with images of his surprise houseguest filling his dreams. Visions of her soaking wet, yet equally enticing in sweats. What would it be like to peel those clothes from her body?

Restless, he'd finally given up sleep just before dawn and gone to the barn to burn off energy.

His cowboy boots reverberated on the cement floor as he approached Juniper's stall. Grabbing the supple brown leather halter and lead, he made his way into the stall of his newest horse.

Juniper, a young dapple gray mare, stretched her neck, giving her tangled mane a shake. She sniffed his hand, her whiskers softly touching his palm. The horse exhaled warm breath against his fingertips, a welcome sensation in the cool, damp morning air. Stepping closer, Jesse slipped the cognac halter on her head and led the mare to the crossties, where his brushes were waiting for him.

He never grew tired of this, the connection with his horses and the land. Ranching was more than a job to him. It was a way of life.

Picking up a currycomb, he moved his hand in circular patterns. Excess hair and dirt gathered in the brush.

Other horses poked their heads from stalls. The barn held two rows of twelve stalls. Buddy, his first gelding, lazily chewed on hay, dropping bits of straw onto the ground. Flash, a muscular chestnut quarter horse, loosed a whinny. Beneath his hands, Juniper sucked in a breath before belting out an answering noise.

Satisfied, Flash moved back into his well-kept stall.

The routine grounded Jesse, reminding him of his reasons for using the matchmaker for a practical choice.

Practical.

That was the mantra he said to himself as he picked up the hard brush. His hand moved in time to the rain pelting the tin roof.

Images of his sexy houseguest kept interrupting his thoughts. *Practical. Practical. Practical.*

How many times would he need to say that until it sank into his brain? He surveyed the barn, wondering if he would need to groom every horse today to refocus himself.

Of course, that was the opposite of practical.

After finishing up with Juniper, he led the mare back to her stall and gave her the carrot he'd shoved in his pocket earlier. The mare crunched her treat, flicking her ears forward in something that seemed like thanks.

Latching her stall, he started to leave the barn. He pushed his Stetson down on his head to keep the cold rain from pelting his ears as he made his way back to the ranch house. The cold nipped at his hands as he moved past the pool, his boots trekking through the muddy earth as he closed the distance to the green door of the back entrance. The matchmaking prospects certainly wouldn't be arriving today, or the next, if the weather didn't ease up soon.

After wicking the rain off his Stetson, he hung his hat on a hook and discarded his leather jacket and mud-drenched boots. The hall led to the kitchen, where he found Esme sitting in front of the fireplace in the lotus position. A plated pastry and coffee mug rested on the mahogany end table to her left.

Damn.

His heart hammered.

Hair drawn up into a sleek ponytail and skin dewy in the firelight, she looked enticing, even in a long slouchy sweater and floral leggings his sister had left behind. Somehow, the pink sweater hinted at her curves, and the floral leggings made her look oddly polished.

His athletic socks still warmed her feet, and he realized he'd have to find her suitable footwear.

Something practical. The word echoed again as he reached for another mug from the open shelf.

"I've had your car towed to my mechanic." He poured himself black coffee, allowing himself to taste the bitter cocoa and fruit undertones. "Carl—who towed your vehicle—said it wouldn't start."

"Oh no, I was afraid of that." She scrunched her nose in dismay. "Because of the flash flood?"

"Most likely." He was drawn to her, this bewitching and beautiful woman. He dropped into the brocade chair on the other side of the fireplace. "If Carl can make it here on his four-wheeler, he'll bring your luggage. Otherwise, you'll have to make do with my sister's clothes for a while longer." He'd offered them to her last night. "I'll see if I can find some rain boots that fit you."

Esme's delicate fingers moved like sultry smoke as she removed her thin phone from where it was tucked under her thigh. "I'll put in a request for a rental car for when the rain lets up. Hopefully they'll have something available."

He stretched his legs out in front of him, powerful legs encased in denim. "You might as well save yourself the time."

"Why?" She hesitated. "Is there a problem?"

"This time of year, with the holidays and all, rentals are all booked for weeks." He flashed her his best bad-boy grin, even though he'd officially hung up his bad-boy ways. "I could lend you a vehicle."

"That would be so helpful." She placed her phone beside her on the armchair. "Thank you."

He watched her through narrowed eyes, unable to

resist. "I have an extra truck. It's twenty-two years old, but runs great. Carl's a super mechanic."

She fidgeted with the end of her blond ponytail, rubbing the strands between her fingers, clearly caught off guard by his offer. "Oh, uh, yes, thank you."

He narrowed his gaze, assessing the impossibly posh woman in front of him. "You've never driven one, have you?"

She arched an eyebrow. "Actually, I learned on an ancient stick-shift truck at Daddy's ranch. A Ford so ancient I figured no one would notice if I added an extra dent or two."

"Touché." He lifted his mug, toasting in her direction.

She eyed him intuitively as the flames licked upward in the fireplace. "You were teasing me."

"Perhaps."

She raised a finger to her lips. "Shhhh. Don't tell your three potential brides that."

A begrudging laugh barked free and before he could second guess himself, he said, "Maybe if the rain lets up this afternoon, we'll get enough of a break to chop down a Christmas tree. That is, if you want to come along?"

"Sure," she said, already launching to her feet. "As long as you don't expect me to load it into the truck."

She flashed him a sassy wink.

"You can just stand there and look pretty." And the thing was, he meant it.

So much for keeping his distance. But something about this woman tempted him more than he wanted to admit.

* * *

Jesse's flirtatious words still echoed in Esme's ears two hours later. Steering the conversation toward her father and the club was tougher than she'd expected.

But she was determined to keep her cool. Slow and steady was her best option. And thanks to their current project sorting Christmas ornaments while waiting for a break in the rain to get a tree, she would have the time she needed.

Despite the rain, light beamed through the floor-to-ceiling windows on two of the four walls of the great room. That, coupled with the cathedral ceilings, made the petal-white room feel impossibly airy.

Which was good considering all the boxes of Christmas ornaments that flanked the white love seat and leather couch. She'd moved the glass-and-wood table in order to create room for the bins Jesse had brought down from the attic, noting as he did so that these were only the tip of the iceberg.

To set the mood and to gain control, Esme queued up her favorite Christmas playlist from her phone, connecting it to the Bluetooth surround-sound system. A hazy, warbly '50s-era carolers version of "Here We Come A-Wassailing" filled the room.

There.

The start of Christmas. And the real start of her mission.

They opened the first box of ornaments. Reaching into the box, she pulled out two silver bells, one with Jesse's name engraved on it, the other with the name Janet etched on it. "Your sister, right?"

"Yes, we split the decorations between us. Somehow

I must have missed giving her that one." His brow furrowed and he tilted his head to the side, inspecting the silver bells. For a moment, she wondered if he'd pull out his phone and snap a picture to send to his sister. But his hands made no move for the phone in his pocket.

"How long until you get to see her over Christmas?" A little prying, but curiosity filled her as she laid the ornaments down with care onto the sofa.

"Like I said, my family wasn't tight-knit," he said, not that it answered her question. "My parents didn't get along. They're gone now." His face hardened, tight lines pulling at the corners of his mouth.

"I'm sorry for your loss. My mother died ten years ago and I still miss her dreadfully." She fidgeted with the thin bracelet her mother had given her so long ago.

Her mom—Tamara—had been a kind and loving mother. Esme knew her parents hadn't married out of romance, and seeing their unhappiness only made her all the more determined not to settle for less than a fully committed heart.

The loss of her mom made Esme cling all the harder to the rest of her family. She couldn't imagine what she would do without them. Her dad and her siblings meant the world to her. Christmases were big, boisterous events for them. Sometimes it had been a challenge to get Roarke to join in, but she and her sisters had worked to wear him down. She had high hopes for him this year, now that he'd found happiness with his new love, Annabel. "That's got to be tough for you and your sister, having lost both parents. I can see how maybe it would have brought you two closer to each other."

She pulled out an ornament tucked in protective

paper. Glitter twinkled as she removed the wrapping to reveal a reindeer towing a sleigh.

"Janet's great, and I do love her, of course. It about killed me to think I might lose her when her appendix burst. But she's well now, thank God." A sigh racked him and he scrubbed a hand over his face.

"That had to be so scary." She stopped unpacking ornaments, searching his face, cradling the sleigh in her hand. "You'll have a lot to celebrate together over Christmas, with her recovery."

He ran his fingers through his blond hair, then rubbed along the back of his neck. "It's unlikely we'll see each other. We don't have much in common. She's a lot younger than I am, and, well, we just have our own lives now."

Jesse looked away and pulled out a snow globe, full of glitter around a tree, a nutcracker and a ballerina. A wistful shadow played across his face.

His thumb stroking the smooth glass, he flipped over the trinket and wound it up. "The Dance of the Sugar Plum Fairy" played as a snowstorm enveloped the little scene.

Biting her lip, she couldn't help but be moved by such a glimpse of nostalgia in this rough-and-tumble man. She stood, reaching a hand to touch his shoulder, then stopping short. "But perhaps the ornaments remind you of happy memories?"

"Yeah, they do." He set the globe on the mantel. "And I look forward to making memories with my own kids one day."

Well, that was sure a splash of cold water, reminding her of his plans. She pulled a smile and tugged at the hem of the pink sweater. "Your sister has nice taste in clothes."

He angled his head. "Are you being sarcastic, Ms. Prada?"

"It's not office wear, but it's fun for ranch work, soft and cheerful."

"That's nice you can appreciate a less flashy style."

"I'm not a snob." She handed him a longhorn ornament.

"Really?" He took the decoration, their fingers brushing.

Her skin tingled even after he'd pulled away. "You don't have to sound so surprised."

The snow globe stopped playing just as the song drifting through the speakers subsided. For a moment, silence filled the great room.

Desire danced in the air, an electricity between them as he moved closer to her. "Would it soften the sting to your ego if I told you how hot you look no matter what you're wearing?"

Music started on her phone again, orchestral carols stroking the air.

She closed her hand into a fist, trying to will away the lingering sensation of that simple touch. "And what about those three bridal prospects of yours, one of whom will give you babies to make Christmas memories with?"

He canted back, nodding tightly. "You're right. It's totally inappropriate of me. I mean it when I say I want to be a family man, and all that entails."

"The epitome of a Texas Cattleman's Club fella."

"Yes, exactly that." His gaze held hers, setting

her skin on fire with just the stroke of his eyes on her face.

Even knowing it was unwise and there were so many reasons they were wrong for each other, she still felt herself sway toward him. His hand lifted slowly, reaching out to tuck her ponytail back over her shoulder. Then his fingers slid to cup the back of her head. Goose bumps of awareness spread over her and she wanted this moment, this connection. Just one kiss.

With luck, it wouldn't even be a very good kiss and she could refocus on her plans to repair her father's reputation. So giving in to temptation was the right thing to do. Or at least that's what she could tell herself as she angled forward the rest of the way for her lips to meet his.

And damn, it was very far from being a bad kiss.

Four

Jesse had expected the kiss to be good. Esme was a sexy woman, after all.

He had not expected that his senses would be set on fire at the first brush of her lips against his. A connection he fully intended to deepen. And explore.

Sliding his arms around her, he drew Esme to his chest, angling his mouth over hers, his tongue tracing the seam of her lips until they parted and…

Thoughts fled until only sensation remained. The soft give of her breasts against his chest. The glide of her hair through his fingers as he cupped the back of her head. He could smell the scent of shampoo and wondered what perfume she chose. What would be in her suitcase once the weather cleared enough to retrieve it. He wanted to feel and learn more about her. More than just the kiss.

Although it was still one helluva kiss.

She tasted of coffee and mint and something innately *her.*

Music hummed softly in the background and rain came down in sheets outside, all almost drowned out by the hammering of his speeding pulse. A breathy sigh whispered from her and he groaned, surrendering to this moment with her.

He swept a hand behind her, brushing away the ornaments and paper, clearing a space to recline her back in the thick woven rug. Her arms twined around his neck and she arched closer, skimming her mouth over his neck up to nip his earlobe.

Irresistible.

Her breasts pressed against his chest in a sweet temptation, her foot stroking the back of his leg as her thighs parted ever so slightly. He'd wanted her since the first time he saw her on the side of the road. The fierce desire for her swept him away as surely as the storm sweeping over the landscape. Until the power of it was ringing in his ears.

Except…

"Your phone," she gasped softly, her breath warm against his skin. "I think that's your phone ringing."

And it was. The text message sound dinged a couple more times. Each successive ring called him back to reality. And each ring raised the level of surprise more and more of what had just occurred. The surprise of the heat that passed between their bodies.

Damn. How could he have lost control so fully? His focus narrowed sharply as he angled off her, swiping his cell off the coffee table. Multiple texts scrolled across the screen and he cursed under his breath.

"Is something wrong?" she asked, elbowing up, her cheeks flushed, her hair tousled from his hands.

She quickly straightened her clothes. The moment had passed. Even if he could stay. Which he couldn't.

He pocketed his phone. "That was my foreman. He and the rest of my crew are cut off from the barn by the rain. I've got to get to the animals." He paused, stroking a finger down her face lightly. "I'm sorry to leave abruptly."

"It's okay. You're needed," she assured him, smiling but inching back. She crossed her arms somewhat protectively around her stomach and chest, as if she were Alice in Wonderland shrinking before his eyes. "And it's not like the kiss was anything more than an impulsive mistake for both of us."

Ouch. That stung more than a little. Because as far as he was concerned, it was a steamy, soul-searing kiss that he wouldn't mind repeating.

But she was right. He'd had no business losing control with her. "If you need anything, call me." He pulled a card from his wallet and passed it over quickly. "All right? Promise?"

"Absolutely." She eased to her feet, backing away. "I should call my sister and check in again anyway." She turned from him, her sun-gold hair glistening.

He reached for her hand, stopping her, not sure what he planned to say until the words fell out of his mouth. "That kiss may have been a mistake, but I don't regret it for a second."

* * *

Hoping her distraction didn't show, Angela Perry half listened to her sister Esme's latest check-in call from Royal while staring out at the Houston skyline from her high-rise condominium. At least they weren't FaceTiming today, so any distraction wouldn't be visible. Esme was going on and on about decorating with Jesse, down to what his decorations looked like.

And yes, Angela was more than ready to embrace the Christmas season, all the way down to the tree behind her with freshly wrapped gifts. She'd had one helluva tough year, caught in the middle of the feud between her father and Ryder Currin. Maybe that was a part of why she was having trouble mustering too much enthusiasm for Esme's call.

Their father's latest ploy to become the president of the Houston branch of the Texas Cattleman's Club was frustrating. Ryder certainly wasn't using a PR expert to sway votes.

Worry gnawed at Angela over what might happen if her father lost. Would he withdraw his recently extended blessing over her dating Ryder again?

A roll of nausea rippled through her. Pain, recent and still tender, colored her memories. Breaking off the engagement had just about broken her heart—and his. Taking a risk on becoming a couple again had been scary.

Though she knew Ryder was her future, emotions still ran high. Angela chewed the inside of her lip, a habit she picked up as a child when nerves got the best of her during school competitions or when she needed an anchor back to the world. Not that this was the best way to cope.

But it was a way.

And she sure as hell needed something right now.

"Angela?" Her sister's voice snapped her out of her reverie. "I'm rambling, aren't I?"

"Not at all," Angela lied, more than aware of how Esme sometimes felt excluded by her sisters. Angela loved both of her sisters, but in her heart of hearts, she knew there was a difference with her twin bond to Melinda. Not that she would ever admit as much to Esme. "I appreciate your checking in and I'll be sure to pass along the update to the rest of the family."

"Thank you. I hope I have something more concrete to share before long."

Hearing Ryder stirring about in the kitchen, Angela figured she'd better cut this conversation short before her sister freaked out that something may have been overheard. "Stay safe and good luck with Jesse Stevens."

She signed off just as Ryder stepped from the kitchen into the living room, carrying a wooden tray of meats, cheeses and olives. He was such a wonderful man. And sexy.

If she didn't already know him, she would have never guessed he had three adult children. Like Brad Pitt, Ryder looked better and better with age.

Even in faded blue jeans and a chambray shirt, Ryder looked like he'd stepped off some movie set. Short, dark blond hair framed his tanned face. Blue eyes as bright as a Texas summer sky met her gaze, just as warm as a summer day, too.

As he yawned, his square, cut jawline moved. Even in these little gestures, he was handsome. He stretched, walking toward her in socks. His well-worn brown boots still took up residence by the fireplace.

Theirs had a been rocky relationship, made more than a little difficult since their families had been bitter rivals for years. Ryder had been a lowly ranch hand on the ranch outside Houston where Sterling Perry—an old-money Houston heir—was briefly the foreman during his engagement to Harrington York's daughter.

As part of a business and social alliance, Harrington had offered his daughter Tamara's hand in marriage to Sterling Perry, as long as Sterling agreed to learn the ranch business from the inside and then live there after he married. When Harrington had died, Sterling had seen Ryder comforting Tamara and assumed they were having an affair, even though Tamara was a decade older.

Discovering that Harrington had willed a key piece of oil-laden land to Ryder had only added fuel to fire, even though Sterling had inherited the bulk of the estate. When over two decades later, Ryder and Angela became an item, Sterling had been enraged. His fury had led to Angela and Ryder breaking up. Finding their way back together had been a long, heartbreaking journey.

But here they were, trying again with the hope of the Christmas season urging them on.

"You're so thoughtful." She extended her legs, wriggling her toes in front of the fire. The rain was making even a Texas winter cold. "I'm starving."

His gaze lingered on her legs for a second beyond casual interest before he set the tray on the end table and sat beside her, his jeans and chambray shirt covering those honed muscles of his. “How’s your sister doing?”

Thinking back to the drawn-out conversation with Esme, she tilted her head from side to side. “She’s still flooded in at Jesse Stevens’s place.”

She decided he didn’t need to hear all about the decorations.

“Well, I guess that’s convenient for your father.”

She struggled to hide a wince, concern firing anew. “Please don’t say you mean that in a negative way.”

He held up his hands, his blue eyes widening. “I get that your dad wants to be the president of the new Texas Cattleman’s Club chapter. And we all know that your father can be…determined when he sets his mind to something. Just look at how hard he pushed to break us up.”

Angela’s mouth tightened at the truth of his words.

However, it hadn’t helped that an executive at Ryder’s oil corporation had been the one spreading rumors about her father and a Ponzi scheme that had almost destroyed Perry Holdings.

Bringing that up wouldn’t be wise at the moment. So she settled on, “But my father relented about us.”

“You’re right.” Shifting his weight, he leaned toward her. “Then he promptly sent your sister to Royal to tip the scales in his favor,” he added, his face showing lines of stress and concern.

“It’s not like he sent her to seduce Jesse. She’s a highly qualified PR executive.”

“She’s a daddy’s girl,” he muttered. His jaw became rock solid. Tense.

"And your daughters aren't?" Angela knew otherwise. Both girls loved their dad. And he loved them. He was so proud of Annabel's makeover business, Fairy Godmother. And Maya, his adopted daughter. Things had been in turmoil with them since Maya had demanded more information on her birth parents. But the eighteen-year-old had never doubted her dad's love.

Angela chewed on her lip until she tasted iron. She felt her stomach knotting. "You and my father have hated each other for a long time. I know that's not going to magically go away just because you and I are an item. I only want the two of you to try."

"He and I have come to a truce—"

"It feels more like a temporary cease fire."

A wry grin tucked into his face. "For your sake, we're offering a united, powerful front to get to the bottom of what's going on."

"And after that's been solved?" She didn't want to think about losing Ryder or her father.

"Well, one of us is going to be leading the new chapter. If it's him, I'll be polite. If it's me…?"

She didn't want any part of this conversation anymore. And she had a damn good idea of how to distract them both. She angled toward him, smoothing the collar of his chambray shirt. "Let's stop talking about my father."

"Sure. If you're done with this—" he gestured to the tray of snacks "—then we can head out to finish up the last of your shopping. Although I can't imagine you have more to buy."

"Or we could skip the shopping." She shifted to straddle him, tugging at his shirt.

Grin kicking up the sides of his mouth, he cupped her hips, his eyes smoldering. "Excellent idea."

After her phone call with Angela, Esme had grown restless. It hadn't escaped her notice that her sister sounded breathless and a bit distracted. Ryder Currin's fault, no doubt.

She was happy for her sister, but also concerned for her dad. He was getting older, and this club presidency meant the world to him.

Determined not to waste time, she'd finished getting dressed in clothes left behind by Jesse's sister. She'd even managed to find a pair of rain boots that fit if she put on three pairs of socks. At the thought of seeing her handsome host, her nerves pattered as fast as the rain.

Yesterday she would have sworn she wouldn't be venturing out into the rain again anytime soon. And here she was, pushing out of the door and running through the storm in an oversize slicker that wasn't much more attractive than the sweats she'd worn last night.

Sure, he could most certainly handle things in the barn on his own, but he had saved her. And kissed her.

Who was she trying to kid?

She wanted to spend more time with him. To persuade him for her dad and because he was an interesting, charismatic man. She couldn't remember when she'd been this drawn to anyone this quickly.

She wanted to see if the chemistry of that kiss had been a fluke.

A well-appointed barn stood guardian before a small

patch of trees. As the cold rain continued to pelt down, she widened her stride and dashed for the door.

Once her boots crossed the threshold, she whisked the rain off her body. Drips melted into the floor as her breath slowed. Then she quieted to watch Jesse, unnoticed for the moment.

Hands wringing her damp hair, Esme held her breath as Jesse's muscled form gently stroked a bay horse. Even from a few feet away, she saw the whites of the horse's eyes and the flaring nostrils.

Something had spooked the bay, who kept tossing his head skyward on the crossties, front hooves picking up and down as if he might bolt. Jesse's practiced hand stroked the horse's neck as he spoke impossibly softly in an attempt to soothe the still-frightened animal.

Electricity danced in the air again. Sure, she hadn't anticipated being drawn to him at all. The kiss from earlier drifted back into her mind as this softer-but-still-powerful Jesse filled her vision.

As if sensing her, the bay craned his neck around, nostrils flaring once again, scenting her. Jesse was alerted to her presence and turned around.

"Well, hello, I didn't expect to see you out here. In case you hadn't noticed, there's a crazy-strong storm raging out there."

Grinning, she hung up the slicker on an empty peg along the wall. "I did notice, thank you, and it seemed to me that perhaps you could use some help."

He angled his head to the side, studying her through narrowed eyes. "You realize this isn't glamorous, right?"

"I know what I'm getting in for. I grew up on a ranch, something you seem to keep forgetting. Just because I don't choose to continue that way of life doesn't mean I magically forgot all I learned." Her arms folded across her chest.

"Okay, then," he conceded. "I welcome the extra set of hands. Especially ones so knowledgeable."

She took that as a challenge. A half smile tugging on her lips, she raised a brow. "Point me in the direction of what still needs accomplishing."

After he'd given her a quick rundown of what he'd done thus far—currycombing, hard brush and soft brush on Ace, the bay on the crossties—he launched into how the bay needed to have his hoof wrapped to deal with an abscess.

Reaching back over a decade, Esme remembered when her own buckskin mare had abscessed. If she were being honest, the flow of the care stayed with her but the particulars faded into the background.

Approaching the horse, she offered the palm of her hand to Ace. Sniffing gingerly, the horse's whiskers tickled her palm. But he visibly settled, a great sigh releasing the tightness in his neck. The crossties hung in loose loops for the first time.

"You're a natural." Jesse's eyes showed surprise as she stroked the horse's leg, feeling for the heat of the infection.

Warmth danced on her cheeks, but she willed a casual wink to keep her mind off how close her body was to Jesse's. "Sometimes I get lucky."

Standing up, she looked at the supplies he'd gathered. He bent over, asking the horse to raise the injured foot with a click of his tongue and a tap on the ankle bone. Ace, shifting his weight, complied.

Eyeing the pile, she recognized the Betadine bottle and handed it to him.

"So the city girl does remember her origins after all." He laughed, cradling the hoof as he poured the antiseptic on it.

His muscles rippled with a strength that took her breath away. Which was especially impressive given that she'd spent her life around cowboys, had seen plenty. But he was in a class of his own.

He was more than a figurehead ranch owner.

"Just here for the assist. What is the next step? I'm afraid this is where it gets fuzzy for me."

Looking up from the hoof, he smiled, nodding toward the supply bucket. "I need a pad and tape."

She nodded, handing him the last bit he needed to ensure the horse would heal properly. While he wrapped the horse's hoof, she spoke quietly to Ace, stroking his silky neck until the horse's eyes became heavy.

He finished checking his medical work and then carefully placed the wrapped hoof down. In a fluid movement, he snapped the lead line onto the leather halter and unhooked the crossties. Leading Ace back to his stall, he fished a treat out of his pocket, which the horse happily munched.

After closing the stall door, Jesse led her down the aisle to the wooden door of the barn office. The space was lit by overhead lighting and a blinking Christmas tree in the corner near a sturdy wood desk, scarred from use and full of papers. It had a different vibe than the expertly decorated house and pristine horse stalls. And how ironic that he'd put a Christmas tree in here, but not in his home yet.

She wondered if this might be a peek into his core personality, less constrained, less intent on being analytically perfect in his approach to everything.

He opened a stainless steel refrigerator tucked behind the desk and pulled out two water bottles, one for each of them.

Extending one bottle to her, he leaned on the desk's edge. "Did you reach your sister?"

"I did. You probably think it's strange how often she and I talk—given that you said you're not close to Janet."

"I think if you're both happy with your relationship, then that's awesome." He gestured for her to sit in the leather office chair. "I wish I'd had a houseful of siblings."

"And that's why you've got these three blind dates coming to meet you," she said, trying very hard not to notice how amazing the chair smelled, carrying the hint of him in the leather, like being wrapped in his arms.

"That's the plan." He shook his head wryly. "You were *not* a part of my plan."

"Sorry?"

"I'm not," he said enigmatically, continuing before she had a chance to question him. "You were incredible in there with the horses. Thank you, Esme."

She fidgeted with the bracelet on her wrist. The one from her mom that she couldn't ever remember being without. A small fidget of comfort. "I only did what was needed."

"But you *knew* what was needed, sometimes before I had a chance to ask. That's impressive." He nodded.

"Yes, I know. You grew up on a ranch, but not everyone pays attention. And it's not as if you needed to work."

Helping on the ranch had been yet another way she'd tried to impress her father, only to see he hadn't noticed because, to her surprise, he didn't like the lifestyle. He didn't even like horses, which blew her away because even the city girl in her loved the horses.

All the same, here she was again, still trying to prove she was indispensable. "What's going to happen with the Houston chapter of the Cattleman's Club?" she asked, blurting out what was on her mind.

"I can't predict the election," he said noncommittally.

"Do you think my dad has a chance?" Was she wasting her time here? What if Jesse said no and she would have to leave the second the rain stopped?

"Sure, he has a chance."

"But so does Ryder Currin."

He shrugged.

She sighed, the truth slipping out, frustration and fear of failure weakening her defenses. "I wish someone else was running. If Dad's going to lose, it's going to be so much tougher for him to swallow seeing Ryder at the helm."

"I thought they'd reconciled."

Had she said too much? Would that ongoing battle be a problem for the charter chapter? "They're making an effort for my sister. But they've hated each other for a long time. It's tough to believe they once worked together."

Except her father had known he would marry his boss's daughter. Which was ironic since her father didn't even enjoy ranching, not the way Jesse did. The way Ryder Currin did, too, for that matter.

All a moot point. Her father would make a good president for the new club. Winning would also make it much easier for her dad to accept Ryder with Angela.

And if her dad knew the turn things had taken with Jesse Stevens and that kiss?

Even the word flamed through her, leading her gaze to slide back to Jesse. His eyes met hers quizzically, then knowingly. Heat glinted in his expression.

The air crackled with awareness between them and she couldn't will herself to break away. The tip of her tongue moved over her top lip in an unconscious invitation.

Still seated on the edge of the desk, Jesse angled toward her, his hand sliding to cup the back of her neck. He angled his mouth over hers, and desire radiated through her, driving her to her feet. She looped her arms around his neck and held him close, and somehow, it wasn't nearly close enough. She ached for more of him, all of him. She couldn't stop the sigh of desire from escaping her lips.

A low rumble of pleasure vibrated his chest against hers a second before he swept his arm across his desk. Binders crashed to the floor, papers fluttering before they fell to rest. His arms hooked under her bottom, lifting her and setting her on the sleek mahogany surface.

Surprise flickered through her, excited her, spurred her to demand more, to throw caution to the wind and see how far they could take things. An invitation he seemed to understand, since he lowered her against the desk, then lay over her.

Her world narrowed to the music of the moment.

Her heart hammering in her ears.

Rain drumming on the roof.

A car roaring up the drive…

A car?

She froze, her skin chilling with realization. Jesse angled back, his head turning, his brow furrowed. He started toward the window and she bolted to her feet, making it there only a step behind Jesse.

An SUV was racing up the drive, rainwater sloshing from behind the speeding vehicle all the way to the front porch. She took one look at the sensible four-wheel drive with a cowgirl-hat-wearing woman stepping out from behind the wheel, and Esme knew.

In spite of the weather, the first of those matchmaking candidates had arrived.

Five

In all of his imaginings, this was not how he'd anticipated meeting his potential future bride. With the taste of another woman still on his lips, the exotic scent of her clinging to his shirt.

Papers were strewn all over the floor because he'd been a heartbeat away from taking Esme right here, right now, on his desk. Practical plans for his future be damned.

Jesse scrubbed a hand over his face, exhaling hard over the latest arrival. He should be relieved. The woman pulling up to the house could be his wife one day. According to the matchmaker, he had one in three odds this was it.

Yet Jesse couldn't help but be frustrated over her timing. He'd been enjoying the afternoon with Esme. She'd surprised him again today. Not just with showing up to help, but by being completely unaffected by mud and dung and hard work. He couldn't deny he'd been very impressed. But he also knew he couldn't fall for her. She was all about her job, her glamorous lifestyle, and didn't seem the least bit interested in marriage and children. Or so it appeared from the way she'd reacted to him saying that's what he wanted, his reason for reaching out to the matchmaker.

"Well," Esme said, backing away from the window, rain boots squeaking on the floor with a reminder of all her help, "this is awkward."

Her husky voice turning airy, he could feel the attempt at humor and he appreciated the effort to downplay the situation. But it didn't alleviate it enough.

And it wasn't going to get easier.

He looked out the window at the newcomer again. Given the number of paw print stickers on her back window, he guessed, "That must be Amaryllis Davis. She's a veterinarian, only lives about an hour away."

"Amaryllis? Her name is Amaryllis?" Esme bit her bottom lip for a moment, scrunching her nose before continuing, "Forget I said that. My name's Esme, for goodness' sake. I have no room to tease anyone over what a mama chooses for a name."

He knew he should say something to smooth over this moment, but he didn't have a clue. Never could he have imagined himself in this position. "I'm sorry about the timing."

It was probably the lamest sentence he could offer her. But no other words formed. Comforting her with his touch would cross a line. Again. And he knew he needed to reel back his emotions. Tuck them away. Focus on the future. On finding his perfect mate.

"You were honest from the start about the matchmaking prospects." Her beautiful face tensed into unreadable lines. She shook her head, honey-blond hair rippling in the office light.

He stared at her for a handful of heartbeats. Not long really, since his pulse was racing from being near Esme. It was so damn wrong that he wanted to steal one last kiss from her. That he was wondering what might have happened if he'd met Esme before contacting that matchmaker.

Those thoughts weren't fair to Esme or the woman outside. Or the other two candidates on the way.

Still, he had trouble shutting them down.

With his current luck, they would probably show up early, too.

Esme inched back a step, increasing the distance between them. "You should go meet her without me. I'll just hang here and text my sister." She waved him off like it was no big deal, but her eyes told another story. "I need to firm up plans to meet my sisters for brunch with Angela's friend Tatiana."

"You're sure?" he asked one last time. "We'll talk as soon as… Well, once we see if she's staying or not. You aren't going to leave yet, are you?"

A hopeful question. One he shouldn't ask. One he had to. He straightened the papers on his desk and picked up the binders, looking up at her.

Slender hands twirled her long blond hair. He noticed her chipped manicure. She cleared her throat. "I don't have a car and I'm guessing you didn't leave the keys in the old truck."

Her levity during an awkward moment just made her all the more appealing. And he'd only known her for a day. He told himself it was infatuation. Chemistry. Not the stuff practical unions were made of.

Looking down at the scattered ranch documents, he knew the more practical path was the path that continued forward with his plan. Secure a woman who shared his goal to raise a family. Someone who believed in the legacy he wanted to build.

Steeling his resolve, he nodded and turned to leave. To meet the woman the matchmaker had called his 98 percent perfect mate.

Grudges were a bitch. And she knew that better than most. Even if she kept a smile on her face so that no one would guess the person behind all the Perry and Currin grief was actually a woman.

How sexist of them to keep assuming only a man could take them down.

She sat at the conference table in Perry Holdings headquarters in Houston and knew she should be content. Happy even. Her job here at Perry Holdings gave her the money and prestige she'd burned for as a child growing up in poverty.

Listening to all of these entitled blue bloods at work made her blood boil with resentment over all they took for granted. Hearing them bandy about plans to spoil their children at Christmas with extravagant gifts and vacations reopened old wounds and depthless anger. It took all her theater training from college to keep her face neutral. To check the fire that burned in her chest. That resentment had become unbearable when she'd learned how the Perrys and Currins had cheated her out of a chance for a better life.

She eased back in the massive conference chair, the offices radiating the aura of elegance-meets-the-West. Perry Holdings had four floors in a downtown Houston skyscraper. But this could have been her father's business, his success. His *power.*

Or Currin Oil, with its five floors in an elegant brick office building in a more industrial neighborhood on the outskirts of Houston. At least the meeting was finally shifting from discussion of buying diamond earrings for a baby to starting the business meeting.

Such as it was.

Schooling her face to feign interest in the outrageously long discussion about the recent fluctuation in stock prices, she drummed her fingers impatiently along her leg under the table. Bracketed by Ethan Barringer and Roarke Perry, she hoped they wouldn't notice her nerves. She worked to ground herself by fingering the texture of her Chanel linen business suit, the hem just grazing the top of her knees. None other than her boss, Sterling Perry, led the meeting. He was so arrogant, all smiles now that the cloud of suspicion had shifted from him.

But she wasn't surrendering. Not yet. Not ever.

Understanding about the detriment of grudges didn't stop the burning need to take down everyone in the Perry and Currin families. And they had no idea how close danger had been, still was. They were all so damned arrogant that way. They didn't understand what it was like to grow up a joke, her status always one giant step behind that of her so-called friend.

And now, here she sat, right under Sterling Perry's unsuspecting nose.

He was so arrogant, so full of himself in his expensive suits with cowboy shirts and Stetsons when rumor had it he didn't really even enjoy ranching. But he was a formidable businessman, smart and intimidating.

She had barely believed her luck when he'd promoted her to the vice president position. Of course, that arrogance of his made him so confident in his decisions that he'd missed the obvious these past months. Even when it was uncovered that Willem Inwood spread the rumors about Perry that threatened to tank stocks, no one had suspected her of playing a part.

It would almost be amusing how little they suspected her, if only her situation wasn't so dire, her goals finally so close she could almost taste success.

The catalyst for her grudge had come about so unexpectedly, in a quiet moment. She had been nostalgically going through her late dad's things in her attic when she discovered an old letter, from her father to her mother. He'd promised that he would change, that things would get better. She had been stunned to read that her father planned to ask the dying Harrington York for help. The man had promised him a tract of land on the outskirts of Houston that was reputed to be rich in oil.

Harrington York, whose daughter was married to none other than Sterling Perry.

Once a wealthy titan like Harrington and his son-in-law Sterling, her father drank and gambled and got himself into trouble, losing his fortune. But she'd known her dad wanted to reform and that land would have given him a second chance to do just that. But Angela's grandfather Harrington must have changed his mind because when he died that land went to Ryder Currin, who'd developed an oil empire from it. Currin, a nobody ranch hand rumored to be having an affair with Harrington's daughter, Tamara, Sterling's wife. Such pervasive gossip that Sterling's youngest offspring, Roarke, had submitted to a paternity test with Ryder Currin.

Negative.

But still.

Good Lord, these people were like an episode of a reality show. And she had paid the price for their selfishness.

Her mother had never reconciled with her dad, and her life fell apart. She'd lost everything because of Harrington's false promises, and the way the Currins and Perrys had greedily done what was best for them. Her temple throbbed at the thought of how fast her father had been forgotten. How fast her life had taken a downward spiral.

She had even, very reluctantly, given up her baby. She'd had no support system to help her raise her daughter, not like someone at this table would have had. Bitterness soured in her mouth, growing stronger every day.

Within a few years, her father drank himself to death, leaving behind a second wife and a son who she had refused to acknowledge as her brother.

Until this opportunity arose.

She didn't feel guilty about using him in her scheme. Why should she? He had a similar lack of conscience.

Her brother was an easy mark because he'd always wanted the relationship with his sister that she'd denied him since birth. Her half brother had been more than eager to bring down the man "responsible" for destroying their father's future.

Her hands closed into fists under the table. There was still a chance her carefully laid plans could still unravel. Willem was in jail. Staying silent, sure. For now. Eventually the prosecutor would find the sweet-spot offer that would make Willem sing.

And then it would all be over. Job lost. Friends gone. Possible jail time for her, too, based on the roll of the dice. No amount of deep breaths could will away panic over the undeniable.

Because once they knew it was she—Tatiana Havery, Willem's half sister, Angela Perry's "best friend"—who'd orchestrated everything? Her time would have run out to make her enemies pay.

Esme was running low on patience. With herself, primarily.

She stood at the kitchen island, chopping a salad and wondering why and how she'd assumed control of entertaining matchmaking contestant number one—Amaryllis, the veterinarian, who was likely perfect for Jesse. Esme diced radishes faster and faster, struggling to appear unaffected by the brunette on the barstool.

Would she be the one Jesse chose for his perfect mate? She seemed right on the surface, given her career. Even Amaryllis's car was a better fit than Esme's destroyed Porsche.

The knife slipped, barely missing her thumb.

Jesse's dating life was not her business. It had no bearing on the situation with her father. She'd just shared a couple of kisses with Jesse Stevens, nothing more. Okay, so it had been, quite possibly, the best kiss of her life. All the more reason she should stay in her suite and work since he had plans to marry and propagate with a stranger.

But curiosity had her out here playing chef on the off chance of finding out why this woman was completely wrong for Jesse.

Radishes reduced to edible rubble, she moved on to cucumbers, still trying to study the woman without being obvious. The last thing she wanted was for Amaryllis to notice. Or worse yet, for Jesse to come back inside and catch her in an unguarded moment. He likely wouldn't be much longer talking to the ranch hands who'd made it back, thanks to their four-wheelers.

When Jesse had asked Amaryllis how she'd managed the drive in spite of the weather, she'd informed him she'd had lots of experience driving in all kinds of storms. After all, her work as a vet extended to farm animals. She'd navigated worse roads to assist in a delivery. Being punctual was important, she'd added, tapping her wristwatch. She had committed to being here at a certain time and she kept her commitments.

No spinning out in a sports car on a washed-out road for her, apparently.

Amaryllis sounded…too perfect.

Even from here, Amaryllis sat too straight. Like a rod shot through her back. Neatly trimmed nails painted a pale pink fiddled with her hair. The first bachelorette glanced down at her watch, then looked impatiently at the kitchen threshold.

Amaryllis broke any stereotypes Esme'd had about vets dressing in baggy scrubs even on their off days. A fitted lavender button-up shirt outlined her curves. Without so much as looking at Esme, the woman scrolled through her phone, pausing to type every so often. She delicately crossed her legs, clad in a pattern of thin black-and-gray pinstripes, as she ignored Esme's presence.

Esme skillfully scraped the chopped vegetables into a large pottery bowl before turning her attention to the grilled chicken breasts waiting to be sliced. "So what made you sign up for a matchmaker? If you don't mind my asking." The words came out of her mouth before her filter could catch them. Slicing the chicken breast into even strips, she waved her free hand. "Wait. Forget I said anything. It's none of my business."

Since walking into this house, she'd lost all damn control of herself. Frustration grew in her chest, and she continued the rhythmic slicing, attempting an air of casual sophistication and disinterest that Esme knew lingered somewhere inside her.

"I'm not ashamed at all. Ask away." Amaryllis pulled out a gold compact from her leather bag. Looking at herself in her reflection, the brunette fluffed her hair and then turned her attention to Esme. Unruffled and precise. "I'm a large-animal veterinarian, which means I spent almost every waking hour of my twenties studying. And now's not much better. I'm a workaholic who loves her job. There's not much chance for me to meet people who aren't affiliated with my practice."

Esme nodded, dumping the chicken into the bowl. Shifting her weight from left to right foot, she shrugged her shoulders, tension growing the longer the woman stayed.

"I would think that would actually give you plenty of opportunities to meet people who share interests with you. You didn't have to drive all the way out here to meet a rancher."

Was she trying to make Amaryllis leave?

Jesse wouldn't appreciate having his plans upset. And it wasn't that she actually had a problem with matchmakers. Plenty of her friends used dating websites, quite successfully. She'd even dipped her toes into those waters a couple of times.

She knew her questions were pushy and not even necessary, but she couldn't make herself stop.

Brows raising, Amaryllis pinned Esme with a matter-of-fact stare that threatened to shut down the conversation. "In my small town, the options are limited. This is the most efficient use of my time."

Amaryllis was too...practical for Jesse. Even though he proclaimed he was going this route for logical reasons, she could tell by his messy desk, it was all an act. He had a freer spirit than he wanted to admit.

"And you don't care that he has two other women coming?" The question sucked the air from the kitchen.

Amaryllis blinked fast, her lips going tight. Apparently, it did matter to her. And Esme felt bad for bringing it up. This really wasn't her business. But something like satisfaction clung to her regret for sharing Jesse's plans.

Which only made her feel worse. Confused her, too.

How did this happen? Esme felt the weight of why she was actually at Jesse Stevens's house crash on her shoulders. Her father's future as the president of the Texas Cattleman's Club. Not to scare away Jesse's suitors.

"I'm sorry," Esme said quickly, shoving aside the bowl and racing to the other side of the island. "That wasn't my place. Talk to Jesse. He'll be back in a moment. I'll just get out of your way."

"I should be leaving." The lady vet moved faster toward the door, tugging her rain jacket on with each step.

Oh, hell. What had she done? She'd ruined everything. This wasn't going to help her father at all. She should have reined in her jealousy, damn it.

"He's a great guy." Esme fast-walked after her, her socked feet slippery against the tiled floor. "I can give you pointers on him, make up for the fact that I shouldn't have said anything."

Amaryllis turned quickly, her eyebrows shooting up in surprise. "So you're going to apologize for meddling by meddling some more?" With a bark of bitter laughter, she shook her head, securing her purse strap over her shoulder. Anger and embarrassment flared in the woman's brown irises. Looking her up and down with an X-ray stare, the woman pressed her lips together. "Wow, you're a piece of work."

Before Esme could think of a suitable response, the door was slamming. Esme tried to formulate a recovery plan. It was her forte, after all. But then she heard the sound of a car engine starting, tires crunching.

Any hope for salvaging the damage she'd caused extinguished as the engine sound faded.

Guilt pinched. Hard. She sagged back against the counter. She'd had no right to be jealous. But the feeling was still there all the same.

Why?

Did she have feelings for Jesse she was unwilling to explore? Yes, she was undeniably attracted to him. And they did have a lot in common, like having been brought up on a ranch. A strong work ethic. Humor.

But she certainly wasn't putting herself on the list of marriage candidates. She wasn't even sure she wanted to have children. Jesse hadn't hidden his plans for the future. In spite of her upbringing, she was a city girl, an executive who loved five-hundred-dollar shoes, in spite of the muck boots she'd worn earlier today.

That seemed like a lifetime ago.

The door opened again and Esme straightened. Had Amaryllis come back? No, the footfalls were too distinctly masculine.

Jesse stepped into the kitchen, sweeping off his Stetson. "Where's Amaryllis?"

Esme cleared her throat, knowing this could hurt her father's bid for a favor from Jesse, but unable to offer anything but the truth and a vow to herself that she would do better with the next two candidates. "I have a confession to make."

Six

A confession? Frowning, Jesse tossed his Stetson onto the kitchen island, keeping his eyes firmly on Esme's face and off the sight of her in jeggings and a long white button-down shirt.

Hey, wait, was that his?

He cleared his throat. "It's okay that you took my shirt."

She blinked uncomprehendingly for a moment. "Your shirt." She looked down and tugged the hem. "It was in the laundry. I hope you don't mind."

"No need to confess about riffling through my clothes. And with luck, your suitcase will be here tonight…or tomorrow." Would she be spending another night?

Not that it should matter. Not with his potential mates coming. Still, he selfishly craved more time.

Esme pursed her lips, her hand moving to the tall glass filled with ice and water. As she swirled the ice against the glass, he watched her grow more tense, her shoulders rising, her jaw clenching.

Her hand shook as she gripped her glass. "That's not my confession. You asked about Amaryllis. She's gone. As in left the property."

Tilting her head, she gestured to the now-empty driveway.

Running a hand through his hair, he tried to make sense of what she was telling him. Had he offended the lady vet somehow? "Where's she going? The Cozy Inn and the Cimarron Rose bed-and-breakfast are probably full with Christmas travelers."

Esme opened her mouth as if to speak, then clamped it shut. He took a step toward her, looking for some clarity.

"She's gone-gone. As in left town, not coming back." Esme crossed her arms over her chest defensively. "She wasn't right for you."

He frowned, surprised and confused. "When I went outside, she seemed quite eager to get to know each other better over dinner. What made her change her mind?" When she didn't answer right away, suspicion nipped at him. "Or should I ask *who* changed her mind? Esme?"

"That's my confession." She inhaled deeply, then blurted, "I let it slip that two other women are coming."

Even from here, he could see the whites of her fingertips as she gripped her water glass.

He rocked back on his boot heels. "That shouldn't have been a surprise to her, though. We both went through a matchmaker. Nothing's exclusive until we decide to date."

She couldn't help but think again how her mother had married her father because it was a practical match that pleased her family. Maybe that had something to do with why she and her siblings had stayed single for so long.

"How very…progressive of you." She nudged the salt grinder closer to the pepper mill.

"I take that to mean you're a romantic, all about the hearts and flowers and being swept off your feet."

"There's no need to make fun of me. I'm very sorry I chased off your new girlfriend. Oops. Not girlfriend. Your potential wife." She winced, resting her hand on his arm. "Wait, scratch that. I'm trying to apologize, not dig myself in deeper."

That small touch sent sensations zinging through him. Her eyes widened with that same awareness he felt, the undeniable attraction.

Then realization dawned. Esme was jealous of the women being sent by the matchmaker, had likely even chased Amaryllis off. That gave him more of a kick than it should, especially when she'd made it clear she wasn't looking for the same things as him in a relationship. Hadn't she?

"So if you don't want me seeing Amaryllis," he mused, heat flaring over his skin at her nearness, "does that mean you want to take that kiss further?"

Her lips worked silently for a moment, color rising in her cheeks. Her chest rose and fell faster, the curves of her breasts enticing. His hands itched to explore.

"You're egotistical." She stepped back. Away from him? Or away from temptation?

He wasn't going to let her off the hook that easily.

"And you like me." The realization was satisfying as hell.

"You're infuriating. And more importantly, you have two more women due here, when?" she asked with a challenge in her voice. She pointed to the window, at the cloudless sky.

"Tomorrow, most likely. The weather app on my phone showed that roads are starting to clear." Esme would be able to leave. "They were supposed to come today, but they texted while I was finishing up in the barn to say they're waiting, just to be safe."

Her jaw dropped. "You scheduled all three women today? At once?"

"I told you Amaryllis already knew about the others. She's a practical, down-to-earth woman."

He needed practical. Stable.

Esme's eyes fluttered closed, then opened again, sparking.

"Knowing about the other women is different than not caring. She had her hopes up, Jesse. You can mock romanticism all you want. It means something to some people, though. It clearly meant something to that woman who ran like hell from the prospect of being a party of some lineup of women for you to pick from."

"What if I were a part of a lineup of men for her?"

"I would find that sad, too," she said without hesitation.

"It doesn't seem like you approve of matchmakers."

She shook her head, her silken hair gliding over her

shoulders. "You misunderstand. I have no problem with a matchmaker. I just think the way you're going about it is..."

"Is what?" he asked, more curious than he should be about how this woman's mind worked. "Spit it out."

"Fine." She braced her shoulders, her chin jutting. "I think it's a recipe for disaster. For heartache. Whatever you want to call it—romantic or practical—it just doesn't seem like something that will work long-term. Not that my opinion matters at all. It's your life."

Her criticism stung. He wanted a family of his own and put a lot of thought into how to approach this. And she just shot it all down in an instant as she stood in judgment of him. "You sure are being confrontational for a person who wants to persuade me your dad should lead that new chapter."

"I'm emotional. I can't make a spreadsheet of my feelings like you do." She grabbed her empty glass and stalked to the sink. "But no worries from here on out. I'll be sure the next two candidates hear only glowing things about you from me."

She stormed across the kitchen and toward the main part of the house without another word, anger crackling off her. His eyes were drawn to the sway of her hips as she walked away. Even after she was gone, her fragrance lingered.

As did his thoughts of what would have happened if Esme had been on that list.

Even two hours later, Esme couldn't believe what she'd said to Jesse. She was normally a calm professional. She was a middle-child peacemaker.

Not today, though.

She'd been hiding out here in her room since their argument, sitting in the middle of the bed and trying to make out a Christmas shopping list. A totally fruitless endeavor since her mind kept wandering back to their fight in the kitchen and how she'd wanted him to…

To what? She hugged the fat pillow, the high-thread-count cotton sensual against her skin.

Sighing, she had to admit the truth. She'd wanted Jesse to agree with her, then sweep her into his arms and kiss her until her knees melted.

The scent of something cooking, something fragrant and full of spices, teased her nose. She glanced at her clock and saw it was approaching suppertime. Would the time apart have hit the reset button for him as it had for her?

There was only one way to find out.

She tossed aside the pillow and slid off the bed, smoothing the shirt, his shirt that she'd pulled from the laundry. Her footfalls soft against the floor, she drew closer until she found Jesse standing at the dark stainless steel stove, stirring a pot of what looked like…

"Is that beef stew?" she asked, gripping and rubbing her wrist, a go-to gesture from when she had heated arguments with her sisters. A self-soothing gesture to calm herself. Not that Jesse knew that. But muscle memory was a powerful thing, and she needed all the smoothing-over vibes she could get.

He glanced back over his shoulder. "It is. Corn bread's in the oven."

"I would have thought you had staff to help you."

After all, he had a bunkhouse for ranch hands, and

he'd mentioned a foreman. But his house was huge and quiet.

He continued stirring, pausing for a moment to smell the deep notes of pepper billowing off the steam. "I do, but they clean and leave. It's just me so they don't need to come often. And I cook for myself."

She stepped closer, dropping her grip on her wrist. "I'm sorry for what I said earlier. It's your life. You know what you want. And that's more than most people in the world."

"Thank you. Apology accepted."

"Does that mean I'm invited to supper?"

"I'm not going to starve you." He tasted the stew and her mouth watered. For him. "My mechanic said he'll get to your car in the morning for a better diagnostic. Unless you have family or friends you want to come get you now. If the rain gets much heavier, the roads could wash out even worse."

Leave? So soon? Apparently, he still was angry, and she couldn't blame him. "Are you asking me to go now? I'm not sure my family could get here safely. But I can still go. There must be lodging somewhere."

"No, that's not what I'm saying. Like I said before, I'm sure everything's booked anyway, given it's the Christmas season." His mouth kicked up into a smile. "And you're chasing women off my property who will need a place to stay since the rain picked up again."

He leaned to pull the corn bread out of the oven, and she couldn't help but check out his butt. No female with a pulse would be able to deny how fine it was, denim cupping the perfect curve in a way that made her long to touch.

She squeezed her hands into fists on the kitchen island.

"Woman," she reminded him. "I've only chased off one woman."

He chuckled softly. "The week is young, Esme."

"It would help if you weren't so funny." Leaning against the cool granite countertop, she shook her head, taking in the subtle pull of his muscles as he stirred the stew.

"And it would help me if you weren't so sexy smart," he retorted.

"What does 'sexy smart' mean?"

He eyed her with a smoky gaze. "You have a brain that rivals your body. Smart women are sexy."

Her skin tingled with awareness. "Thank you for noticing…both. I worry because I work for my father that people may think I don't deserve the job. I try twice as hard to prove myself."

"Word around the club is that you're fierce at what you do. Have you ever thought about looking into switching companies?"

She'd thought of leaving—just once. But duty bound her to protect all that her father had built. Had sacrificed for. She couldn't walk away from the legacy.

"It's the family business. Plenty of relatives work together."

"Okay, fair enough." He leaned back. "So what do you say I dish up dinner and then you can tell me why your father is the best candidate to lead the new chapter of the Texas Cattleman's Club."

Surprise rippled through her. "Really? That simple? You're just asking me?"

"I am. I'll be looking into Ryder Currin. A few other possibilities, too."

"So my dad didn't need to send me here," she said softly.

"It shows how much he wants it. That means something. I get that he's excited about the new chapter. We all are." He passed her a bowl. "Now let's eat."

Companionably, they dished up their dinner, her mind scrolling through what she wanted to say.

Because yes, this club meant a lot to every one of them and she didn't want to say anything to mar the opening.

She could already envision the parties they would have there. The site had been chosen with care, a historic former luxury boutique hotel that fell into disrepair, now almost finished being renovated by Perry Construction. A gorgeous three-story building on a corner downtown. There were suites on the top floor for the president and chairman of the board. The second floor was for board members' and officers' offices and conference rooms. And the first floor contained the ballroom, a bar-style café club for members only, and the main meeting hall.

Stepping into Jesse's dining room, she stopped short at the sight of wineglasses and flickering candles. For a stew dinner?

It was incongruous and charming all at once. A smile lit her from the inside out.

More than just charming, actually. It was dreamy. This man had a romantic side, whether he wanted to admit it or not.

And she needed to remind herself that some other

woman would be the recipient of that long-term. Possibly sooner rather than later, depending on what he thought of those next two candidates.

Resolved, she took her seat at the table to start her pitch on why her father was the person to lead the Houston chapter of the Texas Cattleman's Club.

The very last thing she wanted to be discussing with Jesse Stevens.

The next morning, Esme stared at the two newest matchmaking candidates who'd arrived bright and early, within minutes of each other, and were now getting a tour of the barn. The foreman had just pulled Jesse aside to point out some issue with one of the mares.

Esme was surprised Jesse had left her alone with the two new arrivals after how things went with Amaryllis. He welcomed them and introduced her as a business associate in from Houston before he was called away.

Not that he'd gone far. She felt his gaze on her from across the barn. Warning her?

Biting her lip, she forced her attention back to her side of the stables. This go-round, she wouldn't let so much as a whisper of criticism pass her lips. Far from it, she intended to sing his praises. And to do so, she should learn a little more about them, to get a handle on the best way to help them impress Jesse.

So she flung herself into conversation with the two women in the barn, all the years of training to maneuver through intense situations coming into use now. Not that she could have ever imagined her professional training would prove handy while speaking to matchmaking candidates. But she handled Riley Jean Smith and Michelle Mendoza.

Esme turned her attention back to Riley Jean and remembered the woman mentioning something about having a six-year-old. "Where's your son?"

Riley Jean fluffed her long, wavy jet-black hair. "Staying with my mama. She loves special time with Lonnie Mac."

Esme pulled a smile. "That's what grandmothers are for."

Riley Jean scrunched her pixie-like face, blue eyes grave and serious. "She wants me to have time for myself. And honestly, even though the matchmaking company checks out the prospective dates carefully, I wanted to spend time with him on my own, to form my own opinion."

That made sense. Esme cocked her head to the side, as she petted one of the horses whose head poked out from the stall. The sorrel horse stretched beneath her hands, enjoying the attention.

Shaking her head, Riley Jean held up a hand. "Don't take that the wrong way. It's not like I think he's a serial killer or something. I researched him on the internet. You know, just the basics like his social media pages, his professional profile, college records, friends of his… You're single, too. You understand."

Riley Jean touched a hand to Esme's arm in what seemed like a strange act of camaraderie.

Staying on target was going to be a challenge. More than she had thought. With grit and determination, she willed words to her tongue. "Of course you should meet with him first. Sounds like your mother taught you to be a good mama."

"Thank you. I try."

Actually, the woman sounded a little stalkerish with all that checking up on him. Reasonable safety was one thing. Doing a deep dive into the internet was something else altogether.

Esme shifted her attention to the other woman. "So, tell me more about yourself."

Michelle leaned against the stall door—a vision in heeled boots, jeans and a plaid shirt. Dark waves framed her tan face, making her brown eyes all the more striking. "I'm a former runner-up in the Miss Texas pageant, third runner-up."

"You're lovely. I'm surprised you didn't win."

"Me, too," she said with no indication that she grasped how egotistical that sounded. "I got thrown from a horse the week before the competition, hurt my hip, which made walking in heels a real bitch."

Michelle pushed herself off the stall door, offering her palm to the sorrel horse before petting it. From down the barn, the low timbre of Jesse's voice reverberated, though there was no telling what he was saying.

Esme resisted the urge to shout "fire" and send both women running. But she wasn't going to repeat her mistake by chasing them off. She owed her father—and Jesse—more than that. She needed to be better. She hated being ruled by jealousy whether it was about Jesse, her sisters or her dad.

If this was what Jesse wanted, then she would do her best to help make it happen.

Checking to make sure Jesse was still occupied with

ranch business, Esme leaned closer to Riley Jean and Michelle. "I would like to help you both."

Michelle's microbladed eyebrows rose. "Both of us?"

Esme bit back a sigh. "This isn't *The Bachelor* where you're both trying to outdo the other."

Michelle rocked back and forth in her high-heeled boots with a chuckle. "Speak for yourself."

"Okay, that." Esme tapped Michelle on the arm. "He has a good sense of humor. He'll like that about you."

Michelle shook her hair back over her shoulders with a perfect toss. "I considered doing a stand-up comedy routine as my talent but opted for a patriotic tap dance instead."

"Hmm… I'd say go with your first instinct from now on." Esme bit the inside of her cheek. "Riley Jean? I bet you miss your son."

"I do." She touched a heart locket around her neck. "He's the best thing that ever happened to me, and he's everything to me since my husband died. Do you want to see Lonnie Mac's picture?"

Riley Jean opened the locket to reveal a photo of a gap-toothed boy. A kid who would probably love to have Jesse's attention.

"Cute kid," Esme said, in spite of herself. "Having a family is very important to Jesse. He really wants kids."

A reminder she needed to take to heart.

"Whoa, hold on," Riley Jean protested. "That's getting ahead of things. I only just showed up."

Esme felt the crisis boiling and knew she had to do her best to douse it. "I just meant it's okay to talk about your son. I've seen single-mom friends of mine hold back sharing about their kids for fear it'll chase the guy away. That's not the case here."

Riley Jean smiled impishly. "That's all good to know. Thank you."

Esme fidgeted with the ends of her sleeves, ready for this to be over but knowing there was still a task in front of her. "PR is my chosen profession. It's all about taking the facts and putting the right spin on things."

Michelle looked her up and down. A moment passed before she opened up her bubble gum–pink lips. "I have one last question."

Esme nodded. "Sure. Shoot."

"Why aren't you going after Jesse when you clearly know—and admire—so much about him?"

Surprise slammed into her. A fair question. She looked down the barn to where he worked with a horse. He was so handsome, even covered in dirt, his muscles apparent as he gripped the horse's hoof for more treatment for the abscess.

He was earthy, handsome and, yes, "sexy smart."

As if Jesse sensed her looking at him, he glanced over at her. His green eyes glinted and he smiled. She smiled back. How could she not?

Michelle's sigh and a creak of leather across the room drew Esme's attention back. Riley Jean was gathering her purse and Michelle was tugging on her jacket.

Oh, damn.

Esme straightened quickly and double-timed after them, barely catching them at the barn door. "Where are you going? Did I say something wrong?"

Michelle tucked her head to the side with a half

smile. "Honey, you didn't have to say a word. Your body language said it all. You've got it bad for that man."

Riley Jean nodded. "And by the steamy look he just smoked your way, he has it bad for you, too."

Did he?

She looked over at him quickly, and uh-oh, he was already striding toward her, no doubt because of the rapidly departing women. How had they gotten so far ahead of her already? Panic nipped at her as she called out, "Wait."

But Michelle and Riley Jean were deep in conversation as they moved toward their vehicles, heads tilted together.

"What's going on?" Jesse asked as he closed the distance between them.

Esme met him at the open barn door, chilly air from outside blasting through. "I swear I didn't do a thing to chase them off. In fact, I told them great things about you."

He turned from the door back to her, steam—the sensual kind—smoking from him in palpable waves. "Like what?"

She couldn't believe her ears. She gave him her full attention as the women drove off. Her pulse picked up speed. "You're not angry over them leaving?"

He planted a hand on the doorframe beside her. "Surprisingly, no. Not at all." He stroked back a strand of her hair, drawing two fingers down the lock. "My focus is exactly where it should be."

Butterflies churned in her stomach and she realized, truly realized and acknowledged for the first time, that there was something between them that just couldn't be ignored. Breathless and dry-mouthed, she couldn't deny that she wanted him.

Before she could have second thoughts that could rob her of exploring those feelings, she said, "That's really convenient."

He worked that lock of her hair around his finger, slowly drawing her closer. "How so?"

"Because," she blurted, the words tumbling out of her mouth faster than she intended, "I was thinking perhaps I could try out to be one of your dates."

Seven

Jesse stared at Esme in shock.

Surely he couldn't have heard her correctly. Although the surge of passion shooting through him shouted how much he hoped he had. He wasn't even disappointed to see the three supposedly perfect candidates bail. His thoughts were too wrapped up in Esme.

"Try out?" he asked, pulling the barn door closed, sealing them back inside, a few stray pieces of hay crunching under his boots. "What exactly do you mean by that? Audition to be my wife?"

"That might be a bit of a quick leap down the aisle. But a test run as your girlfriend—your wife, if you will—could give me the chance to see if I really like it." She shifted in her boots. Her blond hair fell over her blouse, hinting at her curves.

"You're certain of what you're suggesting? After everything you said about the matchmaking process?" His brow raised as he leaned against the stall door. Duke poked his head out of the stall, tilting it sideways. The horse chuffed, knocking his muzzle into Jesse.

A wide grin broke across Esme's face, lighting her eyes. She reached up to ruffle Duke's forelock.

"Part of me feels like that's all I want for Christmas," she said earnestly, her blue eyes sparkling. "To be honest, the other part of me isn't sure about anything, particularly life on a ranch and one that's not even near my relatives."

He liked that family was important to her. How ironic that until now he hadn't thought of that being a core part of who she was. So much so that she'd risked her life coming out here in a horrible storm just because her father had asked for her help. He started to churn over the possibility of chucking the matchmaker notion and giving an earnest shot at seeing where the attraction to Esme led.

"And you're okay with this, even though we barely know each other?"

"Seriously? You're asking me that?" She snorted on a laugh. "You were willing to consider marrying someone you'd never even met in person."

"Fair statement." He cupped her shoulders, then slid his hands down her arms, linking fingers.

"Although now that I think about it, your matchmaker had you fill out a profile. So let's do that."

"You want to take a survey now?"

"Not a written one. We can do it verbally." She

leaned closer, the heat of her breath a tempting caress. "Organically."

"Hmm, sounds intriguing. Do you want to go back to the house or to the office?"

She inclined her head, voice husky. "Your office. It's closer."

His heart rate picked up the pace. "After you, ma'am."

He gestured toward his office, following her inside. The Christmas tree lit the room well enough, so he didn't turn on the overhead light.

Esme settled onto the leather sofa, leaving space for him. "I'll start easy. What's your favorite music?"

"Country, acoustic." He sat beside her, stretching his arms along the back of the couch, his fingers brushing against her. "Simple but rich."

"Mmm, sexy answer. I can imagine long, slow kisses with guitar music in the background." Her eyes flamed, lighting an answering fire in him. "I like soft rock, old classics. And there's common ground there to be found in coffeehouse styles of the tunes."

"Favorite author?"

Esme tapped her fingers along a stack of magazines on the table beside the couch. "Jane Austen. Favorite movie?"

"*True Grit*, the original. All Stetsons, all the time." Watching Westerns was a ritual he'd started with his grandfather long ago. Funny how he hadn't thought about that until now.

"What's an absolute no-no in a relationship?"

Her question surprised him, but his answer was easy and earnest. "Lying."

A pained wince twitched at her face. Lines of worry

etched her brow. It made him wonder what had happened in her past to cause them. And made him want to ensure it would never happen again.

She braced her shoulders. "Agreed."

Good. "If you could live anywhere other than Texas, where would it be?"

"There is nowhere other than Texas." Tucking her feet beneath her, she preened like a cat.

He threw back his head and laughed, full-out. He liked the way she could draw that from him. "Ah, perfect answer. Your turn."

Esme pursed her lips. "When was the last time you cried?" Then she shook her head. "Never mind. I don't really expect you to respond to that. Male machismo being what it is."

She might say it didn't matter, but she must have asked for a reason. He'd already gleaned that her father was a controlling type. Certainly, Sterling Perry had a reputation of being all business, all flash. No substance?

Had that question been a Freudian slip? Was Esme looking for more from the people in her life?

Regardless, he had no problem offering her an honest answer. He looked past his desk to a nondescript piece of tack on the wall. "The day my horse Apollo died. I'd had him since I was a kid. I still keep his leather halter hanging there." He pointed to the wall. "I won't be putting it on another horse."

"I'm so sorry for that loss. It sounds like Apollo was an amazing friend to you."

Apollo had gotten him through every tough time in high school. He'd left it all behind when he rode. "I told you my family wasn't close. That led me to spend most of my time in the stables. Everyone there brought me up, taught me a good work ethic, taught me about life."

"You're truly tugging at my heart here."

He traced a finger along her cheekbone, just under her eye. "When was the last time you cried?"

"When my shoe broke in the rain." She angled to nip his finger.

He chuckled, his hand cupping her shoulder and drawing her closer. "Have you considered designer boots? I bet you would rock them."

She flattened her hands on his chest, her palms warm. "Well, thank you for the lovely compliment, cowboy."

"I think we're finding we have more in common here than we expected." Her scent tempted him, enticed him, sending blood surging south.

"And we didn't even need the matchmaker." She stroked sensual circles on his chest that seared through his flannel shirt.

"And you do realize a part of being a wife means being in my bed?"

Her hands slid up his chest to loop around his neck. "That's the part I'm most looking forward to."

Esme didn't consider herself an impulsive person, but she'd never been more certain of anything. She wanted to make love to Jesse Stevens. Here, now, in this office that felt so much more like the essence of him than his perfectly decorated home he'd put together with a laser focus on creating some mythical family.

Reality was better than dreams.

Reality with *this* man.

She met him halfway for the kiss, not that far to move as they were both already angling forward. The hot sweep of his tongue along hers was bold and hungry. His spicy scent filled her every breath. Everything about the moment seared into her senses in a way she knew she would replay in memory again and again.

His fingers speared through her hair, massaging along her scalp as he drew her head closer. She sank deeper into the kiss and delicious sensations licked along her spine. She glided her fingers down his back and tugged the tails of his shirt from the waist of his jeans, tunneling up to stroke the muscled expanse of his back.

A frenzy burned at her even as she ached to savor every touch, taste, caress. Drawing the moment out sharpened the edge of desire, dulled the edge of time until she whispered against his mouth, "I'm ready to show you my sexy brain."

He chuckled, his hands gliding down to clasp her hips. "Oh really?"

"Yes, and more."

He growled softly in appreciation. "I'm looking forward to it."

"You'll reciprocate, of course."

He angled back to meet her gaze. "Am I moving too fast for you?"

She struggled to gather her thoughts and how to express herself when she still had so many questions herself. "To be honest, I've never felt this much for someone so quickly. So yes, my head is spinning more than a little, but I'm sure. Very sure that this is what I want."

"For what it's worth," he said, "even with the whole matchmaker gig, this is moving at lightning speed for me, too."

"But you're sure?" she repeated.

"Absolutely. I want you. Here. Now."

"All I needed to hear."

As soon as she said the words, he slid from the couch to kneel in front of her, the lit tree glimmering behind him.

Between kisses, he eased her sweater over her head, breaking briefly to tug it off and toss it aside. The air was cool against her flesh, then warm as he touched her again, unhooking her bra, freeing her for his touch and gaze. He peeled down her jeggings, his hands warm, launching butterflies in her stomach and goose bumps along her skin.

He reclined her back onto the sofa, his lips grazing her neck, nuzzling aside her sweater to nip along her collarbone. He was definitely overdressed, and she intended to fix that. Immediately. She made quick work of the buttons on his shirt, shoving the flannel off his broad shoulders, flinging it aside. Then… Wow… Just wow… His chest was on display, a feast for her eyes and hands. She arched up for another kiss, desire pulsing through her, demanding more. Of this moment. Of him.

She tucked her hands into his jeans pocket and whispered against his mouth. "Birth control?"

"Yes, I have it."

"So glad." She teased his bottom lip between her teeth.

"Me, too." He rested his forehead against hers for a moment before rolling to his feet.

He fished out his wallet, withdrew a condom and set it on the coffee table on top of a stack of farming magazines.

She swung her legs off the sofa and reached for him, unfastening his jeans. Easing the zipper down. Revealing the steely length of him. She stroked up, then down again. His hands gripped her shoulders, his chest rising and falling faster until he kicked aside his jeans and boxers. He angled back down to join her, stretching out over her in a delicious weight, his bare body meeting hers. She passed him the condom and quickly, he was ready.

And she was more than ready.

His gaze held hers as he slid inside her, filling her in a slow, deliberate stroke. Holding. The sensation of being connected for the first time was so intense, a ripple shimmered through her. Then he moved, and she moved with him, instinct taking over.

His mouth grazed her ear, her neck, before settling, yes, on her breast. Need tightened through her, sending her arching up. Her nails scored down his back lightly, although it was a struggle not to dig her fingers in deeply, anchor them both even more firmly.

She drew her foot up his calf and a husky moan rumbled in his chest. She'd known the attraction between them was strong, but she still hadn't expected the chemistry to be this intense, more than she'd felt with anyone before. Soon, too soon, she felt release building. And as much as she wanted to hold back, to wait, the bliss increased, growing more intense until her head was flung back with the force of her orgasm. Feeling Jesse's hoarse groans of completion heat her skin sent aftershocks along her already-sensitive nerves. Every sense was heightened, honed to right now.

His head was buried in her neck, his breath ragged, until with a hefty exhale, he rolled to his side, taking her with him. He eased a hand away to pull a blanket from the back of the sofa and over them, holding her close, staying silent other than the sound of their hearts galloping in sync.

As she drifted off to sleep, her walls and defenses down, she couldn't escape the niggling voice telling her that this had been a dangerous idea.

And already she wanted him again.

Their interview that afternoon had gone beyond anything he'd imagined. He could certainly check "sexually compatible" off his list. Their lovemaking still lingered in his mind. He already craved her again.

Jesse paced in the sunroom off his bedroom suite, glass walls overlooking his property. In the landscape lights the pool glimmered, spa waters churning. The bunkhouse glowed in the distance. Christmas lights glinted along the split-rail fences, marking the lines of his property out in the distance.

Space, waiting to be filled.

For a moment, he allowed himself to envision what the future might look like. And what it might look like with Esme in it. He dropped into one of the wingbacks, a glass of whiskey in his hand. His memory was full of images of her asleep in his bed, hugging a pillow, her honey-blond hair fanned around her. He wanted to make the most of his time with her, and it would be helpful to know how much time he had before he would have to make some trips up to Houston. It would help to find out about the state of the roads.

Checking the time, he found it just shy of midnight. He didn't want to wake anyone up…but then, his friend was a night owl. He typed out a text to his friend Nathan Battle, the sheriff of Royal.

Are you awake? If not, I'll catch up in the morning.

Seconds after he hit Send, the phone rang, Nathan's number flashing.

Jesse answered. "Thanks for calling. Hope I'm not disturbing you."

"Everyone's asleep or playing video games. What can I do for you?" Nathan was an imposing leader for their police force, with a soft spot for his wife, Amanda, and their children.

Jesse moved out onto the balcony. A few stars peeked out of the nighttime clouds. "How're the roads looking?"

"We have a couple of rural routes that are washed out and a damaged bridge. But we've marked enough detours for people to get around."

"I imagine you've had your hands full."

"Amanda's been on me to take a vacation once this is over." Nathan's wife owned the Royal Diner, an informal eatery where small-town Texas gossip got spread.

"Sounds like you're married to a wise woman." Nathan and Amanda had the kind of rock-solid marriage that was an advertisement for matrimony.

"I'm a lucky bastard," his gravelly voice echoed over the phone line. "But you didn't call me for a weather report. If you wanted to know about the state of the roads you could have phoned anyone in the department."

"What do you think of all the jockeying for power going on over in Houston to decide who's going to head the new club?" Of all his friends, Nathan was like a brother to Jesse. He'd served as sound counsel for years.

"I think we've been lucky to have our group stay local here for a long time. We've got a good town here and the club has made great strides since admitting women. The Texas Cattleman's Club stands for community and family, honor and friendship, a cohesive force to support each other and do good in the community."

Though his friend couldn't see, he still found himself nodding in agreement. For all those reasons he took his role in the Texas Cattleman's Club seriously. "I agree."

"Choosing the person to set the tone in Houston is important. We don't want our brand to be turned into some kind of social club or to lose its values. Houston isn't Royal. It's going to take a strong leader to guide all those larger-than-life personalities."

"Solid insights." His throat tightened. He hesitated.

A yawn echoed from the other end of the phone. "Do you mind if I ask why we're discussing this?"

Shooting a glance at his bed and finding Esme stirring just a bit, he moved farther out onto the balcony and kept his voice low. "I've got an unexpected guest here. Sterling Perry's daughter. She's come to town to lobby for her father."

"What do you think?"

He blinked. How in the hell did he answer that? "What do I think of *her*? Esme's brilliant."

"Uh-huh." Nathan chuckled.

"Uh-huh what?"

Nathan laughed softly again. "My friend, I've been in this job a very long time and that's taught me how to read a person's tone. The sound always tells more than the words. And your tone tells me you are head over ass infatuated with her."

"And if I am? But she's the epitome of Houston glamour." Opposite of everything he thought he wanted during the whole matchmaking process. And yet he couldn't help but feel drawn to her.

"Glamour isn't a bad thing. You've been to enough galas at the club—tuxedos and gowns and jewels. I defy you to find any event more high-end than ours."

"Good point. Esme would enjoy that." He envisioned her in a floor-length ball gown. Dancing. Their bodies in sync as they moved to the music.

"And since you contacted that matchmaker, I assume your interest is still for something lasting. A wife and family?"

"My plans haven't changed."

"Then my advice? Pursue her. Find out if what you're feeling for her is the real thing."

Before Nathan had even finished signing off, Jesse's mind was already churning with ideas and excitement.

Dinner out. Maybe they could even double-date with his neighbor Cord and his girlfriend, Zoe. Cord would be relocating to Houston soon and Jesse was going to miss him. But then, connections in Houston would also give him a reason to see Esme. Houston might have massive department stores, but Royal offered top-notch specialty niche shops, and he wouldn't mind having Esme along as he finished his Christmas shopping. And he still had a tree to chop down for all those decorations and an old-school string of lights like he remembered from childhood.

Full of plans, he pushed to his feet. He intended to show her just how amazing life could be here. That the town of Royal had everything to offer for a full social calendar.

And he very much looked forward to wooing her all the way back to his bed.

Eight

The past two weeks had been a blur of bliss for Esme, a time of discovery, getting to know Jesse, their differences fading in the face of so many shared interests, laughs and kisses. They'd spent nearly every moment together, going on dates, buying last-minute Christmas gifts and adding to the scant wardrobe in her suitcase. Touring his land, decorating his Christmas tree, making love in front of the fire.

He'd learned she had a weakness for flowers and could eat her way to the bottom of a bowl of popcorn. Heavily buttered. She sang Christmas carols with gusto, her pitch questionable, her enthusiasm undeniable.

Her equestrian skills were some of the best he'd ever seen. She was fire in motion on a horse.

Esme was a sensual woman who took pleasure in experiencing life.

Their nights had been spent passionately exploring in a lengthy quest to discover what made the other unravel with desire.

But she knew their time together was drawing to a close. She would have to return to Houston and her job. She'd delayed as long as she could.

Tomorrow, she was due to go back to Houston. Key members of the Royal chapter—including Jesse—would be touring the new club's building renovations. Afterward, there would be a meeting with those Royal players, held at the Houston site.

Cases would be made for who should be the new president. Had she done enough good during her time here? Heaven knew, she'd been focused more on her relationship with Jesse than on her father's bid for power.

She shoved aside the pinch of guilt. There was nothing she could do about that now, and she wouldn't let it steal the joy of this last evening with Jesse.

Tonight, they were enjoying a five-star dinner at the Texas Cattleman's Club—the original branch—in Royal. Music from a string quartet filled the room with classical Christmas melodies.

Looking around, no one would guess the place had suffered a devastating tornado, the fiercest to hit Royal in nearly eighty years. They'd rebuilt, better than ever. Pride surged in her heart at this community, the bonds made in this space. No wonder Jesse felt like these people were family. His comfort here showed in his easy manner, his way of greeting friends who stopped by their table.

The club was housed in a large, rambling single-story building made of dark stone and wood. The interior decor consisted of mostly dark wood floors, leather upholstered furniture and super-high ceilings.

Hunting trophies and historical artifacts adorned the paneled walls. Her favorite was the tooth of an ancient relative of a horse. As a child, she'd been delighted to know herds of horselike creatures roamed the lands she called home. She'd even had her own horse tooth in a small shadow box that always felt strangely comforting to her. That the Royal club boasted a similar horse tooth gave a sense of continuity between the two spaces. A slice of home for her. In addition to the elegant formal dining hall, there were several private meeting rooms and a great room for both public and private Texas Cattleman's Club events.

During her tour of the place prior to being seated for dinner, she'd been most surprised to discover the club had a childcare center for club members and employees, the laughter and squeals broadcasting how much the kids enjoyed the setup.

To see how inclusive the Texas Cattleman's Club had become warmed her even on the somewhat chilly Texas evening.

And of course, that was just the inside. Outdoors there was a stable, a pool, tennis courts and even a playground. Her mind was spinning.

She pulled her attention back to the table, tapered candles flickering in the middle of an arrangement of white poinsettias and holly.

She spooned up the last of her chocolate trifle. "Thank you, Jesse. This is the perfect end to an incredible meal, from the lobster bisque to the filet mignon."

"I'm glad you enjoyed yourself." He stretched a leg out. He'd worn his good boots with the suit.

"This has been an amazing two weeks."

He clasped her hand across the table. "I agree. I don't want things to end just because we're going to Houston."

Her chest grew tight. It was ironic how excitement and anxiety could make such a tangle. "I feel the same." Not wanting to risk wrecking their evening by wading into deep waters too soon, she said, "I'm looking forward to you meeting my family."

"I'm sure they'll be glad to have you back," he said with a pensive look in his green eyes.

She reached for her wine, avoiding his gaze, not ready to have the Houston-versus-Royal discussion yet. She sipped the after-dinner wine, then set the crystal glass on the table again. Her fingers tapped nervously along the gold beading at the glass stem, syncing with the Christmas carol playing softly.

The silence between her and Jesse stretched until she looked up self-consciously, pulling her hand away from the glass and clenching her fingers. She nodded toward the string quartet. "'Silent Night.' It was my mother's favorite carol."

"You must miss her a lot this time of year."

"Very much." She blinked back tears. "We all do. Even my dad, although their marriage wasn't the best. She married him out of duty. He married her for power. It's no surprise things didn't work out well at all."

"Is that why you reacted so strongly to the matchmaker idea?" he asked insightfully.

She could only nod, not trusting her voice.

He clasped her hand again. "Thank you for telling me that."

"Thank you for listening." She swallowed down a lump in her throat, then drew in a shaky breath. "Okay, that's enough serious talk for one night. I just want to enjoy this night of Royal's finest. In fact, I'm thinking we should order more dessert to take home and enjoy later."

"That sounds like an excellent idea. How about you choose for the both of us and surprise me?" Jesse placed his linen napkin by his plate. "And while you're doing that, I need to have a quick word with my friend Cord. I won't be long."

"Take your time." She smiled, soaking up the sight of him in a charcoal-gray suit and festive red tie.

"You really are incredible." Jesse's gaze smoked over her from across the table, lingering on the plunging neckline of the emerald velvet dress she'd chosen in one of the specialty boutiques at the Courtyard Shops. He dropped a kiss on her lips before stepping away.

Her toes curled in her Valentino heels. Tingles spread through her all the way down to her fresh pedicure.

The day had been deliciously pampering from start to finish. While Jesse had had business to attend to at his lawyer's, he'd suggested she spend the day at Royal's Saint Tropez Salon. She hadn't expected such a luxurious, high-end spa in a small town. She'd felt petty for judging so quickly.

Her appointment at the salon had afforded her time for reflection. Something about lavender-scented towels and rubs peeled away stress. And the relative silence had helped. It had forced contemplation. Forced reflection.

Truth be told, these weeks with Jesse had dominated that reflection. How wrong she'd been about him. The silly but serendipitous circumstances of their meeting. How lucky they'd both been to find each other because of the chaos of the storm. Ironic, she'd mused, for a man who craved stability and practicality.

She'd met so many incredible people over the past couple of weeks, some of whom were seated in the dining room tonight. She smiled in response to Megan and Whit Daltry. Megan ran the local animal rescue, Safe Haven. Jesse had brought Esme along when he'd dropped off a donation to help with the rescue's three horses recently taken in. Esme had been amazed at the large operation, one that was apparently growing exponentially under Megan's leadership.

Megan and Whit were dining with Natalie and Max St. Cloud, a fascinating couple. Even though Max was a tech genius billionaire, his wife still owned and operated the Cimarron Rose bed-and-breakfast, with a small bridal dress shop attached. Both couples' children were enjoying a Christmas-themed movie night in the childcare center.

Her heart tugged at the memory of glimpsing those sweet little faces when Jesse had taken a detour there to pass out Christmas candy. They all clearly knew and adored him. And she couldn't deny being enticed by the notion of a baby of her own someday, and celebrating family Christmases.

A cleared throat pulled her attention back. She found Zoe Warren, Cord's girlfriend, standing by the table. The towering brunette looked stunning in a simple gold sheath dress. Esme had enjoyed getting to know her and Cord during a lunch at the Royal Diner.

Zoe smiled genuinely. Drink in hand, she gestured to the table. “I hope I’m not interrupting your dinner.”

“Not at all. I’m glad you came over.” Esme stood quickly and then greeted her with a welcoming hug. “Have a seat. It looks like our dates are deep in a conversation that isn’t close to wrapping up.”

“Thank you. I would like that.” Zoe settled into a chair beside her. “I enjoyed our lunch the other day.”

A phantom gurgle tickled her stomach, even though she was far from hungry. Lunch with Zoe the other day had been at a small, vaguely yellowing local spot. Esme had her doubts as she crossed through the metal door. But after sitting down, her senses had been delighted. She felt as if she’d stumbled upon a contender for one of those reality television shows about stellar restaurants with questionable exteriors.

And the diner’s food—she’d ordered the chicken-fried steak and a glass of sweet tea—had been every bit as wonderful as the interior. “The Royal Diner is one of those fun finds off the beaten path of major cities.”

Zoe sipped her champagne, bubbles climbing up the crystal flute. “It’s incredible how Amanda and Nathan Battle juggle two such busy careers with family life. I’ve lost count of how many children they have.”

Esme toyed with the stem of her wineglass pensively. “It sounds like they have it all.”

“That they do.” Zoe grinned, motioning to the waiter who was walking by with a tray of champagne. She took another flute before looking back at Esme. “So how are you liking the rest of Royal?”

"Surprisingly very much. It's not Houston, of course," Esme said with a shrug, unworried about judgment since the woman was from Houston, as well, "but I've found there's much more offered here than I expected. It's a unique mix of a small town with some big-city amenities."

"It's quite a haven." Zoe glanced over at her handsome dark-haired boyfriend, concern furrowing her forehead. "I worry he's going to miss Royal and all his friends here. But he insists he's committed to making a move to Houston for me. He's bought the loveliest ranch on the outskirts of town. He's making such a big sacrifice for me. For us."

Zoe was a police detective in Houston. Her investigation into Vincent Hamm's murder had brought her here to Royal. Esme and her family owed Zoe a debt of gratitude, the cop's progress going a long way to help shift the cloud of suspicion off Sterling Perry.

Esme toyed with the placement of her silver dessert spoon. "How incredible that he's willing to move for you."

"We're in love." She looked toward her boyfriend, her face full of emotion. "We found a compromise, because the option of being apart was more than we could bear."

Esme's gaze skated to Jesse deep in conversation with his friend and she wondered…

If Cord was willing to relocate to Houston, might Jesse be willing to make the move, as well? Tomorrow would be pivotal for more than her father.

Her own future with Jesse rode on their trip to Houston.

* * *

Ryder Currin paced through the Houston building of the Texas Cattleman's Club, checking last-minute touches to the structure's renovations before the contingent from Royal arrived tomorrow. Angela walked alongside him, making her own notes in her tablet, the scent of paint heavy in the air. He could hardly believe the plans for starting this Houston branch were coming to fruition. Ryder had been instrumental in bringing the chapter to Houston, and yes, he craved the position as president. He wanted to lead the organization through this transitional time.

But would that ambition threaten his second chance with Angela, given how much her father wanted the same thing?

Telling himself it was pointless to borrow trouble, he pulled his attention back to the building, his boot steps echoing up to the soaring ceiling.

The location and architectural style for the Houston chapter's future home was very different from the Royal club. It had seemed an insurmountable project at first, since the historic former luxury boutique hotel had fallen into disrepair. But all their plans for renovation were coming together, thanks to Perry Construction. The three-story edifice had always been stunning on the outside. Now the inside matched.

The location was practical for so many reasons, including the fact that three doors down was the Houston Galleria Hotel, a medium-sized luxury hotel where members could stay when in town.

Angela's high heels clicked on the floor as she walked ahead of him, caught up in her notes. This club was important to her, too. Ryder understood she was caught in a tough position with both him and her father wanting the lead position here. He didn't want anything to interfere with this second chance they had. He would withdraw if it came to that, but she'd insisted this should play out as the club decided.

He just wanted to make sure there was no negative blowback as they rolled out the official grand opening with a New Year's Eve bash. Press releases for the event had been delayed with Esme Perry out of town for so long.

They'd all been thrown for a loop when Angela's sister had decided to stay in Royal even after the storm passed. And of course, Sterling had been all too willing to accommodate time off work so his daughter could spend more time currying family favor.

Ryder was a man who abided by the rules, so this flagrant lobbying really chapped his hide. It just wasn't fair play.

Angela made everything more complicated. He loved her. Deeply. Truly. In a way that made his soul sing, something he hadn't expected to happen again after his wife Elinah had died. He didn't underestimate how important it was to get this right with Angela. His first marriage had ended in divorce. He couldn't regret the union since his son, Xander, had come from that relationship. But his breakup with Penny was still a failure that marked him.

One he wouldn't allow himself to repeat.

The rumors that he'd had feelings for Angela's mom were true. But he'd never acted on those feelings because of respect for rules and fair play. Honor meant something to him. Besides, his second marriage had shown him what real love was. Elinah. A part of his heart would always belong to her. Their time together had been the best, years that gave him his daughter Annabel and then they'd adopted Maya. Losing Elinah to cancer had almost destroyed him.

He wouldn't go through that heartbreak again. He would do whatever it took to keep he and Angela's love safe. There'd be no repeat of their breakup. Already he could envision her living in his home. His log-style mansion wasn't as fancy as the Perry place. He'd grown up poor and had never been comfortable with ostentation.

Still, the place had been plenty roomy to bring up his children with space to spare. And for more children?

Ryder looked at Angela. He saw the weight that seemed to press down on her, to change her normal happy expression. He hated to see her sad. "I'm sorry your sister missed the brunch she had planned with you, Melinda, Tatiana and my girls."

He was, truly, although secretly he was always antsy when Angela or his daughter Maya spent time with Tatiana. The woman was a shark with the power to upset their lives.

"The brunch will still happen, I'm sure." A brief flash of disappointment flickered in Angela's eyes before she schooled her features. "We haven't set a specific date. Just sometime whenever Esme gets back."

She noticed a paint droplet on a nearby marble plant stand and Ryder watched her as she worked to eradicate it.

"Well, keep me in the loop." A glint caught his eyes.

Stooping down, he picked up a stray nail from beneath a windowsill and pocketed it. Still so much to do.

"About my sister's return?"

Shrugging, he ran a hand through his hair and then stopped at the nape of his neck. "Sure, and the brunch."

Muffled noises grabbed his attention. Shouting and angry voices. He locked eyes with Angela. Her brow furrowed in confusion.

His daughter Maya shouldered past the painters putting last-minute touches on some trim. She raced toward him in a flurry of color with her bold yellow coat and her vibrant red hair. His youngest child had never been one to get lost in the shuffle of day-to-day life.

"Dad, I have to talk to you," she demanded, her raised voice echoing upward as she crashed into the room. Panting and distraught, she wasn't budging.

"Well, hello to you, too, Maya. It's good to see you. Angela and I are almost through here—"

"No, Dad. Not later. Now. There are so many rumors flying around about our family, too many secrets. I can't—I won't—wait any longer. I'm eighteen. It's time we finally had this talk." She stomped her foot in exasperation, but her eyes were filled with tears.

Regret hit him in the chest, that he'd brought his daughter to this level of anxiety.

Angela clasped his arm, a welcome touch when Maya's outburst had him reeling. "I've got plenty to occupy me. Please, take as long as you need."

She gave his arm a final squeeze before walking off toward a pile of plaster dust beneath a gilded mirror, snapping photos with her tablet.

"Thank you," he said, appreciating that she understood and accepted how important his children were to him. He tucked an arm around his daughter's shoulders and guided her to the café area free of painters.

Maya gasped for air beside him, her shoulders shaking in a way that telegraphed how close she was to losing it. He'd put enough bandages over skinned knees and listened to enough of her high school drama to read the signs.

He guided her to a club chair and dropped into another one across from her. "What's going on, Maya? These rumors about the family business have been circulating for a while now. What made today so upsetting?"

Maya closed her eyes tightly. Took a deep breath.

Then another.

Ryder could see her mouth moving as she counted to ten before she opened her eyes. His fire-haired child had always struggled to rein in her emotions.

"It's been building up for a long time, and then when the invitations went out for the mother-daughter tea today…" She picked at the wrist of her yellow coat. "I need you to tell me the truth, once and for all."

A sigh all but deflated him. Hearing about the mother-daughter tea sucker punched him, even after all these years since Elinah died. He would always miss her. She'd been a loving wife and mother. He'd tried to make up for what his children had lost…but it was an impossible void to fill.

Then a dark thought hit him. Maya was asking about her biological mother. He'd promised to tell her when she was eighteen and he'd put it off long enough. The pit in his gut grew deeper.

"The truth?" he asked, stalling to give himself time to collect his thoughts for a conversation that would undoubtedly prove difficult. Those secrets had been a heavy weight on the shoulders of a man who prided himself on honesty and honor.

"About my biological parents." Her eyes were clear, her tone steely. "No more delaying. Tell me now, or I'm never going to talk to you again."

There was no missing the vehemence in her voice. Her arms crossed tightly over her chest in a protective hug as she bit down on her lip. Ryder could feel fear and anger radiate from her in waves.

She'd asked in the past, but never pushed. They'd done a kind of dance with the subject, her pressing, then backing away as if she was afraid of the truth.

And there was reason to be wary, the same reason he'd held back telling her until she was old enough to handle the truth. But she was eighteen now, no denying that.

He took her hands in his and thought back to the first time he'd held her and she'd wrapped him around her little finger. He loved all of his children equally, but he'd always felt more protective of his little girl. He wished he could spare her the heartache the truth about her mother might bring.

"Before I start, I want you to know how much I love you."

"I love you, too, Dad." She squeezed his hands. "Now quit stalling." Brows lowering, she fixed him with a stare he recognized. His stare. The one he used to signal he meant business.

"Your biological grandfather was a man named

Sam. Eighteen years ago, he showed up on my doorstep out of the blue one night. Sam's daughter was barely twenty and she'd just given birth to a sickly—" his voice hitched "—but so very beautiful baby girl."

"And my father?"

Here was where things started getting tougher. "He abandoned your mother." He paused for a moment to let that part soak in before continuing. "Your mother was in no position to be a mother. Sam talked her into letting him find a good home for the baby. He said his daughter vowed she loved her baby but knew she couldn't care for a child. He provided documents from both your biological mother and father that signed away their rights to you."

She deflated, tears streaming down her face, her body shaking from the impact of the news. This was a story he wished he never had to burden her with, but he knew she had the right to know. It didn't make the telling any easier, though. He'd give anything to take away the pain snaking its way onto Maya's face. To stop the quiver in her lips.

And his gut knotted since there was still a second shoe to drop once his daughter found out her mother was someone she knew.

"Maya, honey, I'm sorry." He wanted to gather her into a hug and promise everything would be all right, the way he'd done when she was growing up. When she'd trusted him to fight those battles for her. "Sam was drunk three-quarters of the time and had gambled away anything left of the family money."

"But why did he choose you?" The sentence came

out in a rasp. A voice of a much younger Maya cracking through as a sob racked her.

It broke him.

"Harrington York—Sterling Perry's father-in-law—willed me a small parcel of land. Land that Sam swore York had promised to him one day. But the land went to me and that was the start of my oil business."

Ryder hated to paint her biological grandfather in a bad light, but Maya wanted to know the truth and he wouldn't lie to her any longer. "Sam harbored a grudge against the Perrys and me because of that. He told me that I owed him for what happened and this was my chance to repay him by making sure the baby was raised by a wealthy family in a closed private adoption."

As much as Ryder had hated the way the man had gone about things, he couldn't let Havery walk out the door with that infant. The man couldn't be trusted. Ryder hadn't cared about anything else but making sure the baby had a good home.

That she felt loved. Damn it, that still was the only thing that mattered to him in all of this.

He took a deep breath and finished the story. "Sam swore that his daughter—Tatiana Havery—didn't want to know where you went."

"Tatiana Havery?" Maya's face crumpled as the name sank in, as she realized that her birth mother was someone who moved in their world and their lives.

Her shoulders shook harder, sobs racking her. Ryder opened his arms and—thank God—she flew into his hug without hesitation to cry it out. A lump lodged in his throat, too, and neither of them said a word until her tears slowed.

Then she eased back, swiping her wrists under her eyes. "Thank you for telling me, Dad. I'm going to need some time to digest all of this."

Feeling helpless to right this for his child, Ryder watched her rush away, her red hair rippling behind her, hair she'd inherited from her mother. Sighing hard, Ryder sagged back in the chair. He hoped he hadn't lost Maya forever for not telling her the truth sooner.

This whole situation had spun out of control so damn quickly. He rubbed a hand over his suit jacket lapel, still damp from his daughter's tears.

He didn't like or trust Tatiana one bit. But she was also Angela's best friend. And he'd been keeping Maya's parentage a secret from her, too, even when they were engaged, since Tatiana herself was unaware that Maya was hers. If Ryder wanted to have a real chance at a future with Angela, he couldn't hold back about that any longer. He just prayed it wouldn't be the end of them.

Time was definitely running out for him to tell Angela that eighteen years ago he'd adopted Tatiana's child. And he had to pray Angela and his daughter would understand.

Because he loved them both too much to lose either of them.

Nine

Drawing Esme toward his bedroom after their dinner at the club, Jesse didn't want anything to ruin their last night together in Royal. She was excited about returning to Houston, though he wasn't sure he shared that excitement.

Hell, who was he kidding? He wasn't happy about her departure at all, even though he would make the trip with her to review the new clubhouse. Having her here on the ranch had felt too damn right, increasingly so every day they spent together. In spite of what she seemed to think, she fit here. From the way she helped with the ranch to how she blended in with the community, she belonged.

And when she'd looked at the children in the club's childcare center with such tenderness and even a hint of longing, his last reservation had slid away. He wanted her to make that audition for the role of wife to be a permanent one. Which meant he would have to persuade her to come back to Royal. If not permanently, at least for a while.

One step at a time.

Closing the door to his suite behind them, he flipped on the sconces near the headboard, dimming them low as he turned to soak in the sight of Esme shouldering off the sleeve of her green velvet dress. She looked so beautiful tonight and for a moment, he let himself be mesmerized by the sight of her undressing, until she stood barefoot in a black lace bra-and-panties set. It had been all he could do to keep his hands off her during dinner.

With careful precision, she laid the green velvet dress over the back of the chaise longue as he shrugged off his jacket. Before he laid it aside, however, he pulled an envelope from the pocket and stepped closer to her. "I have something for you."

"A gift? Thank you." She looked up in surprise as she took off her chandelier earrings, the jewels throwing multicolored prisms onto her creamy skin. "But it isn't Christmas yet. I don't open my presents until the actual day."

Doing nothing more than standing with her jewelry cupped in her delicate, manicured hands, she made his heart beat faster. A blonde goddess set against the warm brown tones of his bed. Where he longed to be with her.

"It's a 'just because' gift, something you'll need before the twenty-fifth." He pulled out two tickets and fanned them between his fingers.

She set aside her earrings on the mahogany chest of drawers. “Tickets?”

Her voice was neutral. Not a good sign, but he pressed ahead all the same.

“To *A Christmas Carol*. Royal may not be Houston, but we have a good community theater. I thought we could go this weekend after we return from Houston.”

And he waited.

“I’m surprised.” She smiled, stepping into his arms and wrapping her own around his neck. “This is very thoughtful. Thank you.”

She kissed him, long and deep, with a familiarity woven from their past two weeks as lovers. The caress of her fingers along the back of his neck was cool, the press of her breasts a sweet temptation against his chest.

Much longer and he would have her against the wall before he’d locked in her return to Royal.

He angled back, stroking her blond hair over her shoulders with a caress down her spine. “Would you rather do something in Houston? I have no problem going back to the drawing board. We could make the plans together.”

“You’re asking me to come back here for Christmas?” Blue eyes searched his.

He couldn’t quite make out the hesitation or confusion he saw brimming in her face. He prided himself on being an adept observer of body language. Except he couldn’t hold on to a thought long enough to press his agenda, not with his mind scrambled by Esme’s touch, the press of her breasts against his chest.

“Yes, I’m asking you to come back.”

“Let’s worry about the future later. You’re welcome

to pamper me right now any other ways that come to mind. I'll be much nicer about accepting your present," she said with an unmistakable invitation in her siren's voice as she tugged him toward the bed, walking backward.

And he didn't need any encouragement to follow, his gaze drawn like a magnet to the sway of her hips. The narrow indent of her waist. The long, smooth line of her thighs. By the time he tumbled with her onto the mattress, he couldn't think about anything but pleasuring her. Making her remember how this connection they shared could burn away everything else.

Tunneling his fingers into her hair, he angled her head to kiss her long and slow, deeply and thoroughly. He took his time lowering the strap of her bra, cupping each breast in turn, savoring the shivers that went through her. He liked the feel of her hands on him as she peeled off his shirt, stripped off his belt.

By the time he moved lower to kiss his way down her shoulder, they were both breathing hard, the whisper of exhales mingling with the slide of fabric across the duvet as they swept away the rest of their clothes. Fevered touches gave way to more demanding kisses. His. Hers.

He felt the taut need in her movements as her hips nudged his thighs. Obliging her unspoken demand, he curved a palm over her hip and traced his way to the juncture of her thighs, and he teased her there.

Fingernails bit into his shoulders, a welcome counterpoint to his own need firing through him. He sensed how close she was to finding her release, so he stayed right with her, whispering into her ear how much he wanted her.

When the soft shudders racked her body, the sense of triumph was almost as fierce as his own desire. He didn't let go for long moments, helping her find every last sweet sensation from her orgasm.

As she stilled, he angled back to glimpse her, to memorize this moment. Her flushed cheeks. Her lips swollen from his kisses. A protective surge fired through him.

He never tired of seeing her in his bed.

Her bed, too, now.

For how long?

He brushed aside the thought that threatened to steal this perfect moment from them both. He refused to accept it could be the last time he had her in his home. Having her stay in Houston was unacceptable.

All the same, there was a frenzy between them tonight. She reached into the bedside table and passed him a condom, urging him to hurry, her voice breathless and encouraging as she sheathed him. Her touch was slow and deliberate. Knowing and tempting.

"Jesse…"

She didn't need to ask him twice.

He rolled her under him in a smooth sweep, sliding inside with a sense of home. Her legs glided up and around his hips, holding him, syncing them both into a perfect rhythm. Flesh against flesh. Heartbeats racing against each other.

They'd made love in every room of his house in every position and still each time with her was as exciting as the first. And while he wasn't a romantic, there was something special between them. Something unique. He would be a fool to let it go. To let her go.

Purring her pleasure, she urged him to his back and straddled him. She rode him, fanning the blaze inside him that begged for release.

His hands dug into her hips, guiding her faster as he thrust upward. Even as his eyes grew heavy with the need to seal in this moment, he couldn't tear his gaze away from the sight of her over him. Her blond hair over her shoulders and along her breasts. Her chest rising and falling faster. Her pale flesh flushing. Her release was close. He knew her body that well now. And seeing her orgasm was the sexiest thing he'd ever experienced.

So much so, it sent him crashing into his own climax, sensation surging through him as he plunged into her. It was more than sex. It was— He stopped the thought short, too dazed to let his mind travel that path. She'd already rocked his world beyond measure in a few short weeks.

His life had been forever changed by the rainstorm that had landed her on his doorstep. And now everything was riding on their trip to Houston and being able to persuade her to leave it all behind.

Because he couldn't imagine his life without her.

Tatiana was seething over the board meeting about to take place, bigwigs from Royal in Houston to represent the charter chapter of the Texas Cattleman's Club.

And she wasn't welcome.

She tried her damnedest to scrub out any trace of the woman she was before she rose to power in Perry Holdings. She'd shed family mementos. Opted for all new things. Posh designer fixtures. Symbolic, partly, of creating the life she wanted. It still counted for nothing. Got her nowhere. As if not being born into the world of the Perrys meant she could never fully enter the rarefied realm of Houston's wealthiest society.

Angela called herself a friend, but hadn't gotten Tatiana a ticket to the inner circle. No matter how much money she made, how high she rose in the Perry firm, she was still an outsider. She'd never felt that more than today. Her fist clenched around a crystal paperweight. Waterford. For once, though, her designer-decorated town house brought her no comfort. She struggled against the urge to hurl the paperweight through the window.

Instead, she strode over to her white Christmas tree decorated with monochrome lights, with silver tinsel and pale blue ornaments. Normally, the twinkling delighted her. An anchor in an ocean of chaos. Today, even as she straightened the ornaments, Christmas magic held nothing for her.

Her doorbell rang, the high-pitched bell chimes cutting her thoughts short and launching a wave of panic through her. Could it be the police? She had spent the past nine months looking over her shoulder. She wasn't sure how much more of this she could take.

With a deep breath, she steadied her nerves and scraped her red hair back into a sleek ponytail. Not a strand of hair out of place.

She looked through the peephole.

It wasn't the police. Far from it. A stranger, a teenager, stood in the corridor. Her long red hair and mustard-yellow coat were definitely not cop material, even if she'd been older.

Curious, Tatiana opened the door. "Yes, what can I do for you…"

She let her question drift off, a hint for the teen to introduce herself.

"Maya," she said, jamming her fists into her yellow coat. "My name is Maya Currin."

Currin? Maya Currin, as in Ryder's daughter? Tatiana had heard Angela talk about her future stepdaughter. But other than that, Tatiana had had no contact with the Currin family all these years.

But something brought the girl here today and Maya could use a distraction. "Come in, dear. What can I do for you?"

Maya stepped over the threshold warily, her hyperfocus on Tatiana unnerving. Just as she considered asking the girl to leave, Maya turned her attention to the condo, walking to the massive wall of glass, flattening her palm against it.

"I'm Ryder Currin's youngest. I've been away at college for my freshman year, but I'm home for Christmas."

The girl looked around the apartment, staring unabashedly, her gaze lingering on the white plush sofa.

What the hell was going on? Was the girl unhinged? "Are you looking for someone?"

A shaky sigh rocked through her before she continued. "I've always known I was adopted. My father always swore he would tell me about my biological family once I turned eighteen, but he's been putting it off. Until yesterday, when I insisted." She turned back to

Tatiana. "I stayed awake all night working up the nerve to confront you."

Tatiana's scalp tingled with premonition. This conversation couldn't be headed where she thought… Still, she started shaking, staring at this beautiful girl with red hair and brown eyes.

Practically a mini version of her.

Tears misted her eyes as the undeniable truth hit home. "Are you my daughter?"

She didn't even need Maya to respond. She knew. Could sense it between them. Her heart fractured all over again at the time they'd spent apart. And how close her child had been all this time.

Kept from her by Ryder Currin.

Maya nodded slowly. "Yes. My father can confirm it."

Fat tears rolled down Maya's face and she flew into Tatiana's arms with zero hesitation. The one thing that was hers, that no one could take from her. Tatiana held her tight with a possessive urgency. Her child. Grown, safe and beautiful. She'd led the pampered childhood Tatiana hadn't had. If only Maya's childhood hadn't been with that horrid Ryder Currin.

Regret threatened to level her. The choices she'd made had been impossible. Unfair. The reality of how much she'd lost stood in front of her now, a haunting reminder of how truly she'd been robbed.

"I wanted to keep you. I loved you so much." Tatiana held her hands tightly, hardly able to believe she was truly touching her baby girl. "But I had no money. I was alone. My father was on his last legs healthwise." A nice way to gloss over her father's alcoholism. "I begged him to let me give you to a good family to raise."

And her father had promised her he would. Then he'd turned around and given her baby to Ryder Currin. The betrayal cut deeper than any other.

Fury rose in her, only tempered by the joy of meeting Maya.

"Thank you for letting me in and telling me," Maya said. "There are so many questions I want to ask, but I have to get back to my dad. I—I—" The teen stuttered with nerves. "I hope we can get to know each other."

Tatiana's broken heart warmed, and she was filled with pride over this beautiful child she had created. "I would love that."

She hugged her daughter again, transported back to the day she'd held the infant bundle in her arms, her heart broken, her life wrecked. The memories lingered long after she'd escorted Maya to the door, leaning against the frame to watch her child walk to the elevator, step inside and disappear from view.

Overwhelmed by emotion, Tatiana backed into her condo and leaned against the closed door, unable to think straight. The man she despised was raising the daughter she'd always loved. It wasn't fair. Her whole damn life wasn't fair right now.

For the first time since she'd decorated her apartment, she felt weighed down in this space, in spite of the pristine white decor she'd chosen for a sense of freedom, of a fresh start unsullied by the past. Normally, it soothed her, giving her a sense of control.

Instead, right now the piercing all-white motif made her feel as though she'd been trapped in a hospital, about to undergo surgery. Except the surgery was a painful montage of every moment in her life that went so damn wrong.

She couldn't escape the cornered feeling that her brother might give her up to avoid jail time. The more she thought about it, the more freaked out she became until she surrendered to the fear. Racing around the condo, she threw a haphazard collection into her suitcase, then frantically searched for her passport. She had to leave the country. Now.

But…

How could she? Her daughter, her baby girl, was here in Houston. And after all this time, she had the chance to get to know her. Her mind whirled all over the place with questions. Had Angela known about this? All this time? That her boyfriend had been raising Tatiana's daughter?

The fury raged. Angela had to have known. The bitch.

Someone had to pay for all Tatiana had been through. Angela had a golden life, full of advantages from being Sterling Perry's child, and now from being with Ryder Currin. Both men disgusted Tatiana. They'd stolen that parcel of land from her father. If he hadn't been cheated, then her family wouldn't have fallen apart. She wanted Sterling and Ryder to hurt as much as she did right now, as much as she'd always hurt when she'd thought of her daughter.

Her fury focused on the perfect way to make both men suffer. By taking from them someone precious. Angela. If Angela were to die…

Tatiana's hand tightened around the paperweight

again, the crystal cool in her grip, like a rock in her hand with enough heft to bash in a head. She forced her hold to relax. Whatever happened next was totally in her control.

She'd killed once. She could do so again.

Esme could hardly believe she was back in Houston. Home. And that Jesse was with her.

It seemed like a lifetime ago that she'd left for Royal. So much had changed since then, hell-bent on making a difference for her dad. She still wanted that for him. In fact, she looked forward to seeing the two most special men in her life—Jesse and her dad—making a difference in the club.

Her family, Jesse, even her brother and sisters.

The gathering would be like a family reunion.

Her suede pumps click-clacked musically against the tile floor in the Houston club building. A tour of the facility had gone well, and now they were meeting in a conference room. Every reverberation made her feel more at home, more comfortable with her newfound happiness. As she turned the corner, she saw a familiar silhouette.

Angela dressed with her pitch-perfect fashion sense in a black-and-white A-line dress with a small clutch. Her sister noticed her nearly at the same moment. A wide grin pulled the corners of her mouth skyward.

With determined steps, Esme closed the distance between her and Angela, wrapping her older sister in a tight hug. She'd missed her and wanted to share the latest news about the burgeoning relationship with Jesse. She just knew Jesse and Ryder would enjoy each other's company, too, both such down-to-earth men with a love of the land. So much joy and hope for the future coursed through her heart. But as she eased back and looked more fully at her sister, she could sense something was off with Angela.

"What's going on?" Esme prodded gently. Possibilities cartwheeled through her mind.

At the simple question, Angela's face paled. Deeper concern rose in Esme's chest, and she maneuvered them to one of the decorative palms out of earshot of the people milling in the halls as guests from Royal began arriving at the Houston chapter clubhouse for the tour of the new facility.

A somewhat nervous laugh trembled from Angela's lips. That's when Esme knew something serious had happened. Top of the list of her guesses? "Are you and Ryder okay?"

If that man had hurt her sister again, Esme would never forgive him.

"Well…that's a million-dollar question. I'm still reeling. Prepare yourself. Turns out Maya, Ryder's adopted daughter, is actually Tatiana's daughter. Tatiana. My best friend. And Tatiana never told me." Angela's voice shook. "She never even hinted she gave up a baby. And Ryder… I just… I just can't believe he didn't tell me before now. I'm trying not to feel betrayed. But it's just… a lot of information to digest."

Esme blinked. Then she immediately scanned the room for Ryder Currin, who was deep in conversation with a group of people down the hall. That bastard had actually once been engaged to Angela and hadn't opened up about his life—about something that would have a deep impact on his fiancée. Sure, his children were all adults now, but they would have been Angela's stepchildren, an important connection. He'd expected Angela to give her all to a relationship, yet he'd held back about this tie to her best friend.

And where did that leave them now?

Her sister's breakup with Ryder had been rough. That was no secret. They'd fought for their relationship, though, made it back to a promising forever. But she imagined information like this didn't do a lot in the way of bolstering trust in a relationship that still needed healing.

Esme schooled her features into PR neutrality. The last thing Angela needed was Esme's anger piled on top of all the turmoil she must be feeling. Esme just wanted to be here for her sister. "Are you having second thoughts about being with Ryder?"

Angela wrung her hands until her knuckles turned pale, nerves clearly rising hard and fast. "I know that I love him."

Esme pulled her gaze from her distraught sister to Ryder Currin again. Did the man love Angela as much? Was he the man Angela deserved? He inclined his head to the rancher he chatted with, his black Stetson obscuring his face.

Esme wished she had the answers and assurance. Love was a risky prospect. Even thinking about a future with Jesse was scary—and exciting. There was so much potential for heartbreak and failure. And opportunity for happiness.

She turned back to her sister. "What can I do for you?"

Her sister let out a breath. "Just be here for me. Be

my sister." She pressed a trembling hand to her chest, the absence of her engagement ring so very sad. The tan line even remained. Faint, but there, if one looked close enough. "I can't say this hasn't thrown me. I feel like I barely know him."

Throat bobbing, Angela's voice trailed off.

Esme struggled for the right words. Just being there somehow didn't seem like enough. "I realize this is unbelievably hard. I'm here whenever you need to talk."

Never had she been more grateful for her siblings to support one another, to continue the family bond. They needed one another.

Jesse was right that family was everything. And if he moved here, he could share in all of hers.

Esme squeezed Angela's hand in more unspoken support.

"I'll be okay. I'm glad you're home." Angela squeezed back in understanding, the sibling connection never more tangible. Esme felt like finally she and her sister had related without any barrier, no more being an outsider to Angela and Melinda's twin bond.

She wasn't going to let that go and hoped the same progress could be made with Melinda.

Esme made a mental note to talk to her sister more about this later, and they made their way into the conference room. Esme was drawn into a conversation about the press releases she needed to send out while someone tapped Angela with a question about the order of events. Giving her sister one last glance before they parted ways, Esme had to admire Angela's strength through so much adversity.

Then, turning her attention from the influx of people

on-site for the meeting, Esme took a moment to admire the renovations. There was still some work to complete before the holiday party a couple of days before Christmas, much less in time for the official opening at the huge New Year's Eve blowout gala.

But it was still already an impressive conference room, from the lengthy wooden table to the massive chairs all around. Crystal pitchers of water were placed strategically, but she was too nervous.

She was actually listening to her first Texas Cattleman's Club business meeting, with all the influential players on hand, including the current Royal chapter president and board members. Familiar faces, new friends even, after her time at Jesse's. Cord and Sheriff Battle sat on either side of her father. Ryder Currin scowled from the other side of the table where he sat with Angela. It saddened Esme that her sister seemed a gulf away, but they would mend that with time. Angela had to understand Esme's reasons for rooting for their father.

Then the gavel sounded, startling Esme and pulling her upright just as the meeting was called to order.

Ten

Echoes of Houston traffic pierced the walls of the historic site of the new Texas Cattleman's Club. One of the many reasons Jesse avoided Houston. Too much traffic. Too many people. Too many buildings.

Not enough sounds of crickets and birdsong. Not enough roaming horses and cattle. Not enough intentional living. He wouldn't even know it was Christmastime here, the only nod to the season the massive tree in the lobby.

He couldn't wait to get Esme back to Royal where they could celebrate the holiday together, under the spruce he'd cut down himself. The one they'd decorated together in front of the fireplace, sharing memories from their childhoods as they did so.

The sooner he finished this meeting, the sooner he could hit the road with her. Jesse hung back in the meeting room, the rest of the board from the Royal chapter seated around the conference table listening to pitches for leadership positions. Leaning against the wall, he studied the players. There were more contenders than just Sterling Perry and Ryder Currin to consider for the role. Venture capitalist Camden McNeal. Or Lucas Ford, an investigator and security mogul. Plus there was a wild card in the mix with Cord Galicia moving from Royal to Houston. He could well be a strong candidate to see the club through the start-up, since he had firsthand experience with the inner workings of the Royal chapter.

Jesse couldn't quite comprehend how his neighbor was going to make big-city life work. Even living on the outskirts of Houston. The hum, bustle and lights of the urban area radiated outward in palpable bands.

Jesse was already feeling claustrophobic, ready to get back home. To take Esme to that Christmas play and continue his campaign to persuade her to move.

Settling his weight onto the heels of his best pair of boots—a thoughtful gift from his sister three Christmases ago—Jesse scanned the crowd. He attempted to read the reactions of his fellow members. It seemed he was not the only one keeping a tight rein on his emotions during the candidates' speeches. Members listened attentively, doing their part to hear the unique plans each potential president would do his best to execute.

As Ryder Currin finished his pitch to run the new club and returned to his seat beside Angela, Esme took the floor. Apparently, Sterling intended to let his daughter put her PR skills to work and do the talking for him.

Jesse worked to keep his face neutral, which was tough to do with Esme using all of her job savvy to lobby for her father. She was poised. Articulate. Convincing.

Damn. This woman enchanted him. Seeing her here today was more proof of her sexy-smart charm. He couldn't even detect a trace of nerves as she adjusted the microphone at the lectern to make herself better heard. Of all the places he'd seen her, she looked like she was born to be in the spotlight.

Crossing his arms over his chest as he leaned against the back wall, he focused on Esme in action. She looked stunning in her sleek black power suit. Her sky-high heels reminded him of meeting her for the first time, her broken shoes sinking into the mud, her beautiful blond hair soaked. She'd been a drowned rat, but somehow managed to keep her composure.

That charisma was in full wattage today, and not just her poise, but her keen mind. Her father watched her with unmistakable pride. Jesse took the measure of the man from a different perspective now, as Esme's dad, rather than just an infamous figure in the news.

Sterling had aged well, his brown hair graying at the temples. His blue eyes were the same shade as Esme's, and he also seemed to share her appreciation of style. His suit had a custom cut, his cowboy boots expensive without even a scuff. He may have worked as foreman of the ranch to prove himself to his father-in-law decades ago, but Jesse doubted Sterling was much of a hands-on ranch owner these days.

He looked 100 percent a powerhouse Texas businessman. And that's how Esme was pitching her dad to the Royal chapter board. As a successful, ambitious entrepreneur who'd expanded beyond just the ranch. Always striving for perfection, her father didn't know the meaning of the word "enough." Perry Holdings included real estate as well as banking, property management and construction.

In fact, Perry Holdings was responsible for the stunning renovations of this very building, with the help of Ethan Barringer, CEO of Perry Construction. Originally from Royal, Ethan made for a nice connection between the two worlds in tackling this project.

Esme painted her father as a visionary who knew how to put together a winning team, this historic building a symbol of his plan to grow the Houston branch of the Texas Cattleman's Club into the future.

In total Perry Holdings PR mode, Esme had them eating out of the palm of her hand.

Jesse realized *this* was the essence of who Esme really was. A city woman. A businesswoman. And no matter how sweet it had been to have her in his bed, in his house—in his life—he couldn't escape the deep-seated sense that eventually she would be miserable out on his ranch, far from the work she obviously did so well.

She completed her presentation and returned to sit beside her father. His smile of appreciation and pride brought a light to Esme's eyes. Even her sister nodded approval during the applause from across the room.

Esme blinked fast, a sheen of tears in her eyes. She was clearly choked up. Emotional.

She'd warned him about that, about her romantic side. She had a heart that was easily touched, and he'd grown to appreciate that about her. But how could he justify taking Esme from these people she loved? He recognized how selfish it would be. From a job she was born to perform. His freshly formed dreams of building a life with her at his side faded. He cared for her too much. His heart ached already at the thought of saying goodbye. But he wanted her to have the life that would make her happy.

Unable to take another moment of this meeting, Jesse ducked out into the hall, his focus homed in on the exit, on getting away from there as quickly as possible. Just as he reached the door, he heard the sound of fast-clicking high heels on the floor, growing closer.

"Jesse," Esme called. "Jesse, where are you going?"

He turned in the lobby—empty save for a towering Christmas tree—and the sight of her glowing smile poleaxed him. He swallowed down a lump in his throat, unable to push past the emotion.

She reached him and rested her palm on his chest. "What did you think of my presentation? I really think it went well, but I don't want to be overly optimistic. Still, I think a celebration is in order. Dinner out at my favorite Houston hot spot. My treat."

She looked so happy. So hopeful. The knowledge ate away at him.

"Esme." He clasped her hand and removed it from his chest. "I have something to tell you."

Her smile faded as she glanced down at the way their hands were suspended in air. "You look serious. Is something wrong?"

Everything. He'd made a huge mistake thinking he could change her, that he could transplant her to his world and mold her into the kind of woman he'd always imagined at his side. To do that would be a disservice to the bright, beautiful, smart woman she was.

So even though it hurt like hell, he forced himself to say the words that would send her out of his life for good. The quicker the better. Rip that bandage right off. He did his best to take a page out of her book. Keep his tone neutral. Final. Definitive. Sure. "I've made my decision about a wife candidate. And I'm sorry, but it's not you."

Her gasp of surprise cut through the silence between them. Shock froze her features, followed by a wash of pain in her eyes at his rejection of all they'd shared over the past couple of weeks. That glimpse into her heart damn near broke his, but he told himself she would be happier this way.

Living her own dreams instead of his.

Then her shoulders went back, her chin tipped with pride. A feral smile brushed over her lips though pain shone in her pretty blue eyes. "Congratulations," she said bitterly. "I'm glad you got exactly what you wanted."

She adjusted her jacket, sweeping her blond locks over her shoulders. Without another word, she brushed past him, striding past the towering Christmas tree and out the door.

And out of his life.

Weary, physically and emotionally, Angela punched in the code to her condominium. Latches releasing, she pushed inside, ready to put the events of the last twenty-four hours behind her. Far, far behind her. She needed space and a moment to breathe and process. Once inside, she dropped her purse on the floor and reached to turn on the lights.

She startled in surprise, the shock followed by a twinge of fear. Someone was huddled on her sofa. Fear slammed into her chest and constricted her breathing. She'd seen enough crime shows to know victims usually had a small, narrow window of escape. She reached for the doorknob behind her, quietly…

Then recognized the female curled up on her couch among the holiday throw pillows and sighed in relief. Her jagged heartbeat returning to normal, she laid a hand on her chest, her linen dress rough against her fingertips. "Esme, you scared me for a moment."

Her youngest sister looked up, her eyes red from crying as she hugged a red velvet throw pillow with a silver embroidered reindeer. "I hope you don't mind that I used your spare key. I couldn't bear to be alone."

Fresh sobs rolled out of Esme. Her normally perfect makeup was smeared across her face. She looked so different from the woman who had just delivered a fiery and impassioned speech on behalf of her father. Something was seriously wrong for Esme to display such unfettered emotion.

Worry filling her, Angela crossed into the living room and nudged aside the ceramic snowman to reach the box of tissues on the coffee table. "What's wrong?"

Esme drew in a ragged breath, gripping the velvet pillow tassels. "It's over between Jesse and me."

Angela's eyebrows raised in surprise. But then she pushed aside her thousand questions to be there for her sister. Reaching a protective arm around her sister, she gripped Esme in a side hug. "Oh, sis, I'm so sorry."

"We haven't even known each other long." Her face was lined with pain. "It shouldn't hurt this much."

"Our hearts aren't tied to time." She understood too well about love and heartbreak because of her rocky relationship with Ryder. Angela stroked her sister's shoulder, attempting to soothe her as much as she could.

Wishing she could take her pain away.

Losing their mother early on had forced them to be close. And Angela was grateful for that closeness. But at times like this, her heart ached for their mother. What would Tamara have said to soothe Esme? To soothe Angela, even? She tipped her head closer to Esme's, doing her best to comfort.

Clutching a tissue, Esme blew her nose. Tears still leaked down her face. In a cracked tone, she continued.

"Thank you for understanding, for not writing me off as histrionic."

"Of course not. I'm glad you reached out to me. You shouldn't be alone." She plucked another tissue from the box and passed it over.

Her cell phone rang from her purse back at the door. She glanced at it, but looked away fast, not wanting her sister to feel like she had anything other than Angela's full attention. It was rare that Esme showed vulnerability to her. She had always seemed a bit jealous of Angela and Melinda's bond.

Esme dabbed at her eyes. "Please take the call. It'll give me a chance to pull myself together."

"If you're sure..." Angela hesitated.

"Absolutely." She nodded, standing and grabbing her purse.

"Okay, then, but I'll make it quick. Don't go anywhere." She retrieved her own purse and fished out her phone. Her eyes scanned the screen. Tatiana? Angela still hadn't quite wrapped her brain around the fact that her friend had given up a baby for adoption and never told her about it. She would have wanted to help, even if just to listen. Maybe that's what this call was about.

She answered. "Hello, Tatiana, what can I do for you?"

"Angela, I need you." Tatiana sobbed hard on the other end of the phone.

She bit the bullet and plunged right in, her gut telling her the timing of Tatiana being this upset couldn't be a coincidence after Ryder's conversation with his youngest child. "Is this about Maya Currin…about your daughter?"

"Yes," Tatiana whispered. "That's exactly what this is about. And I really need to talk to you. Everything is so out of control. My half brother's in prison and he's clearly mentally unstable. He's been threatening to say all sorts of awful things about me."

"I'm so sorry you're going through that. Let's meet for breakfast in the morning."

Tatiana hiccuped on another sob. "I need to talk to you now. In person."

Angela glanced to her still-hurting sister standing at the kitchen counter wiping her tears around her eyeliner. Shaking her head, she answered her friend. "I'm afraid I—"

Esme turned, her brave face on. "It's okay. Go. I know she's your friend and it's okay."

"But you're my sister." She wanted to be with Esme.

To find out why things had ended so quickly between her and a man she'd been so excited about.

"Thank you," Esme said with a watery smile. "How about we go over together?"

Angela nodded, relieved not to be torn between her sister and her friend. Of course she would choose Esme, but with Willem in jail, Tatiana didn't have any family left.

Other than Maya.

Her heart pinched at the thought. "Tatiana, Esme and I can come over right now. Just let us know where you are."

Angela reached for a notepad and jotted down the location and time. The new club. In a half hour. So simple, she wondered why she'd bothered to write it. She was such a jumble of emotions today.

But it helped take her mind off her own relationship to be there for others.

Angela ended the call and turned to her sister. "We can talk in my car on the way over." Then she grabbed her purse and went to the door.

Esme followed close on her heels. "Getting to be with you helps. Even if we don't talk. I just don't want to be alone right now."

Taking Esme at her word, when Angela got to her car, she turned on soft Christmas carols. Esme sat silently beside her, her head resting against the window, her sniffles further and further apart.

Angela's cell phone rang a couple of times with calls from Ryder, but she wasn't ready to talk to him, not yet. The third time he called, she sent him straight to voice mail and turned off her cell. She couldn't handle another emotional conversation sidetracking her tonight. It felt like the whole world was falling apart.

A half hour later, Angela pulled up outside the back entrance of the club, the historic building rather foreboding at night. While Christmas lights lined the street and lit up the other buildings, the club was pitch-black inside, the only illumination a Christmas tree in the lobby. She was glad she'd brought someone along with her. Tatiana's car was parked in back, too, so she had to be inside the building already. Why would she be sitting in the dark?

Arriving at the back door, Angela tapped in the security code, something Tatiana would know, too, since she was with Perry Holdings.

"Tatiana," Angela called as she walked inside, her sister following a step behind.

A faint light shone from the back parlor, the dim glow giving the place a creepy vibe that reminded her that the body of the murdered Perry Holdings assistant had been found in this building. Of course she had to think of that now, when she was already uneasy.

"Tatiana?" she called again, reaching for a switch to flip on the lights.

Tatiana stepped into view, her red hair in wild disarray. A step closer and she was bathed in light.

And her arms were extended, a gun held with steady hands.

Esme gasped behind her. Shocked and confused, Angela couldn't figure out what her friend was doing.

Tatiana waved the gun, gesturing toward the parlor. "Both of you. In there."

What the hell was going on? Was Tatiana unhinged?

Angela cast a quick glance at her stunned sister. She wasn't sure how they were going to get out of this, but she had to believe they would figure something out.

Angela kept her voice low even though her heart pounded so very hard with fear. She needed to stay calm. Stay in control of her emotions and de-escalate the situation. Giving herself completely over to fear would only immobilize her. Which might interfere with any way to keep her and Esme safe.

Her hands clenching so hard her nails cut into her palms, Angela struggled for the right words for a situation she never could have imagined happening. "Tatiana, my friend, whatever you're feeling, I understand—"

"Shut up," Tatiana shouted.

Angela snapped her jaw shut. She tried to get a read on the events quickly spiraling out of control. The woman who stood before them might as well have been a stranger. Her expression, her tone, her actions... Angela didn't recognize any of them.

"You're not my friend, Angela, and you can't have any clue what I'm feeling, or what I've been through. Showing up here with your sister when I said I needed you? You've just proven what I already knew. Perrys always look out for Perrys and to hell with the rest of us."

Fear for her sister constricted her throat.

If only she hadn't brought Esme along, she wouldn't be in danger. "Esme has nothing to do with whatever grudge you have against me. It's not fair to keep her—"

Tatiana closed herself inside the empty parlor with them, the gleam in her eyes vicious. "Nothing in my life has been fair. My father lost everything because the land he was promised by your grandfather went to that idiot Ryder Currin instead. And your sister Melinda gets to have a baby when I had to give up mine."

Tatiana Havery was a madwoman, and Angela had never seen it. Never known. She felt stupid and foolish, all the more so because she couldn't focus on getting out of this situation. Panic clogged her airways, making it hard to breathe.

Esme took a step forward with the signature calm that stood her in good stead at work. "What can we do to make this right for you now?"

She was buying them time. Angela looked around the room, taking in the high windows and lack of furnishings. Tried to formulate a plan that didn't end in death and gunshots. And so far, she came up empty.

She wanted Ryder. Why hadn't she taken his call in the car? If something happened to her and she never got to speak to him again… The hurt of that made her legs wobble beneath her.

Tatiana's gaze swung wildly to her. "It's too late. I thought I was going to get my revenge by bringing down the Perrys and Currins for taking what was rightfully my father's. Yes, I was responsible for spreading all those rumors with the help of my brother. And it was working, too." She pointed the gun back and forth between them. "But then that stupid Vincent Hamm overheard one of our conversations. So I had to kill him."

Angela swallowed down a knot of horror as she looked around and realized that Tatiana had brought them to this building, where Hamm's body had been dumped, with a grisly purpose. And there was nothing in this empty room to defend herself with. She gripped her purse harder, trying to remember what was inside, what might be used as a weapon, all the while trying to keep track of what Tatiana was saying.

"I tried to pin the murder on your father but of course Mr. 'Teflon' Perry got away with it. The Perrys and Currins get everything and my family got nothing. That land would have given my dad a fresh start."

But Tatiana's father had lost everything because of his addiction. He'd gone broke just as Tatiana finished boarding school. She must have had her baby not too long after that.

"Tatiana," Esme said softly, "I remember your dad. We were all so sad when he died in that accident. It had to have been hard for you."

"Accident?" Tatiana shrieked. "It wasn't an accident. He killed himself. Because of your family…and that vile Ryder Currin, who got the land my father should have had. And now Ryder has my daughter, too?"

Esme backed up a step, no longer the conciliatory, smooth businesswoman.

Angela agreed. Talking wasn't going to work. Tatiana was crazed, her speech dripping with bitterness and hatred. She had already made up her mind to murder them.

Angela's purse slid from her shoulder, hitting the floor with a thud. Her cell phone skittered out, a reminder of all those missed calls from Ryder. She would give anything to hear his voice one more time. But she was never going to see Ryder again, never have the chance to hold him, tell him how much she loved him.

She reached for Esme's hand, needing to feel her

sister's presence. Wanting to offer whatever love and comfort she could.

Tatiana's face spread in an evil smile. "It's time Sterling Perry and Ryder Currin learn what it feels like to have their hearts torn out by losing what's dearest to them."

Eleven

Ryder tossed his uneaten supper in the sink.

The dish clanked, the sound jarring in his too-still, too-quiet home on Currin Ranch.

Damn it, he was tired of being ignored. He'd phoned Angela repeatedly since the meeting ended and she wasn't answering. She hadn't called back, much less sent a text in response to his voice mails.

Angela was going to have to talk to him eventually, so it might as well be now. The longer silence stretched between them, the tougher it would be to bridge that gap.

Sure, she'd sat at his side during the meeting, but other than that, she hadn't spoken to him since he'd told her about Tatiana being Maya's biological mother. Angela hadn't even allowed him to apologize for keeping the secret from her. She'd just walked away, refusing to talk to him.

He could see how it would seem that he didn't trust her not to tell Tatiana—her best friend—where her baby had gone. He couldn't help but wonder if he'd kept the information from her because on some level, he had still been holding back from committing.

Whatever the reason, he owed her an apology. They had been engaged. He should have honored that commitment he'd made to Angela. It hadn't been fair to expect her to build a relationship with Maya without all the facts.

He stalked to the foyer to snag his jacket and pluck his keys out of the carved wood bowl in the entryway. He pulled open the door and stopped short. Maya stood on the other side, her keys in hand.

Given how upset she'd been, he hadn't expected to see her so soon. Except she didn't look at all distressed. In fact, she had a hopeful gleam in her tired eyes. All that emotion in a short time must have been draining.

She pushed past him into the house, turning back to him, tentative but with a growing excitement building. "Guess what?"

Shrugging, he tried to imagine. A boy, maybe? Final grades were posted and she made the president's list? Anything was possible. "I haven't a clue."

"I went to see my birth mother," she blurted. "I told her I'm her daughter."

He went cold inside. He'd figured she would want to meet Tatiana, but he hadn't thought it would happen this soon, before she really had the chance to think through all the implications of the meeting. To prepare herself for her birth mother's potential reactions. He wanted Maya to be happy, but he also wanted to protect her from hurt. What if Tatiana didn't want Maya in her life?

Although based on the happiness on his daughter's face, it seemed the meeting had gone well. "What did Tatiana say?"

"She was so shocked." Maya's hands moved a million miles a minute as she spoke. "She definitely had no idea that you were raising her biological daughter."

It had been her own family's stipulation. Ryder had kept it a secret for good reason.

"And?" Questions piled up inside him, blanketed with a deep sense of foreboding. He could never place his concern, but something about Tatiana had always sent his senses skidding.

"She was glad to meet me. She said she'd never stopped loving me. She cried." Maya swiped away a fresh stream of tears rolling down her cheeks. "She seemed happy, but something in her face made me really believe she regretted the decision, too, you know? Like maybe she'd begged her dad not to send me away? She seemed so overwhelmed, I decided to give her some space to digest."

Thinking of Tatiana's pain sent his thoughts spiraling. His daughter continued to share information about the meeting, but Ryder lost track of her words as bits and pieces of what had happened over the past several months swirled through his head. Vincent Hamm's death. His employee Willem Inwood going to prison for his role in a Ponzi scheme, a scheme he'd attempted to blame on Sterling Perry.

Decades of controversy over that one damn piece

of land Harrington York had willed to Ryder, but both Sterling Perry and Sam Havery thought was rightfully theirs. The land had proved to be rich in oil, stoking the bitterness Perry and Havery harbored.

And the oddest piece in this whole puzzle. Inwood was Tatiana's half brother. Ryder had thought it strange Inwood would do something that could jeopardize Tatiana's position at Perry Holdings. But what if they had been colluding to get back at both Ryder and Sterling because of that land?

He could feel the blood drain from his face as he wrapped his brain around the possibility—probability—that Tatiana could have orchestrated those rumors to avenge what happened to her father. For having to give up her baby since she couldn't offer her a future.

An even more horrifying prospect occurred to him. Could she have even killed Vincent?

No. That was a stretch. This was Angela's best friend he was talking about…

Oh God. Angela.

He focused on his daughter again. "Maya, kiddo, I am so glad you're happy." He didn't even want to think of what it would do to his daughter if it turned out her newly found biological mother was a criminal. "I want to hear all about it. But I need to take care of some quick business. Will you wait for me here?"

"Sure, Dad." She backed away, smiling. "It's okay, really. I have tons of things I want to write in my diary so I don't forget anything about this day."

She faded from sight in a flurry of teenage energy and red hair. A surge of protectiveness shot through him. For her. For Angela.

Heaven help anyone who tried to harm his family.

Gathering his keys and wallet, he tried to call Angela again. It went straight to voice mail. He tried Melinda's number, willing her to pick up.

"Hello?" she said, her voice so like Angela's, a shared twin timbre. "What's going on, Ryder?"

His boots ate up the space to the garage. "Is Angela with you? She's not answering her cell and I need to talk to her."

"No, she's not, but I'm at my condo with Slade packing up a few last things before I sell the place." Melinda's condo was in the same building as Angela's. "Do you want me to go check on her?"

"Yes, please."

"I'll call you back from her place if she's not there."

"Thank you." He didn't want to worry Melinda, given her pregnancy, but he also didn't want to waste a minute more.

Waiting for her to phone back felt like an eternity. He threw open the door of his truck and settled behind the wheel, ready to tear out of there if he needed to start a search.

His cell rang from where he'd placed it on the dash. Melinda. He jabbed the screen before the second tone could chime.

"Did you find her?" he asked without preamble.

"She's not here, Ryder." Melinda's answer ramped up his concern. "But I found a note she left behind about some kind of meeting? It says, 'T at the TCC building at 8 p.m.' Does that make any sense to you?"

His grip tightened on the steering wheel. He didn't want to believe the worst. But he knew in his gut, Angela was in grave danger. “Thank you, Melinda. You’ve been a big help.”

Without a second to waste, he peeled out of the garage. Plowing down the drive, he called for backup to meet him at the club.

Houston police detective Zoe Warren.

Royal sheriff Nathan Battle, who, thank God, was still in town.

Ryder knew they wouldn’t question him or write off his suspicions the way someone on the other end of a 911 call might. And sure enough, they agreed without hesitation. Zoe had been with Cord and Jesse, who were coming, as well.

The drive felt like an eternity even though he knew he’d made it in half the usual time. Pulling up behind the TCC building, Ryder didn’t know whether to be relieved or horrified to find Angela’s car parked beside another vehicle. Tatiana Havery’s?

Two more cars swept in, doors opening, as his backup arrived. Sheriff Battle raised a finger to his mouth for silence, then motioned for them to follow him.

Ryder’s heart raced as they entered the building, fast and silent, everything inside him telling him he needed to get to Angela. Now.

Muffled voices echoed down the corridor, female voices. Coming from the parlor.

Ryder bit back bile while the group crept closer. He kept his footfalls quiet as he picked his way forward, praying there wouldn’t be a squeaky floorboard. The voices grew louder, more distinctive.

Tatiana.

Angela.

And Esme?

Nothing about this scene made sense to him. How had it gotten to this point? How had Angela found herself in the crosshairs?

Another rolling wave of protective urges washed over his body. He needed to make sure Angela—and Esme—made it out alive. And in one piece.

Ryder shot a quick look at Jesse Stevens, the Royal rancher who was Cord's close friend. His face was pale, his jaw flexing.

But he looked every bit as hell-bent on getting to the women as Ryder.

The door had a vintage stained glass inset. Shadows moved on the other side, muffled sounds seeping through…

"The Perrys and Currins have to pay for what they did to my father. To me. To my child."

Tatiana.

Every muscle in Ryder tensed for action. He burned to push through that door now and to hell with caution.

Zoe paused, holding up a hand for them to wait. Nathan Battle nodded. This was Zoe's jurisdiction. Her case. Her bust. But Ryder intended to be right on her heels.

Nathan's lips thinned as he checked his weapon. Tension was so thick that it was tangible in the air.

Withdrawing her weapon, Zoe mouthed silently, "One, two…three."

They moved as one, bursting into the room. Ryder's hungry gaze devoured the sight of Angela. Alive.

And held at gunpoint.

"Tatiana," Ryder called, distracting her for a split second, willing to risk taking a shot without hesitation. Angela's life was at stake.

That second's distraction was all it took for Zoe and Nathan to tackle Tatiana while Jesse pushed the two sisters out of the way of any potential gunfire. A single shot went wild and shattered the stained glass.

Then silence.

Sulfur from the gunfire tinged the air.

Adrenaline burned through Ryder as he braced a hand against the wall to keep from sinking to his knees in relief. Angela was safe. Thank God, she was safe. Only a couple of strides away.

"My daughter," Tatiana whimpered as Zoe handcuffed her, reading Tatiana her rights. Glass crunched under their feet on the way out, Tatiana's sobs growing fainter.

But Ryder didn't have the least bit of sympathy for her and didn't intend to waste so much as a single thought for her. His focus was on Angela, barely registering Nathan and Jesse helping Esme to her feet.

Ryder reached for Angela, hauling her close, his heart slamming against his rib cage. "Thank God you're all right. I was so damn scared when I couldn't reach you."

The memory of that interminable drive to the club sucker punched him all over again. He knew with certainty he loved this woman deeply.

"How did you know where to find me? Find us?" Angela looked over at Esme deep in conversation with Nathan Battle. Her sister's arms moved in sweeping gestures, no doubt recounting the story of how they'd wound up at gunpoint. A story he, too, wanted to hear.

An unexpected distance gaped between Esme and Jesse. Maybe they hadn't been as close as everyone thought and it had only been a fling.

Ryder buried his face against the top of Angela's head and breathed in the scent of her shampoo, like an exotic flower. "You left your note with the address and time at your place."

"I'm so glad you made it in time," she whispered, trembling in his arms. "I really believe she would have killed my sister and me."

And if Melinda hadn't discovered that little scrap of paper, he could have lost Angela forever, a blow his heart couldn't have withstood. How could he have let her get away before? Their broken engagement was the biggest mistake of his life.

One he didn't intend to repeat. He would do whatever it took to win her back. To build a life with her. A strong partner, his lover, his love.

With Angela's help, he would need to tread gently with Maya about her birth mother and what had happened over the past months, culminating in the most horrifying night of his life.

Unwinding the events of the last few hours would take patience and finesse. Traits he deeply admired in the woman he loved. The one who made his life so much better.

His eyes held hers. Throat bobbing, he strung together words. Knowing it would never be enough to explain how he felt about her.

"Angela, you have to know I love you. I've known

love before and this is the real thing. Something worth cherishing. And I'll be damned if I'll throw that away again. We're the forever deal. And whatever I need to do to convince you to marry me—"

She pressed her fingers to his mouth, her eyes on him. "Ryder, stop." She eased her hand away. "You don't have to convince me. I love you, too. I want nothing more than to be your wife."

A swell of relief filled him. Along with gratitude for this second chance with Angela.

He pulled out the engagement ring he'd given Angela, a ring he'd kept with him since the day she'd taken it off. "I've kept this with me even though I was the one who called off our engagement. I couldn't seem to let it go, to let *you* go."

"And now you never have to." She smiled up at him, her hand outstretched for him to slide the ring back in place.

Where it would stay for a lifetime.

A week later, Esme stood in the middle of what she'd once thought would be her dream come true—a holiday party held at the beautifully renovated building for the Houston branch of the Texas Cattleman's Club. Tomorrow was Christmas Eve. At the very least, she should be celebrating having survived Tatiana's attack.

She truly was grateful for her family's safety, her father's cleared name. Still, the revelry echoed hollowly around her without Jesse by her side. But she hadn't heard even a word from him since Tatiana held her and Angela hostage.

A harp played Christmas songs as Texas Cattleman's

Club guests from both Houston and Royal filled the room to celebrate the completed renovations. The formal grand opening was scheduled to ring in the New Year, the entire memberships of both chapters invited. Would Jesse attend? Would she have to see him with whatever "perfect" woman he'd chosen? The thought sent her stomach plummeting. Thankfully, so far, he was a no-show tonight.

The attack had drawn Ryder and Angela closer, though. Angela had gone through so much heartache over the last year that this warmed Esme's soul for her. They were so rock solid these days. Things had been difficult for Maya, but Ryder's older two children had been a wall of support, perhaps having gained strength from their own happiness. His son, Xander, who'd mourned the loss of a fiancée two years ago, had even found love again with cowgirl tomboy Frankie Walsh.

She stepped aside for waitstaff walking by with a silver tray of bacon-wrapped prawns, another carrying flutes. Even the champagne didn't tempt her. While she was happy for her sister, watching the in-love couple reminded her of a very real absence in her own life. The pain was made more palpable when Cord and Zoe romantically sipped from each other's champagne flutes.

The jabs to her heart just kept coming.

Cupping her crystal glass of sparkling water, she tucked herself farther away from the partiers. She needed to put in an appearance for her family's sake, but she wanted to remain as inconspicuous as possible. She'd even chosen her clothes with just that in mind, settling on a basic black cocktail dress. Her only nod to the party and the season was her red Gucci heels.

She was still raw inside from Jesse's rejection, heartbroken in a way that grew more painful every day. She felt adrift. After the vibrant days on Jesse's ranch, she found city life noisy and crowded. Even her job felt soulless now that she'd moved beyond seeking her daddy's approval.

Maybe she should buy a ranch of her own, work in philanthropy like her sister Melinda. Her sister might even welcome her help as Melinda's pregnancy progressed. She could spend more time with her husband, Slade.

Esme pressed her palm to her forehead, her thoughts all over the place. She had no idea what to do with her future, couldn't even think straight. She'd been so hopeful she and Jesse could build a life together. Seeing him walk away after the police hauled off Tatiana had been the worst pain she'd ever endured. He'd meant what he'd said about not wanting her.

How could things be so awful and perfect at the same time? Her father and Ryder were continuing to strengthen their reconciliation, much to Angela's joy. Their dad had even managed to repay the investors who'd panicked and lost so much money, an empathetic move that had people wondering if Sterling had become more than an empty suit after all.

After all the bad blood between the two families, it still felt surreal to Esme that her brother, Roarke, was engaged to Ryder's older daughter, Annabel.

Perry Construction CEO Ethan Barringer and his fiancée, Aria, were deep in conversation with Liam Morrow and socialite Chloe Hemsworth, both engaged couples radiating such happiness it made Esme ache all over again. An animated Paisley Ford held court with both of them, no doubt sharing news of the latest wedding fashion from her boutique. Her husband, Lucas, smiled proudly, as supportive of his wife as she was of him.

It seemed the whole room was full of couples, making her recent breakup all the more difficult to bear.

Venture capitalist Camden McNeal, his new bride, Vivianne, at his side, had his phone out showing everyone who would look the family photos of the two of them with their toddler daughter. Esme thought of the childcare center in the Royal TCC building, a benefit the Houston chapter didn't offer. She would have never thought to miss it before knowing Jesse and hearing his plans and yearning for a family.

"Can I get you a refill?"

Her father's voice startled her from her pity party. She hated feeling so morose but couldn't seem to shake herself out of it. "Thanks, Dad. I'm good."

He adjusted his tie, ever the clotheshorse. "You really did a top-notch job over in Royal on behalf of our chapter."

"But I didn't do anything that secures the presidency for you. It's still up in the air who'll lead this chapter."

"I can't deny that I would like the position, but I'm okay with however things shake out." He reached for his whiskey glass and finished off the last swallow without even a wince. "You made all of us look good in Royal and laid the groundwork for a great relationship between us."

The two clubs had worked together to draw up nomination papers for board positions and officers, creating the new club's rules and regulations.

His praise meant a lot to her. "Thanks, Dad. I'm glad you're pleased. But I'm not sure what I did."

"Houston and Royal are two very different towns. Forging a strong tie could have been rocky. But you've helped all of us—in both cities—form new business connections and new friendships."

Uncomfortable with praise she wasn't sure she'd earned, she shook her head emphatically. Pieces of her upswept hair loosened, tumbling in front of her eyes. Coming undone, for a change, gave her strange comfort. "It wasn't as difficult as you make it sound. We aren't really that different, Dad."

"If you believe that, then what's kept you from going back to Royal and that man you're obviously so taken with?"

She stared at him incredulously, surprised he'd noticed. She found herself aching to confide in her father, even knowing he couldn't fix this for her. "Dad, he doesn't want me."

"Huh, could have fooled me. Whenever he looked your way, he seemed besotted." He placed his hands on her shoulders. "And even if he's on the fence about committing, when did a child of mine ever back down without a fight?"

She stared back into her father's eyes, the same color as hers, and let his words sink in, really sink in. About Royal and Houston being similar. About fighting for what she wanted.

He continued, "I made the mistake of paying more

attention to business than to my marriage and I paid the price for that. So have you kids. Learn from my mistakes."

The rare glimpse of vulnerability in her father touched her heart and pushed aside barriers of her own making. She'd enjoyed her time at Jesse's ranch, working alongside him, riding to check the cattle, watching sunsets together on his porch.

Dreams spun into possibility. Esme Perry—a wife, a mother, an entrepreneur. Maybe she could have the best of both worlds by working remotely. Why had she gotten it into her head that she had to wait to establish her career before even considering motherhood? They could also share in the Texas Cattleman's Club world and she would still be connected to her family.

She arched up on her toes to kiss her dad on the cheek, a plan to woo Jesse already forming in her mind. "Thanks, Dad. Do you mind if I borrow that old truck of yours I used to learn to drive? I think my Christmas plans just changed."

"Sure," he answered without hesitation. "Just remember, even restored, that sucker's got a tricky clutch."

With a final look at the room full of her family and friends, at the stunning renovations now complete and the club ready to launch, Esme felt her world settle into place. She would always enjoy Houston, but her heart was in Royal now.

She had fallen head over heels in love with Jesse Stevens. And damn straight, Perrys fought for what they wanted.

The night was still young. If she made good time, she could be in Royal to celebrate Christmas Eve with Jesse.

* * *

Jesse was decidedly lacking in the holiday spirit, in spite of his decked-out house. The decorations only served as a reminder of all he'd left behind in Houston and how he would be spending Christmas Eve alone. He'd called his sister, exchanged holiday greetings, but then she was off to enjoy her vacation.

Why in the hell he'd thought coming to the stables would be better was beyond him. Esme had permeated every part of his world until there was nowhere to step without thinking of her, wanting her. Ghosts of their time together whispered from every corner of his ranch. And he had no idea how to find peace with her absence.

The familiar scents and sounds of his stable at night did little to soothe his restless spirit. He just kept thinking of how he would want to share the moment with Esme.

He stroked Duke's nose, wishing those wise brown eyes could offer him some wisdom. "Well, boy, I've made a mess of things, haven't I?"

The horse whinnied in response, shaking his mane. When he was a kid, he used to do this with Apollo. Tell his horse his secrets, dreams, regrets. The act steadied him. At least, a bit.

"I'm already regretting my decision to let her go." He couldn't sleep. He couldn't eat. His life was empty without her. "This ranch means nothing to me without her."

Never had he imagined a moment where the ranch felt like it wasn't enough for him. Sure, he appreciated his horses, his house, the rolling grounds. But he couldn't help but notice its expanse. How big it was. How empty it was.

Pawing the ground, Duke swung his head toward a mare in the next stall. The Appaloosa mare nickered softly.

Everyone was partnering up. Horses included, it seemed. "I want what my married friends at the Texas Cattleman's Club have. A sense of belonging to a family."

That hadn't changed. He just wanted it all with Esme.

Duke nuzzled Jesse on the shoulder. Those brown eyes stared back at him, catching him up short.

He knew the horse couldn't answer. Not really. Still, the flick of Duke's ear let him know he was listening. Stroking the horse's neck, he kept replaying the memory in his mind of meeting Esme. Of all that life with her seemed to promise. Of all that he'd thrown away.

Jesse's mind circled back around to how this ranch meant nothing without her. How he'd wanted that family with Esme. And everything clicked into place with startling clarity.

For some lame-ass reason, he'd thought that he could only have his dream family here in Royal.

As he rocked back on his boot heels, taking in his stable, thinking about his ranch, he also thought about the club here and the branch starting in Houston. And he realized the heart of that organization beat in either location.

Friends. Family. Community. Home wasn't about a building, or even a plot of land. It was about loving people and having them return that love.

It was still a few minutes shy of Christmas Eve, but there was nothing to say he couldn't make his holiday miracle happen now.

After shooting off a text with instructions for his foreman, Jesse made fast tracks outside, toward the house. He could be packed and on the road in less than ten minutes, but even that felt like an eternity.

Ten minutes later, he settled behind the wheel, a thermos of coffee beside him for the nighttime trip to Houston. Only a few hours separated him and Esme.

Mind made up, he turned the ignition key. He was ready for the journey. He needed to see her. To fight for her. The woman who made every room and space light up with energy and love. He'd been a fool to cast that aside, but he wouldn't let that get in the way of winning her back and healing her heart.

Just as he hit the gas, headlights shone in the distance, barreling down the long drive toward him. He scratched his head, frustrated at what might be a delay. He wasn't expecting anyone.

The vehicle stopped in front of him, his eyes taking a moment to adjust to the bright lights from what appeared to be a restored classic truck with a big red bow on the grille. He held up a hand, blotting out the glare as the door was flung open and a pair of shapely long legs stepped out.

A woman wearing sky-high red leather heels.

Jesse put his truck in Park, a smile building inside and spreading to his face. His heart slugged in his ears, each beat an echo of her name.

Esme.

He didn't know what she was doing in a vintage truck, a magnificent ride that at another time he would have been jonesing to drive. It was on the complete opposite end of the spectrum from her Porsche.

But then, everything about this woman was unpredictable. Perfectly so. He wouldn't have her any other way.

He hit the ground running, his strides eating up the space between them as she ran into his arms, leaping into his embrace. He spun her around, his face buried in her hair, the scent and feel of her filling his senses just as she filled his life.

Easing her to the ground, he sealed his mouth to hers and she met his kiss fully, her hands on either side of his face. No hesitation. He didn't know why she'd forgiven him. He was just glad to his soul that she had.

Jesse skimmed a final kiss over her lips before angling back, enjoying the way the stars were reflected in her eyes. "Nice ride."

"Turns out I'm a fan of trucks and a certain cowboy." She tapped his Stetson.

"And I'm a fan of you." He ran his hand down her sleek blond hair, burying his fingers in the silken strands. "I was just coming to you, but I'm glad we don't have to wait any longer. Every day without you has been miserable. I've been a brooding mess since you left."

"Oh, Jesse," she sighed, looping her arms around his neck. "I've—"

"Shhh." He kissed her quiet. "I need to speak first, especially after you took such a leap to drive all the way here. I didn't mean what I said about wanting someone else to be my wife. I was just afraid I couldn't make you happy here in Royal. So I want you to know I'm willing to move, like Cord is doing."

Eyes dancing, she drew teasing circles along his

back. "Thank you for that beautiful offer, and a couple of weeks ago, I might have been wrongheaded enough to have accepted. But now I know my heart and my future are here in Royal."

He couldn't believe his ears or his luck. More than luck, this was a Christmas miracle beyond any he could have imagined. And right on schedule as the night slid into Christmas Eve.

Jesse looked into the eyes of the woman he knew he would love for the rest of his life. "Merry Christmas, Esme. You're the best gift I could have ever received."

"And Merry Christmas to you, cowboy." She pulled his Stetson off and dropped it on her head. "I can promise you, the celebrating has only just begun."

Epilogue

Esme clutched Jesse's hand, eager to hear the announcement of the Houston chapter's president, the news to be revealed just before the stroke of midnight at the New Year's Eve soiree. She was doing her best to seem even-keeled and not at all on edge.

The ballroom was packed with members from both clubs, wall-to-wall Texas powerhouses mingling under crystal chandeliers. The men were decked out in tuxedos and their best Stetsons. Designer gowns and jewels to rival royalty draped the women.

But no one outshone the man at her side. She stole a look up at Jesse, her heart in her throat. They'd had a blissful Christmas week together before driving to Houston yesterday for this evening's New Year's Eve gala.

Esme had gotten dressed twice tonight. The first

time, Jesse had peeled off her gown and messed her updo. But she didn't mind. Not one bit. She and Jesse had thrown their clothes on quickly, barely making it to the gala on time. Trying to restore order to her hair in the car ride over, she'd given up and brushed it into a sleek, straight fall down her back. She'd smoothed the wrinkles out of her maroon gown with her hands, the silver embellishments glistening in the dash lights.

No one seemed to notice her hastily-put-together look. She slid a smoky-eyed glance up at Jesse. His knowing smile promised a repeat of earlier. An answering heat rose in her.

Her father and Ryder both appeared to be a bundle of nerves, even though they were making nice with each other, Angela smiling between them.

Her sister seemed happy. Genuinely happy. A sight that had been missing for what felt like ages.

And Jesse stepped right up like he'd known them forever. She appreciated how supportive he was of her family as a whole, and hoped to help him grow closer to his sister, Janet.

The music shifted from a fast dance number to a softer tune as the chairwoman for the nomination committee walked around the champagne fountain. Abigail Langley Price, a stunning redhead in a bold sequined gown, had been instrumental in allowing women to join the Texas Cattleman's Club.

Abigail climbed the steps to take the microphone. "Well, I imagine everyone is eager to hear the election results." She paused playfully before continuing, "And I won't keep you in suspense a second longer. I'll start with the board members."

She pulled out a card and slid on cat's-eye reading glasses. She read name after name off the list with a flourish, waiting for the applause to wane after each announcement. And every time neither Ryder nor her father was called, nerves ratcheted higher in Esme's stomach with the growing possibility the president would be one of them.

The woman smiled out at the audience. "There are only two more board positions to fill before I announce the first president of the Texas Cattleman's Club, Houston branch. Are you ready?"

The crowd roared in response. Esme's gaze skittered over to her father. She mouthed "good luck" from across the room. Sterling winked at her, inclining his head before turning his attention back to the stage.

Jesse squeezed her hand, a gesture of warmth and support that flooded her. Made her feel invincible. Like anything and everything was possible.

"There's a bit of a twist. We have a tie for the last two board positions, both having gained equal support. Our last two positions will be filled by… Sterling Perry and Ryder Currin."

Neither man had won the bid for president?

Shock tingled through Esme, a sentiment she suspected she wasn't alone in feeling. Whispers zipped from person to person. If not Sterling or Ryder, then who?

The woman tapped the microphone to regain control of the room. "It is now my honor, as one of the first women to be admitted to the Royal chapter of the Texas Cattleman's Club, to announce your president…" A drumroll rippled from the band, then stopped. "Elected with an overwhelming amount of write-in votes… Angela Perry."

Angela?

Without a second's hesitation, the crowd erupted into deafening applause and shouts of approval. And as Esme thought about it, she couldn't imagine anyone better for the job than her sister. She hoped her father and Ryder would be supportive, as well. Angling to look, she found both men holding their hands high in applause as Angela made her way to the stage.

Her sister was a vision in an off-the-shoulder gown of gold tulle with the tiniest shimmer. "Thank you, everyone, for the vote of confidence." Angela pressed a hand to her chest, breathless with surprise. "I'm stunned, to say the least. But honored and excited to lead the Houston chapter as we launch."

She waited for the applause to die down. "I'm especially pleased to serve with my father and my fiancé on the board."

More applause and cheers rippled through the partiers. Jesse let out a whoop. Esme's heart nearly burst as her smile grew even wider.

"I hope you'll indulge me a moment longer as my fiancé and I share some news of our own." Angela held out a hand to Ryder, her engagement ring glinting. She waved for him to join her on stage. He climbed the steps, his face beaming with pride.

Angela looked up at him, their love for each other clear for all to see. "We were given the best Christmas present of all. We're expecting our first child together."

The cheers and applause doubled in a rousing endorsement followed by glasses lifted in toast. Partiers converged around the couple and Esme knew she didn't stand a chance of getting to her sister anytime soon. But that was okay. They had months to celebrate.

Plans were already flowering in her mind for a joint baby shower for both of her sisters. Twins celebrating the births of their first children. Esme was truly happy for them.

Just as she knew they would be happy for her when her day came.

She looked up at Jesse, wondering aloud, "Are you feeling the baby urge? I know you want children. And so do I."

Jesse kissed the inside of her wrist before drawing her hand to rest against his heart. Stars and promises glimmered in those green eyes.

"Someday. But first, I want us to have time together, to get to know each other, to build a foundation for our future." He kissed the tip of her nose. "But at the risk of sounding too practical, I want us to have time to savor falling more and more in love with each other."

"That's beautiful. Underneath all that rancher practicality, you really do have a sentimental heart, full of emotions as messy as your desk."

"My desk?" He cocked his head to the side, a laugh spluttering out.

"No need to look offended. I think all that clutter is endearing." She remembered the time they'd gotten hot and heavy there, a place that had helped her see who Jesse Stevens really was inside.

"Well, then, I'm more than happy to have a messy office."

The countdown to midnight started, the partiers

chiming in until the forty-five-second mark was a thunderous echo of numbers. He pulled her close, swaying with her to the music, then spinning her out onto the balcony.

"How smart of you to have come out here ahead of the crowd to see the fireworks."

"Actually, I brought you out here to tell you how much I love you."

She smiled, her heart full of happiness like a champagne glass full of bubbles. "You've already told me."

"It's something I look forward to telling you every day." He held her tighter. Closer. Their bodies melting into one. Into a promise of forever.

"Now, isn't that convenient? Because I love you, too, and I enjoy telling you again and again." She teased her fingers along the hair at the base of his neck. "I can't believe how lucky we are."

"What a way to ring in the new year."

"And how wonderfully perfect we'll get to share the midnight kiss."

His low growl of approval rumbled between them as he angled down to take her up on that kiss.

A kiss that set her senses on fire. Their love made everything all the more special.

And as she arched up on her toes to press herself even closer, she could have sworn the fireworks had already started.

* * * * *